MW01100428

In a Pig's Ear

In a
Pig's Ear

PAUL BRYERS

BLOOMSBURY

First published 1996
Copyright © 1996 by Paul Bryers
The moral right of the author has been asserted

Bloomsbury Publishing Plc, 2 Soho Square, London W1V 6HB

A CIP catalogue record for this book
is available from the British Library

ISBN 0 7475 2478 5

10 9 8 7 6 5 4 3 2 1

Typeset by Hewer Text Composition Services, Edinburgh
Printed in Great Britain by Clays Ltd, St Ives Plc

To Adam von Trott

ACKNOWLEDGEMENT

For the origin of the name Arthur Pendragon, the author wishes to acknowledge the detective work of Graham Phillips and Martin Keatman in their book *King Arthur: The True Story*, published by Century Random House.

DEMONS AND DAMSELS

The wizard Merlin was, according to legend, the progeny of a fiend from Hell and a virgin from South Wales. The fiend may have been Satan himself though the various learned sources are divided on the subject. The virgin they unanimously elect to have been a novice at a convent in Carmarthen who claimed to have slept through the entire exercise, but then, to borrow a phrase from one more practised in sexual artifice, she would, wouldn't she?

The circumstances of my own conception were remarkably similar to those of the great Merlin, which was why I was called Milan, which is the nearest you can get to it in Czech.

There were some minor discrepancies, of course.

My mother was not, I think, a virgin at the time. Nor was she asleep. There is a film of it, so you can tell. *Die Teufel von Marienbad* it is called, which means, in English, 'The Devils of Marienbad': a tale of witchcraft and demon possession in a convent in Bohemia during the Thirty Years' War. It was made in 1943 during the Nazi occupation and had a limited shelf life, as they say, though I did, in fact, find it on a shelf, some fifty years later, in the archives at the Barandorn studios, just outside Prague. You can see her, my mother, in her nun's costume, writhing on a bed, faking an orgasm. Or in the extremes of agony and despair, it is hard to tell. The fiend is inside her, either in her mind or in that part of her body well out of shot. The shot is a close-up. In the style of the times it is lit from just above the camera and they have used a diffusion filter to soften the image so her complexion appears flawless if a little unreal. But there it is, the moment for ever captured on celluloid, the seed planted. I was born nine months later, almost to the day.

It is possible, of course, that there was a less immaculate connection. Perhaps this was when my father first saw her, on the set. Perhaps her performance put him in the mood for seduction and my mother in the mood to be seduced, though she always denied any participation in the process, other than in the most passive sense.

'I was drugged,' I heard her say once, when I was almost old enough to understand the context. 'He slipped something in my drink.'

Yes, well, it can happen to us all . . .

'His father was a fiend,' she said. 'I can say no more.'

But it was enough.

My mother returned to the studio after I was born but her career had stalled and was never to soar again. I don't think she blamed me for it. I don't think she blamed me for anything. I grew up feeling as loved and cherished as I had no right to expect, though I sometimes caught her regarding me in a certain critical light as though searching for signs of my dark patrimony. I trust she never saw them. I had a sarcastic tongue which I was taught to curb and other 'gifts' which I learned to hide but on the whole I was, so I have been told, a good-natured child. In later years, when I knew the difference, I preferred to think I was the product of her nurturing rather than his nature, though recent events have caused me to revise this opinion somewhat. She had me baptised though she was not herself a practising Christian, just superstitious enough not to want to take any chances.

Baptised a Catholic, then, and versed in the catechism at

the Church of St Michael the Archangel, in Prague. This was before the Communists put a stop to such heresies but, as the Jesuits say, who are more experienced in these matters, 'Give me a child until he is seven . . .'

Of course, I no longer consider myself to be a Catholic, nor would I be so considered by any Catholic of my acquaintance; what Marx and Lenin could not expunge succumbed to the subtler persuasions of Freud and Jung. But not entirely. Never entirely. I carry elements of the faith like old battle scars or secret stigmata of the soul, bleeding my private guilts. I can never rid myself of them, any more than the spectres of the old, cold, Cold War city in which I was raised: the castle of King Karl and the cathedral of St Vitus which would dance before my eyes when the light was right, my mood receptive, in the evening haze above the Hollywood Hills as I drove home along the Franklin Boulevard . . .

But I mustn't ramble. I see I am already losing your attention. The snout is back in the trough, nosing among the slops, the leavings of murderers and rapists, arsonists and thieves, my companions in crime.

I knew I would find you here. I asked the governor as soon as I arrived if there was a farm. And are there pigs? I enquired. I think he was surprised at my interest, which I could tell he did not share.

But Merlin, you see, was incarcerated with a pig when he fell foul of the enchantress Vivien. Some of the stories have them sealed together in a cave, others in an apple tree, for all eternity. My own sentence was rather less harsh, though it leaves plenty of time for us to become acquainted.

Why a pig? A joke, I think. Pigs, in myth, are frequently associated with demons. If you care to examine one of your front feet you will note a small hole beneath the hair, by which they – we – are reputed to enter.

All right, I know . . . What is it that Adam said? Remember

the simple rules of the fairy tale: stick to the story, avoid unnecessary tangents, eschew flashbacks. Begin at the beginning.

So.

Once upon a time there was a tower in the middle of a forest and in the tower there lived a beautiful princess . . .

2

THE TOWER

The forest was a myth: a lie to fool the bombers.

The tower was in the centre of the city but every building still standing had been covered with the hacked-off tops of fir trees in a desperate bid to mislead the raiders in the sky, to persuade them to drop their bombs elsewhere, on someone else. Even the tower was a fake. It had been designed to resemble an ancient fortress of the Teutonic Knights but its walls were of modern ferroconcrete, several metres thick, and on the roof, among the fairy-tale turrets and battlements, there was a battery of the latest anti-aircraft guns from Krupps of Essen. It was called the Flaktower and it was said to be indestructible. Even when the whole of Berlin was a burning ruin the Flaktower held out, less like a medieval donjon to my imagination than a space-age battle station with its guns firing into the sky as if defending the last survivors of a doomed planet from an alien invasion, a war of the worlds.

The tower was as high as a twelve-storey building, though in fact it had only four floors. The first two were bomb shelters linked to the Berlin underground and with room for up to 30,000 people. The floor above was a safe-deposit for the art treasures and archives of the city. Above that there was a hospital.

The beautiful princess worked in the hospital. Her name was Liza and she was a doctor by profession, twenty-seven years old and just qualified. Her father had been a timber baron in the Thüringer Wald but both he and her mother had died in a car crash shortly after the war started and her only brother was killed at Stalingrad. So Liza lived in the Flaktower.

She slept in a little room, like a cell, on the same floor as the hospital. It was intended as a rest room for the duty doctors but Liza appropriated it for herself and because of her condition the other doctors let her stay. She had a narrow bed and a locker and a small washbasin.

I did not mention that she was pregnant? I'm sorry. A beautiful, pregnant princess in a tower. No, I am not lying about the princess bit. Not exactly. Liza's husband, Conrad von Reisenburg, was of ancient lineage. There was a picture of him on the locker, in the uniform of a Luftwaffe *Leutnant* in the 9th Parachute Division. But his titles and his lands had been taken away from him and he had been sent to fight the Russians.

In the spring of 1945, which is when my story begins, the Red Army was closing on Berlin while the English and the Americans continued to bomb it from the air and the only safe places in the city were in the Führerbunker under the garden of the Reich chancellery and in the Flaktower in the Zoo Gardens.

Berlin in the final days . . . There is a challenge for my magic machines, my computers of virtual reality: to recreate such a world. I have fed them the information: the topography, the weight of explosive that fell, the percentage of buildings destroyed, the number of casualties – but what did it feel like to *be* there? To be caught in the middle of a thousand-bomber air raid, or in the food queues in the city centre when the Russian bombardment began and the shells came screaming out of the sky and the horses were stampeding down Unter den Linden with their manes and tails on fire? For this you need imagination, which no computer has. Do you have it, my greedy guzzler? Can you imagine the slaughterhouse, your ultimate destination, can you visualise Hell, which you may yet, on account of your inferior status, avoid?

I have tried.

I have walked through graveyards in Berlin where the stones are scarred and pitted with the wounds and I have tried to imagine what it must have been like to have lived through that time when the air was filled with flying metal. Hiroshima had its mushroom cloud but Berlin had its metallic rain, its slaughtering rain. Every day the American bombers came over, the Liberators and the Flying Fortresses, and by night the British Lancasters and Wellingtons and then, when the Russians came close enough, they finished the job with their tanks and guns, a vast ring of artillery all around the city to make of it a Carthage of fire and smoke, to draw out the air and fill the vacuum with shards of steel. Nothing made of flesh and blood could have lived through that horizontal rain. Nothing did. They all went under the ground and even then they were not safe. Even the dead were not safe. There are stories of the graves being blown open and the corpses resurrected and hurled into the sky and left hanging from the trees.

Even the animals were not safe. The Zoo was destroyed in a single night.

There was a tropical reptile house with a river running through it at first-floor level on a bed of glass so people could walk under it and look up at the exotic fish and the crocodiles swimming above their heads. A British bomb came through the roof and blew it apart. The river erupted through the shattered walls of the building and the fish and the reptiles expired thrashing on the lawns of the Zoo Gardens. The animals were literally blown out of their cages. There were lions skewered with iron bars, roaring in their death throes, wolves eating their own entrails from their torn bodies, a hippopotamus, an animal that could be said to resemble a giant pig, lying in a pool of blood with the fins of an unexploded bomb sticking out of its belly . . .

Ah, I see I have your attention now. Hiroshima passed without a grunt but dead and mutilated animals – the horror!

When the sirens warned of another raid and the steel shutters slid across her little slit of a window, Liza would sit in her darkened room and sing to the baby inside her, or sometimes she would tell it fairy tales: the *Märchen* of the Thüringer Wald where she herself was born. This was how she preserved a sense of peace and calm and order inside her own little world, while in the world outside the lightning would strike from the heavens and the ground would shake and the forest would be engulfed by fire.

When the raid was over, they would bring the casualties into the hospital and she would go and report for duty in the operating theatre. She was working right to the end. When she could no longer cut or saw, they gave her the sewing to do.

She was not the delicate kind of princess. She would not have felt the pea.

Her voice was gentle but physically and emotionally she was tough. She could endure. I have seen pictures of her taken earlier in the war, on holiday in Bavaria. She has shoulder-length blonde hair and a firm jaw tilted up towards the camera. Her smile is quizzical, a little ironic. She looks robust. She has a rucksack on the ground beside her and wears stout walking boots. Though it is a monochrome picture, you can imagine the ruddy complexion. She glows with health.

She would have grown pale in the tower, her unnatural confinement would have taken the bloom from her cheeks. I imagine her with the skin drawn tight across the cheekbones

8

and a shadow under her eyes, as if a thumb pressed into the soft flesh beneath the lids has left a faint smudge or bruise. Her hair is brushed back and tied at her neck with a ribbon. She is constantly herding a maverick strand from her forehead with the tips of her fingers. Her hands are rough, the joints red from constant washing with carbolic soap. She has a small jar of hand cream beside her bed but it is down to the last few centimetres and there will be no more where that came from. She wears no make-up, of course, but her lips appear rouged against the whiteness of her skin. She has a full bottom lip which she catches between her teeth when she is thinking. Her face has a slightly elfin appearance and there is a look in her eyes sometimes, when she is not cutting people up or sewing them together, of the dreamer, of someone whose mind is far, far away.

Why did she stay? There were still trains out of Berlin, until the last few days. It was possible to get a pass, particularly if you were pregnant. Why didn't she leave, as her cousin, Maria Schenke, the actress, urged her? Go south, she said, go to Dresden, they'll never bomb Dresden. She had her duties in the hospital, of course, but what of her duty to the unborn child? (And there speaks the shrill voice of the Catholic in me, the frustrated old priest.) But she had promised Conrad she would stay.

Stay in the tower, he'd said, you'll be safe there, as safe as anywhere, and I'll know where to find you.

He had a dread of losing her among the millions of refugees, of searching and never finding her. But she stayed also because she was too tired to think of going anywhere else. She was exhausted beyond all reason. All her reserves of energy went on the child in her womb. She carried it like a precious flask she was frightened of dropping. It would have been unthinkable to take it into the streets, to wait in the station with thousands of others for a train to the south, while the bombers came over.

And there were drugs in the hospital, and vitamins. It was her very own womb. All she lacked was air and light.

Sometimes, in search of both, she would go up on to the roof, where the guns were. We know that because she told a story about it years later in California.

She was standing on the roof one evening, leaning on the battlements between the guns, when the young Luftwaffe officer who was in command of them came up to talk with her. It was a beautiful evening sky. As the sun was setting on one side of the tower, the moon was rising on the other.

'A fine night,' he said.

And she said, 'Fine for the bombers.'

Most conversations, no matter how they started, tended to drift in the same direction if you were living in Berlin in those days. And he pointed at his guns, proudly perhaps but also to reassure her, and told her that the shells were timed to explode at the same time at the same height to create a lethal 'window' of flak which would destroy any aircraft caught inside it. And there were pompoms and cannon and machine guns in special turrets that jutted out from the battlements to throw up a curtain of fire against any low-flying aircraft that tried to skim in under the window.

And she said, in her soft, gentle voice, that with all these windows and curtains it was amazing that they managed to get a single bomber through and did he think that the damage was caused by all those blazing aircraft falling to the ground?

This remark, I am told, was typical of her. Mockery was her chosen weapon against the regime and those who sustained and supported it, perhaps because she felt as a doctor and a pacifist that it was the only form of resistance possible for her. They must have found it very difficult to deal with. She was exactly the picture of that fair, Nordic beauty they felt they were defending from the dark Asiatic hordes – and pregnant, too.

You grunt.

Perhaps you think that mockery is a pathetically ineffectual response to the obscenity of the Nazis and all they inflicted on the world, but I am not so sure. It has a particular appeal to me. If there had been more mockery earlier . . . but then I am a Czech and you are a pig. I don't suppose it impressed the Russians very much either. They used other weapons to take Berlin.

After they had pounded the city with artillery they sent in the tanks and the mobile howitzers and the trucks with the Katyusha multiple rockets which the Germans called Stalin organs. And then the men with the flame-throwers to burn up the people in the basements and behind them the infantry, and behind the infantry, who were regular front-line troops, came hundreds of thousands of zombies, the living dead who had been freed from the prisoner-of-war camps. The soldiers from Hell.

Can you imagine the mood they were in?

The privations they had endured, can you imagine? The sights they had seen? After their liberation they had swept through hundreds of kilometres of territory that had been occupied by the German army, 'cleansed' by the special forces of the SS. They had seen the corpses hanging from the trees and the multiple gibbets, the living corpses hanging from the barbed wire of the camps, piled into mounds, pitched into shallow graves and covered with a thin sprinkling of lime and earth. They had seen the bones in the gas ovens.

You are grunting again. Irritably this time. I am sorry, I see you want a little nap after your meal and I am disturbing you. Or is it because you can imagine these things as well as I, and you do not need to be told?

Very well. I will stick to my story. To only what is relevant. On the afternoon of 30 April, after ordering the people of Germany to fight to the last, their Führer retired to his private chambers in the bunker under the Reich chancellery and shot himself through the head.

The following day the man he had appointed his successor, Josef Goebbels, emerged from this same bunker with his wife, Mara. He wore his long uniform greatcoat with a hat and scarf and kid-leather gloves and he carried a Walther .38 pistol in his hand. His wife had just murdered their six children, one by one, feeding them drugged chocolates and then crushing a cyanide capsule into their mouths as they slept. She did this so they would not be taken by the Russians, just as some people have their pets killed when they themselves are dying.

They stood for a moment, arm in arm, in the garden. The Russian shells were falling all around, knocking chunks of masonry from the building and sending up great clouds of sulphurous yellow smoke and dust. Mara bit a cyanide capsule and as she slumped, kneeling, to the ground, her husband shot her in the back of the head. Then he swallowed his own capsule, placed the gun against his forehead and pressed the trigger.

Then the SS guards, who had been watching this from the porch over the entrance to the bunker, came out and poured petrol over the bodies and set fire to them. The column of smoke was lost in the pall hanging over the centre of the city.

A few hundred metres away, in the ruins on the edge of the Potsdamer Platz, Liza's husband, Conrad von Reisenburg, was dug in with the remnants of his unit. They could see the Brandenburger Tor still standing amid the ruins, and the Reichstag with a red flag flying from the roof. As it grew darker they could see the searchlights on top of the Flaktower in the Zoo Gardens and the guns on the roof still firing at the Russian aircraft. They did not know about the people in the bunkers under their feet. They did not know that the Führer and his chosen successor were both dead. But at about nine o'clock that evening, something snapped inside Conrad and he stood up and left his post, strolling towards the Zoo Gardens as if he hadn't a care in the world, trailing his rifle by its shoulder strap. Only one of his comrades saw him go. He shouted but Conrad kept walking until he was lost in the smoke and the darkness. They found the body a few weeks later, when they were clearing up the rubble.

The Flaktower continued to resist, even when the Russians brought up heavy howitzers and began to pound the walls from close range. There were more than 60,000 people crammed inside the bomb shelters, twice as many as they were designed to hold, and inside the hospital the doctors continued to operate on the wounded, though they had long since run out of anaesthetic and there was no way of numbing the pain or of disposing of the amputated limbs or the bodies of those who died.

And here, just before midnight, on the first day of May, Liza von Reisenburg had her baby. It was a boy. She called him Adam after her brother who had been killed at Stalingrad.

The next day what was left of the German army in Berlin surrendered to the Russians.

3

YEAR ZERO

Ththe were those who were philosophical. At least the bombing had stopped.

'Better an Ivan on the belly,' they said, 'than a Yank on the head.'

Or so it is said. Perhaps it is a myth. Or perhaps it was said by the ones who had no experience of an Ivan on the belly on behalf of those who had. This is often the case with philosophers.

Personally, I have had no experience of being raped by a Russian in a bad mood. I have seen my country raped but that is different. That is degrading in a different way. It might be said to be metaphysical.

This was a physical thing suffered by a specific number of women, a price extracted for what those special forces had been doing in Poland and Byelorussia and the Ukraine and elsewhere. You may imagine the 'rape' in this context meant more than the insertion of a penis into a vagina.

In the first few weeks of Russian occupation, 90,000 German women were admitted to hospital in Berlin as a result of rape. I do not know if Adam's mother was one of them.

I never met her, you see. Unlike so many of the other characters in my story, she did not whisper her secrets to me, as to a confessor. I do not have that advantage. Even had we met, I do not think that Elizabeth von Reisenburg would have poured out her soul to me. She guarded it too closely.

But her body was a different matter, and more difficult to protect.

Her recent motherhood would not have saved her, any more than her status as a patient, or a doctor. There are recorded instances . . .

They would come into the hospitals, prowling between the beds until they found one that was suitable, and you would have had to be very old and very ill not to be considered suitable.

'*Kommen*,' they would say, a German word they had learned. '*Kommen*,' beckoning with the hand. It was useless to protest.

A doctor was thus taken from the operating theatre. But this, too, could be a myth, who knows? No one knows what happened to Adam's mother, Liza, when the Russians occupied Berlin, no one except Liza and she never spoke of it.

I think she was probably raped, don't you? Let's make her raped.

Why not? There was nothing to protect her, no one. The German army had surrendered, all those Blackshirts and Brownshirts were all dead or in hiding. The only protection was to take a Russian officer as a lover, as her cousin Maria did, but Liza didn't do that, not according to Maria.

The Russians were the sole masters of Berlin for two months. Then they let the other Allies in to share it with them: the leavings. Liza was still working in her tower and it happened to be in the zone they gave to the Americans. Which was how she came to meet Sam.

Captain Sam Epstein of the 2nd Armoured Division which formally entered Berlin on Independence Day, 4 July 1945. Her knight in shining armour, though the armour of a

Sherman tank, I understand, does not shine. And yes, he was Jewish.

His ancestors had come over to America some time early in the century, from somewhere in Russia, I believe, or perhaps from Poland or East Prussia, I forget. Somewhere in Europe, anyway. He came back, though, as an American, properly appalled by this corrupted, disgusting, primitive, barbaric slaughterhouse of his own past and the horrors it was daily disgorging.

And he saw Liza and he said, 'Let me take you away from all this.'

You find that unlikely? After what the Germans had done to the Jews? But she was a beautiful princess, locked up in her tower, and he was a handsome soldier and this is, after all, a fairy tale.

It has great possibilities, don't you think? The story of the young Jewish-American officer and the beautiful aristocratic German doctor with a baby son and a missing husband in Berlin in 1945: Year Zero when the German people buried their past and made a new beginning. But it's not my story, it's Adam's and you'll have to wait to see the movie. All I have to tell you for now is that they were married and went to live in California and lived happily ever after. Or until death did them part, which tends to happen more often in real life.

Sam went to California to finish his law studies which had been interrupted by the war. His family had a practice in Los Angeles and in normal circumstances he would have joined it after graduation but Sam's family were not enchanted by the fairy tale. To them it was more like a horror story and he'd brought home one of the monsters. Not only a German but a Catholic German. So Sam went his own way and took a job with a law firm in Hollywood with a long list of clients in the film industry, and Adam, who had begun life in the wrong place at the wrong time, found himself exactly where he wanted to be. Though at the age of two and a half this might not have been immediately apparent to him.

I have seen a picture of him at that age, taken on a beach shortly after his arrival in America, and he looks as if he doesn't know where the hell he is or how he got there, but I believe this is a characteristic of children aged two and a half. This, too, is a black-and-white photograph but you can tell he was blond, like his mother and with the same slightly elfin look. Apparently he spoke more German, then, than English and as he grew into an all-American boy she continued to teach him her native tongue and many other things about the country of his birth. Her chosen form of indoctrination was the bedtime story, a powerful medium. She told him that it was not true, as he had heard said, that the only good German was a dead German, though confusedly all the good Germans she told him about did turn out to be dead. She told him about her family in Thuringia who were good Germans, all dead. She told him about Conrad, the father he had never seen, and his paternal grandfather, both good, both dead, killed by the bad Germans. She told him about Reisenburg and about the beautiful castle in the forest which his father's family used as a hunting lodge. He had a dim recollection of asking why they didn't go there and of her telling him that it had been stolen by a wicked ogre and that when he grew up to be big and strong he would have to go there and kill the ogre and take it back and live there with a beautiful girl he would make into his princess.

If this is true it is significant, but personally I have my doubts. It is too neat. It sounds like false-memory syndrome to me: something he invented much later and came to believe. He was always inclined to mythologise, to rewrite the script to suit himself, to assume an awareness that probably came much later in life. Possibly he confused it with those other stories she told him, the folk tales of the Thüringer Wald where she was born and raised, which had more than their fair share of ogres and castles and dispossessed princes. She also told him the story of Little Red Riding Hood and the wolf, which originated in the forests of my own homeland, near Marienbad: Mariánské Lázně as we call it in Czech, now that we have reclaimed it. He always maintained that the bit about the wolf eating the grandmother had a particular significance and terror for him, whose own grandparents had all died sudden and violent deaths. He believed this was a powerful formative influence. This I can believe – you only have to look at his films. But I'm rushing ahead again into the future.

First came the horror stories.

Now I am of the opinion, as you will know if you have read the right publications, that horror stories are not necessarily harmful to children. They can, in fact, exert a healthy influence upon them if everything comes out all right in the end and provided they do not become confused with real-life horror. The child lies in bed listening to his mother telling the story and feels a not unpleasurable thrill of terror as the wolf moves in for the kill. But the woodcutter arrives in the nick of time and cuts off the wolf's head and chops open its belly and the grandmother jumps out alive and kicking. The mother kisses the child goodnight and tucks him into his warm bed and he knows it is just a story and feels safe and secure.

This was not the case with Adam. In Adam's case reality and fantasy became dangerously confused. When he was eight years old, Liza Epstein was drowned in a boating accident while on a camping holiday in the Rockies. The body was swept away by the current and they did not recover it for several days. Adam was not permitted to see his dead mother because, he told me later, she had been partly eaten by bears.

19

But this, too, might be a product of his dark imaginings.

When I first met him he told me he could barely remember her and he claimed to know little of his German heritage. But she left him a legacy of fear and enchantment, a darkly complex vision of his own and his country's past. When I met him he was already halfway there: prepared, receptive, open to suggestion.

Picture him at twenty-two, on his first trip to postwar, reconstructed Europe, in the vanguard of the blue-jeaned hordes who were shortly to become its new conquerors. He had his mother's grey-green eyes, moss green like the forest, and his father's blond hair, though worn considerably longer than was the fashion in Nazi Germany or in my own Cold War Prague. He was almost six foot tall with frank, open features and a confident air. People noticed him in the street. You may take it that people did not look this confident or this open in Prague in the late sixties. Nor, if you looked more closely, did Adam. The eyes were curious, yes, but also a little wary, the smile a little too ready: he meant it to be disarming. He wore a brown suede jacket with several political badges in the lapel which advertised his status as a serious participant, a player on the world stage. He did not know it then, but he was about to be pitched into a greater drama than he had imagined and not of his devising.

It was the winter of '67 and he had come to Prague as delegate from the University of Berkeley to an international conference of students which was widely rumoured to be funded by the KGB. We were at that paranoid stage of the Cold War when either the KGB or the CIA were alleged to be the secret paymasters of everything and everyone of significance in the world and quite a few things of no significance at all, like student conferences.

Adam, at this stage in his history, considered himself to be a revolutionary socialist. He was also a romantic. The two are not incompatible and Prague exerted a powerful pull on his romantic imagination.

Picture him, then, as he walks the narrow streets of the ancient city and climbs the endless stairways between the soaring spires and the dark watchtowers with their even darker windows and their hidden watchers . . .

4

THE CARETAKER OF PRAGUE

He is waiting for Christ and his apostles. They come out on the hour every hour, regular as clockwork, and Christ pauses for a moment and waves. Also there is Death and a cock that crows. Adam has been assured of this by the guide. It is five minutes to the hour. He waits patiently outside the old town hall in the middle of the crowd with his eyes fixed on the large hands of the clock. A hatch above the figure XII conceals the apostles. Death, in the form of a skeleton with scythe, waits patiently in the bottom left-hand corner of the picture.

Adam is not so patient. He is, in truth, a little bored. Though not as bored as he'd been in the conference hall, which was why he'd sloped off to join one of the official tours of the city. He has followed his leader through the winding streets of the old town, crossed the Charles Bridge with its black and brooding saints and climbed the ancient stairway to the imperial castle where the Red emperors now rule. It has been something of a disappointment. He has read the history. He knows of the city's violent past and he wants to see the bodies. And if they've cleared the bodies away long ago, he wants to see the lampposts they hanged them from or the windows they pushed them out of. He wants to see the blood on the stones. But all he has seen is stones. And now he is waiting to see Christ.

The minute hand of the great clock jumps a step closer to the hour. Adam becomes aware of a distraction. His immediate neighbours are not looking at the clock. They are looking, with increasing concern, at the sky. The statue of Jan Hus in the middle of the square is pointing his craggy finger at a mass of cloud, the colour of pitch, that advances upon the city like an army out of the east. Within moments it is upon them.

The attack is heralded with a single flash of lightning and an enormous clap of thunder and then the rain comes, all at once with no warning drops, and the crowd scatters, without discipline, regardless of the promptings of their marshals and indifferent to the apostolic procession which has just begun. The disciples glare, Christ blesses, the cock crows, Death wields his scythe, all unnoticed. Humanity, as usual, has other things on its mind.

Adam joins the rush for shelter but there are no welcoming cafés, no shops to linger in, not even a doorway deep enough to provide a meagre cover. The narrow streets have become swollen streams, rushing between baroque canyons, fed by a thousand torrents from gutter and gargoyle. He is swept into a mean quarter of the city, well off the beaten track of the official tours, its streets a little narrower and more sinister, until he emerges into a small square, dark and sombre as a prison yard, flanked by gloomy and neglected apartments. Directly opposite is a church.

It is not a church that features in the guidebooks, even had they not been so clearly biased against this particular form of architecture, and as an attraction it has little to recommend it. The sea-grey stones are stained with rust like the hull of an old battleship, the saintly statues and grotesques have been weathered to a featureless obscurity. But Adam is not overly concerned with its aesthetic merits. He does not notice the statue of St Michael the Archangel, even, with his avenging sword, and would not recognise him if he did. He splashes across the waterlogged square and up the worn stone steps to the sanctuary of the porch.

And there he might have stayed, for the porch provides shelter enough, but something prompts him to try the door and rather to his surprise it opens. He steps in.

The interior is about as comforting as the tomb and almost as chill. But not as lifeless, quite. At the far end of the nave, beside a pyramid of guttering candles, there is a huddle of black shawls. It emits a sound. A mumble jumble of words from deep in the throat with vaguely discernible crooning rhythms. The rosary. The door slams behind him with a loud bang and the chant terminates abruptly. He confronts the white sheep's faces in the gloom. For a moment he imagines he has disturbed a coven of witches at some demonic rite and that they will come flying at him with their sharp talons and their wild hair and force him to flee like poor Tam but without the benefit of a mare. But the faces turn back to the altar and the dirge resumes, stronger than before, though with a new note of anxiety, he thinks, almost of desperation, as if his appearance has reminded them that there is not much time left and they have a lot of praying still to do.

He sits down in a pew near the door, miserably aware of how wet he is. Suede is not a material to be worn in rain. He feels like a chamois leather waiting to be wrung out and wiped across a window. Then he becomes aware of another sound. At first he thinks it must be the rain falling on the roof, but it isn't; it is the rain falling *through* the roof. It streams down the walls in several places and a single constant drip hits the pew in front of him and explodes in a fine spray.

He does not know what makes him stay. The only source of warmth in the entire church appears to be the row of candles in front of the old women. It is like a waiting room for a consultation with Death. Adam does not wish to wait for Death. He wishes Death to take him by surprise, preferably while leading the masses in a reckless charge across the barricades. He does not wish to join these crooning crones in their doleful vigil. The rain outside is infinitely preferable. And yet he sits there, feeling the wet soak through his jeans and into his crutch, too enervated or depressed to move.

He hears the slam of the door again and turns, with the women, to perceive a tall figure in a long raincoat and a broad-brimmed hat, whose arms appear to be threaded through a number of galvanised iron buckets. In one hand it clutches an umbrella, in the other a mop. It looks to Adam like some strange visitation of the rain god, conjured up by his chanting companions. Before his bemused gaze it clanks its way across to the wall, places one of the buckets under the nearest drip and proceeds around the nave, gradually divesting itself of hardware and sloshing the water about with the mop until it reaches the pew immediately in front of him. Dark eyes survey him from beneath the sodden brim of the hat. The face is lean, unshaven, saturnine. It speaks. Unintelligibly.

Adam shakes his head and stammers his phrase for not speaking the language.

'*Deutsch?*' it enquires.

Adam shakes his head again.

'English? American?'

'American,' replies Adam.

The head tilts slightly to one side, throwing a little more light on one eye. Adam is reminded of a blackbird contemplating the tail end of a rather sickly worm and wondering if it is worth the trouble of pulling from the ground.

'You are very wet.'

The apparition clearly has the gift of tongues. Nor does it trouble to whisper. The gravelly voice echoes around the cavernous interior. Adam senses the crabbed disapprobation of the women. He replies, in his own gentler tones, that he came here for shelter.

The eye wanders to the cascading walls – the buckets are a wholly inadequate remedy – and down the length of the aisle to the secret worshippers. It returns to Adam.

'*Kommen*,' he says, forgetfully slipping into German. *Kommen*, beckoning with the hand . . .

Then, in English, 'Yes, come with me. I have a little room across the square where there is a stove. You will be more comfortable there and your clothes will dry.'

Without waiting for a reply, he sets off for the door. After a moment's hesitation, Adam follows, if only to politely decline the offer and seek directions back to his hotel. He joins his would-be benefactor in the porch, confronting the unrelenting rain. Before he can speak, the mop is thrust into his hand.

'Please to hold for me, while I open the umbrella.'

He looks younger than he did inside the church, not much older than Adam, but there is something curiously ageless about his features and each seems to be slightly exaggerated – the long, straight nose, the thick, dark eyebrows, the deep, intense eyes, the wide mouth – as if they are individually determined to be noticed, to make their mark. The overall effect is of a long, rather mournful face, animated by the eyes, like the face of an ascetic monk, Adam thinks, in an icon. Then he smiles and is instantly transformed into something far more human and engaging.

'My name is Milan,' he says, 'Milan Kubanicek.'

And thus we met. The description is Adam's, wrung from him in later years, when we became more intimate. A hungry blackbird, an ascetic monk? Well, I have lost thirteen kilos since I came to this place so perhaps you can see the resemblance. My self-portrait is more Puckish. I prefer the alternative image that came to his mind as we splashed across the waterlogged square under my umbrella. It was of the faun in the book by C. S. Lewis, *The Lion, the Witch and the Wardrobe*, who invites strangers back to his den deep in the forest and feeds them tea and cakes and lulls them to sleep with the playing of a flute so he can betray them to the wolves of the secret police.

My own intentions, I regret, were less honourable.

I led him to an apartment block across the square from the church.

An apartment block. Such a neutral description that invites so many subjective interpretations. The mind plays with fantasies of Manhattan, Paris, even Berlin.

No.

Imagine, instead, a decaying tooth. A carious molar in a mouth that has not seen dentistry for half a century or more.

We entered the main cavity through a portal in a pair of massive wooden doors that had once been painted green. From this tunnel smaller drillings and fissures led off to right and left, with garbage cans placed at intervals for whatever rotting matter was extruded from them, and at the far end there was a courtyard, enclosed on all sides but with a hole into the sky through which the rain poured. To a jaundiced eye, I imagine it looked slightly less charming than the kind of courtyard where KGB torturers led their prisoners when they weren't any fun any more and dispatched them with a single shot in the back of the neck.

My apartment opened directly on to this vista.

'What is this place?' I heard Adam say, with a note of awe, as I jangled my keys. I told him it was owned by the University of Prague and used as accommodation for the students.

'I am the caretaker,' I said.

I opened the door and noted with relief that the fire was still alight in the stove.

'Please,' I said, inviting him in with a gracious gesture. 'You may, if you wish, remove your trousers.'

He did not appear to hear so I let it pass for the time being. I have never been fastidious about such things and the furniture was not so precious that a little damp would hurt.

My quarters were then a single room which combined the functions of kitchen, bedchamber and study. I shared a bathroom with six students on the same floor. But I had made it homely enough, I think, with my books and some photographs and even a few framed prints on the walls.

I opened the cage of the stove and fed it some coal. It was of that quality which, unbeknown to us, was then in the process of polluting half Europe. The small, cheerful glow was instantly stifled. I seized a poker and attacked it as if it were some elemental manifestation of my oppression. A miserable tongue of yellow flame licked at the brown mulch and I shut the door on it and threw the poker down with a curse.

Adam was looking at me with some alarm. I smiled.

'Tea?' I said. I measured a few of my remaining grains into the kettle.

Adam was examining my shelves of books, which included a number of English and German titles.

'Do you make a study of psychology?' he asked, rather as if it might be an eccentric hobby.

'I used to teach it,' I remarked, without irony, 'at the university.'

It was a deliberate conceit and his confusion was gratifying.

'I was dismissed from my position for my failure to appreciate fully the significance and achievements of Marxist-Leninism,' I told him, 'a necessary qualification for the teaching of psychology in our country, or of any other subject, and so I have embarked upon a new career as caretaker, extending my dominions to take in the neighbouring church and a small bakery. I have hopes of obtaining the post of boilerman and chief bottlewasher at the glue factory in Brno when the present incumbent, a cousin, retires in a few years.'

In fact I doubt if my English was quite up to that level of eloquence, or pomposity, at this stage of my development but this was the gist of what I told him.

His confusion increased.

He moved from the books to the photographs. There were one or two of my mother, in her days as a starlet. Not, thankfully, in her nun's costume. This proved a useful diversion for him. I told him about my mother's film career, or at least, those bits I felt were suitable for his ears. He told me then that he lived in Hollywood and that movies were a particular interest of his. He meant, of course, a complete passion.

I encouraged him to talk about himself. Even then, I had that facility. I urged him to draw up his chair to the fire. We became quite cosy, Adam almost garrulous.

'Are you warm yet,' I enquired, during a small pause in the flow, 'or would you like to go to bed?'

He smiled. I expect he thought it was a joke. 'Excuse me?' he said.

I repeated the invitation in what I hoped was a more seductive tone.

He shook his head, still smiling, though a little bemusedly. 'I don't think so,' he said.

I shrugged philosophically, though it was a disappointment. 'I hope you are not offended,' I said.

'Not at all,' he said. But he talked less volubly and a few minutes later he looked at his watch and wondered if he should be returning to his hotel.

'I will show you the way,' I said and put my coat on.

Outside the rain had turned to snow. Great soft white globs of it, not quite bonding yet to the wet streets. Adam was delighted. Snow is less enchanting if you are a caretaker but I took him on a small diversion so we could walk along the river.

The little light was fading from the sky and the floodlights had come on to illuminate the castle on its hill high above the city. This had been the palace of the Winter Queen, the beautiful Elizabeth of Bohemia, daughter of King James of England and Scotland, who had come here as a young bride to reign for a brief season before the Catholics kicked her out. Half of Middle Europe had died in the war to put her back.

I did not tell him this story, then. Instead I told him the story of King Karl and his Big Idea.

King Karl had ruled over vast territories that spread from the Black Sea to the Baltic but they were all in bits and pieces, like a jigsaw that no one could put together, comprising many different peoples, speaking many different languages. So he thought about this problem: what could he do to unite his people? And he came up with the Big Idea. He decided to make a myth, a romantic fairy tale. He built a magnificent castle with two hundred turrets, each capped with a tall spire. And flags, he put out hundreds and hundreds of flags. And he had a splendid crown made for himself and robes spun from cloth of gold and encrusted with jewels. And he surrounded himself with courtiers and made them all into dukes and counts and landgraves and margraves and knights and squires. And he invented a code of chivalry for them to live by and gave them quests and tournaments and even the occasional small war to keep them from growing bored. And he insisted they all live in his palace at a level of magnificence that quickly impoverished them and forced them to live off his bounty, which came from the taxes they paid, and they all competed for the honours that came from being in service to him. And his court became renowned throughout Europe and even the poorest peasant in the most distant province was proud that he belonged to such an empire and had such a famous and magnificent ruler.

This was the story I told Adam as we stood by the river with the snow drifting down in the floodlights. I don't suppose he recognised it as a seminal influence at the time. Besides, he had a far less prosaic reason for remembering this particular evening.

Between the river and Wenceslas Square where he was staying, there is a labyrinth of cobbled streets containing a number of bierkellers. Adam paused for a moment beneath one of the ancient wooden signs. There was a lamp in an iron cage above the door and its light gave a yellow tinge to his features and to the snow that was in his hair. Why do I remember this so clearly, almost thirty years later? Because it was one of those moments on which so much else turned?

And yet if he had not met her then, he could easily have met her back at the hotel, or at the conference centre . . .

There is another story I will tell you, even if you have heard it before. It has been told by Somerset Maugham and also by Boris Karloff in a film by Peter Bogdanovich:

A servant is jostled by a woman in the marketplace in Baghdad and when he turns he sees that she is Death. Death looks at him strangely and raises her hands in what appears to be a threatening gesture. The servant flees in terror to his master's house and borrows his horse and rides like fury for the city of Samarra where he thinks Death will not find him. Meanwhile his master goes to the marketplace and finds Death and asks her, 'Why did you threaten my servant this morning?' And Death replies, 'I did not threaten him. It was only a gesture of surprise for I did not expect to see him in Baghdad. I had an appointment with him tonight in Samarra.'

'I think I'd like a beer,' said Adam. 'Do you have time?'

We went in. A wave of noise and heat. A flight of worn stone steps descending into a sweating vault. I knew the place. It was a favourite haunt of students, had been since the Middle Ages. A bear pit has more elegance. A brass band would have been lost in the din. Waiters steered great trays of beer with one hand, the other scribbling orders on soggy scraps of pad. A number of the inmates mouthed invitations for me to join them and shoved up to make room on the long benches. I enjoyed a certain popularity in those days among a certain set.

I bawled introductions. Two foaming jugs were set before us. Adam was an immediate focus of interest. They began to interrogate him in their brave but mutilated English. Russian was then the second language taught in the schools and English was learned with difficulty and more as an act of adolescent rebellion than out of a desire for self-improvement. I was frequently called upon to translate. Adam found it easier to converse in German, which they spoke more fluently but with less enthusiasm. He leaned over the table, screwing up his face in an agony of incomprehension. Hot, flushed faces swayed towards him out of the smoke, smelling of beer and cheap tobacco. He broke off the engagement to ask the way to the washroom.

I watched him struggle through the crowded tables. Swaying clear of one of the juggernaut waiters, he nudged someone's arm and spilled an appreciable quantity of beer over a youth in a leather jacket. The victim half rose from his seat, raising his arm, his face angry. And then I saw that it was not a man, but a woman. She was as young as anyone in the room, barely eighteen, I thought, and her hair was styled in what was then called an urchin cut in the West. Her face was thin with high cheekbones. Only her eyes and her mouth, which was very full, betrayed her sex.

Adam apologised and she turned back to the table and he

continued on his way to the washroom. And that was that. I was drawn into some shouted conversation and forgot about the incident. But a few minutes later I looked up and saw that Adam had returned and was standing at the woman's table, talking to her and her companions.

After a while he came over to me and said they were delegates to the same conference – from East Germany – and that they were staying at a hotel near to his.

'They're just heading back for supper,' he said, 'so I can go with them if you like.'

I nodded. I gathered this was his preference.

We shook hands.

'If you have any time before you leave Prague,' I said, 'perhaps you would let me show you some parts of the city that are not on the official tours.'

It was a parting gesture, really. I was surprised by his enthusiasm for the idea. We arranged to meet at the clock in the old town square at one o'clock the following day.

When I left the bierkeller, the snow had formed a thick pie crust over the rooftops and was still falling steadily. I felt a disinclination to return to my apartment. Instead I walked to Wenceslas Square and without any conscious design found myself outside the hotel where Adam was staying. I knew I could not go in. I was a marked man and the place would be well watched.

Then, as I stood in the shadows, under a skeletal tree in the centre of the square, I saw Adam come out with a group of what were presumably his fellow delegates. One of them was the woman he had met in the bierkeller. They started a snow fight. The sound of their laughter drifted across to where I stood. Then he took her hand and they ran off down the street. I remember thinking at the time that it was odd that she had so much freedom to mix with Americans. But it was a bitter thought and doubtless came from my loneliness.

5

ESCAPE

I didn't expect him to turn up the next day, but I waited all the same. I was feeling sorry for myself. Also, I had a strong idea I was being watched. This was not unusual, nor even alarming. Mostly you took it for granted and got on with whatever it was you were doing and hoped that if it was illegal, which it probably was, they would lose the paperwork, which they probably did.

Once, years later, I came back to Prague when Havel was president of what was still, then, Czechoslovakia. He still lived in the same apartment he had always lived in, which had been his father's, down by the river opposite an ancient Gothic watertower. One day he took me inside to show me the room where they had watched him for all the years he was an enemy of the people. It was high in the tower behind a locked door. There was a chair by the window and a bed in the corner. There were cigarette butts all over the floor. And on the opposite side from the window they had erected a crude device for the relief of nature which consisted of a tin funnel and a plastic tube which went out of another tiny window above the river. They must have spent years in that room, in shifts, round the clock, simply watching his apartment and smoking and peeing into the tin funnel. Why? Well, I suppose they were keeping track of his visitors. But they would have known them all anyway. Václav told me he would have gladly kept a visitor's book for them if they had asked and people could have signed it with their comments. But then this would have deprived them of their reason for existence. They must have filled whole offices with the paperwork for this one operation alone. I wonder if anyone ever read it.

I mention this partly, of course, to let you know that I was once the consort of presidents, not pigs, but also as an illustration of this feeling we always had of being on a stage with a hidden and hostile audience. It was not always unpleasant. It could, at times, be exhilarating. It dramatised, as it were, our small lives. Well, there was little enough in the way of commercial entertainment. So, when I saw Adam hurrying across the square through the groups of tourists, only ten minutes late, I became affected with a sense of occasion. I felt like putting on a performance, playing to the gallery. There was also an element of self-preservation at work for, despite my attempts at careless disregard, I was conscious of the risk I was taking. One was obliged to report all conversation with foreigners, certainly with Americans. I had no intention of doing so. This was undoubtedly an act of treason. So I studiously ignored Adam's approach until he stood next to me.

'Hello,' he said. 'Sorry I'm late. The last debate went on and on.'

I turned, feigning surprise.

'I am going to give you some directions,' I said. 'Go to the end of the square – ' I turned and pointed. 'Turn right at the church there and you will see two streets facing you. Take the street on the left. It leads to a small cemetery. Please wait for me there.'

He looked a trifle bemused, as well he might.

'Thank me now,' I said, 'and go.'

He thanked me and went. I hung around for a few more minutes and then set off in the opposite direction. It is

36

not difficult to lose a pursuer in the old city and I was well practised in the art. One does, of course, have to accept that the pursuer might have been entirely in one's imagination.

I waited for a moment or two at the gateway to the walled cemetery, looking back down the street, but no one appeared. Adam was waiting for me inside, a solitary figure among the gravestones. I apologised for keeping him waiting and told him I had been shaking off the secret police. He seemed to take this in his stride.

'What is this place?' he asked me.

I told him it was the old Jewish cemetery. It had been here for over four hundred years. You could still see the dates on some of the stones. There was scarcely space to move between them, they were so tightly crammed, sticking up at all angles out of the bare, brown earth. For all those years the Jews of Prague had buried their dead here, generation heaped upon generation. The individuals died but the collective survived. It survived through good years and bad, legitimised beyond question by the continuity of these stones. Then in a few months in 1942, the year of my conception, it was erased, its people removed to a distant concentration camp and obliterated. All that remained were a few empty synagogues, preserved as museums, and this graveyard with its tangle of ossified roots. I had been here before, many times. It was one of those rare places that made me aware of the terrible force that had been unleashed. You felt that the stones cried out to you, a collective cry of the soul from ancestors who had been robbed of their descendants, their worshippers, their mourners. I think I told Adam this, either then or shortly afterwards. I did not then know of his German parentage or of his Jewish stepfather. I did not know of his inherited guilt. I did not know he would enshrine this place in his memory so that his own gestures of atonement would henceforth be made with a conscious genuflection to a circle of weathered stones in a walled cemetery in Prague.

I took him for lunch to the U Golemi where they served grilled carp from the ponds of south Bohemia and a reasonable wine, for the country. He offered to pay. I accepted without shame. My earnings as a caretaker were not substantial and he had made it clear that he was no poor student. He had told me the previous day that his father was a lawyer in Hollywood. Now he told me the rest of the story. It was clear to me, even then, that he had a romantic obsession with his past and with Europe. It was like a love affair that gave him at least as much pain as pleasure but from which it was impossible to extricate himself.

Like his affair with Magda. That was the name of the girl he had met in the bierkeller: Magda Krenkel. I say 'affair'. I'm not sure that this was the correct technical term at this stage of their acquaintance but it was clearly heading that way. She was from Leipzig in East Germany but not, it appeared, a delegate to the conference. She was teaching German conversation to language students at Prague University for a year before she started her own degree course back in Germany.

We met once more before he went back to America. He promised to write. I did not expect him to, but he did. He wrote to say that he planned to return to Prague in the spring. I did not delude myself that I was the attraction. He came to see Magda. But we did spend a couple of days together – at Mariánské Lázně, the town of my birth. My mother had died several years before but we stayed with an old friend of hers who was like an aunt to me. There was a late snow and we went trail skiing in the woods and came home to a log fire and hot spiced beer and potatoes boiled in their skins, which we ate with melted cheese. It was here that he first told me about his German heritage and his mother's life in Berlin in the last days of the war and after, in Year Zero. It was the first time

I gave any conscious thought to that city. The associations, even then, were with Death.

Prague, on the other hand, was the city of life, of rebirth. It was the spring of our liberation, or so we thought, and I had become involved in one of the democratic committees then flourishing in the city. We used to hold our meetings at the writers' and artists' centre in the Manes Building on the river. It was always packed with students and I saw Magda there a few times. We were aware of each other's presence though we never spoke. Some of my friends were suspicious of her. They thought she was an informer, or even an agent of the East German secret police, the Stasi, but I thought then that it was just their prejudice against Germans. It was only later I remembered and wondered if they were right.

Adam was back again for his summer vacation. I was too involved in politics to see much of him even if he had wanted to see me. But when we did meet – for lunch at the Three Ostriches by the Charles Bridge – it was Adam who was preoccupied. I am afraid I was too busy talking politics to notice at first. But when I did and asked him if anything was the matter, he told me that Magda was pregnant.

He was devastated. I gathered that her charms had begun to pall and he had intended to discontinue the affair. Now he didn't know what to do. She was apparently determined to have the child.

I was surprised. I hardly knew her, of course, but she had not seemed to me to be the maternal type and it was much easier then to procure an abortion in Eastern Europe than it was in the West. I am afraid I thought that she was using the pregnancy to maintain her hold over him. I am aware that this is a misogynist view but Magda Krenkel brought out the worst in me.

I told him that if he was not in love with her it would be a disservice to everyone concerned, including the child, if he offered to marry her.

He said, 'So what do I do – fuck off back to LA and leave her to deal with it on her own?'

I said, 'Very well, stay until the baby is born. Longer if you must. But if you don't love her, sooner or later, it will end in tears.'

He said, 'I did think I was in love with her once. Maybe if I stay . . .'

I didn't have to say anything. He knew he was deluding himself but Adam could only play the romantic hero and he would play it to the bitter end.

Fortunately for him, if not for my country, there were other players waiting in the wings with a far more important role to perform. We had our conversation on Monday 19 August. On the morning of the 21st I awoke to the news of the Russian invasion.

I took to the streets with the rest of my friends. We mobbed the metal monsters, hurling our stones at their armoured hides and our eloquence at the men inside them. Both weapons were equally futile. History was against us. We were twenty years premature. You know this story already perhaps and it is not one I wish to recount in any detail; I would be too depressed and there are reasons enough to be depressed in this place without these memories. All that matters here is that on the third day after the invasion I was at the Manes Centre when Adam and Magda showed up. Someone said that the Czech border guards were letting people cross into West Germany and Adam said we should go – he and Magda and I. We could both live with him in Hollywood, he said. He was high on beer and adventure and I was not inclined to take him seriously. But then the arrests began.

Adam bought a motorbike and sidecar. He drove, I rode

pillion. Magda sat in the sidecar with our suitcases. The Three Companions.

We drove to the border and joined a long line of vehicles waiting to cross. It seemed, from what we heard, that the guards were kindly disposed but old habits die hard and they were taking their time letting people through. Magda said she was desperate to use the washroom. Finally, she got out of the sidecar and walked on ahead to the border station. We continued to crawl forwards with the traffic. When it came to our turn, there was still no sign of Magda. Adam parked and went to look for her. After ten minutes or so he came back. He couldn't find her anywhere, he said. He had even been inside the ladies' washroom and there was no sign of her.

I was by then in a state of some considerable agitation. It was growing dark and there was hardly anyone else waiting to go through. I thought this was ominous. Then one of the guards came over and told me there was talk of closing the border. On the road behind us I saw the lights of a convoy of trucks.

Adam said, 'Take the bike. Go.'

I said, 'Adam, I can't drive.'

Adam said, 'Shit.'

It was nearly a kilometre to the West German border post.

I said, 'It's all right. I'll walk.'

I took my suitcase out of the sidecar. It was very heavy, for I had filled it with books. I began to walk. I was conscious of the noise of truck engines and when I looked back I saw the red stars in the harsh floodlights of the border post. I didn't look back again, I just kept on walking, changing my suitcase from hand to hand after every few steps. I believe I was sobbing. It seemed an awfully long way to the lights of the German border post.

I heard the engine noise coming closer.

41

It was Adam on the motorbike. He said, 'Get in.'

I said, 'What about Magda?'

He said, 'I'll go back for her. Get in.'

He dropped me off at the German border and drove straight back. I waited for an hour before I saw the lights of the bike coming back. He was alone. They wouldn't let him in, he said. They'd closed the border and the place was crawling with Russian troops.

Adam wrote to Magda and after a few weeks he had a letter back, mailed from Leipzig. Its tone was cold. She said that when she'd come out of the washroom she couldn't find us. She accused him of abandoning her. She'd been arrested by the Czech police, she said, and sent back to Germany. Adam wrote back. I'm not sure what he said but he told me he would find some way of getting her out to the West.

Her next letter was even colder. She said if he wished to be with her he should come to live in the German Democratic Republic. Otherwise, she was confident the workers' state would provide for a young mother and her child better than any husband in the West.

He wondered if she had been forced to write it, or if this was some kind of revenge for his abandonment of her. I am afraid he was that much of an egotist, even then.

'You did not abandon her,' I said.

'So what happened to her?' he said.

But that I couldn't tell him.

'I could go to Leipzig,' he said.

I did not think there was any real danger of that.

Adam was a romantic but he knew where his future lay and it was not in the German Democratic Republic.

She stopped answering his letters. Eventually they were returned unopened. She had moved from Leipzig leaving no forwarding address. But a few months later she sent him a card, postmarked East Berlin, to say that she'd had a son and that both she and the child were well. He did not know if this was a kindness or a rebuke.

He was racked with guilt but I had my own guilt to deal with at the time. It was the guilt of the survivor for by then I knew that my country was back in the depths of winter and that most of my friends were in prison while I sat in the sunshine beside Sam Epstein's swimming pool in Hollywood . . .

6

THE TERRIBLE HEAD DRAGON

Yes, I went to Hollywood.

Well, where else was I to go? Adam was there and he was my only friend in the world outside Czechoslovakia.

His stepfather, Sam, the former Captain Epstein, was by then one of the top contracts lawyers for the film industry. He fixed me up with a room and some money and a job – teaching psychology part time at UCLA. He knew a professor there who was sympathetic.

There was a lot of sympathy in those days for the poor Czechs, the victims of brutal Soviet aggression whose brief flowering of democracy had been crushed by the Red Army tanks. But to cash in on it you had to be a long way from home. So wasn't I the lucky one? I did very well out of the Czech spring and the cold winter that followed. If you discount the guilt. And even the guilt could be turned to advantage. In an attempt to come to terms with it I went into therapy and ended up a therapist myself and, believe me, there was no more lucrative place in the world to be a therapist than Hollywood in the early seventies.

It was a time when women had discovered feminism and men had begun to discover the feminine side of their nature. This made them more acceptable to women and less harmful to the world but it did not seem to make them any happier.

45

I know this is not the point but it made some of them very unhappy, which is why they came to me. Possibly their unhappiness stemmed from the continuing influence of fifties man, represented by the Incredible Hulk in the movies of that time and persisting in political and commercial life to this day. Or perhaps it went back much further than that. But whatever the reason, the men who came to me were often confused about their role in life and so when I had listened to them I sometimes told them stories.

The story I told most often was about the Wild Man who was found lying at the bottom of a pool in the forest and brought back to the castle and placed in a cage in the courtyard. The king locked the door of the cage and gave the key to the queen, who put it under her pillow. But one day their eight-year-old son was playing in the courtyard with a golden ball and it bounced into the cage of the Wild Man. So the boy asked the Wild Man, would he give him back his ball, and the Wild Man said, 'Only if you let me out of the cage.' The little boy thought about this for a while and eventually he made his mind up and stole the key from under his mother's pillow and let the Wild Man out of his cage, and the Wild Man took him on his shoulder and carried him into the forest.

Well, I need not interpret this story for you, a pig of your sagacity. All I will say is that in some of the legends, Merlin, or Myrddin, was also the Wild Man of the forest, so it is not surprising that I was so fond of recounting it. I am not sure that it did any good but I did my best.

Merlin, my mentor, the demidemon after whom I was named, would have felt quite at home here, I'm sure.

In one of the stories, he attempts to instruct his young protégé, the future king, in various aspects of the human condition. Failing to interest him in his exposition, he turns him first into an owl, then a fish, then an ant, and projects him into the several worlds of these creatures, not to punish him or to teach him natural history but to give him a better understanding of human nature, to learn by analogy.

I thought this was very clever when I read about it but in Hollywood he need not have taken such trouble. He need only have set his sign up on the wall and the entire human menagerie would have beaten a path to his door eager to display every aspect of behaviour, every excess, every inhibition except that of keeping silent.

If I sound cynical, I'm sorry. Some of my clients, I'm sure, came in search of self-knowledge but many more came for less legitimate reasons: because it was fashionable, because I was fashionable, the saturnine Dr Kubanicek from Middle Europe who told fairy stories but more often simply sat and listened and did not interrupt but only nodded and stroked his beard and granted his benign absolution so they could feel better about behaving badly and go out with their souls freshly laundered to sin again . . .

I do sound cynical. Perhaps it is this place. Perhaps it was Hollywood.

Sam sent many of his famous clients to me. The contracts lawyer and the psychotherapist made a profitable partnership. In the land of blind egos, the guide dogs get to chew on the juiciest bones. Headshrinker to the stars, they called me in the scandal sheets during the trial. Or more simply, the Starshrink. They used other names after the verdict but I do not wish to go into that now, except to say that I sometimes wonder if that is why I came to be here. I misused my powers and the spirit who jealously guards them and grants them as a rare gift to his chosen ones was angered and this is how he has chosen to punish me.

But I did not stay in Hollywood all those years for the money. You can snort all you like but I stayed because of

Adam. I was his confidant, his counsellor and, after Sam died, his oldest friend.

Not his therapist, nor, contrary to persistent rumour, his lover.

Adam had his lovers, many of them, all women, and I had mine, not so many but not so exclusive as to gender. I was never promiscuous and, though we failed to convince the jury, I had been celibate for many years prior to the offence. I . . . lost interest. My interest was in other people's affairs. I lived vicariously through the emotional traumas, the neuroses and psychoses of those who came to me for help. And I had Adam, who was closer than any lover.

I am bound to believe that I gave him something he needed and could get from no one else, man or woman. What was it? A distillation of many things but I think the strongest element was a womblike sense of security and of being loved for himself.

Sam once described to me the apartment in the half-derelict Berlin block where Liza lived after she came out of the tower. This was Adam's home for the first two years of his life: one high-ceilinged room six metres by four and a half which combined the functions of living room, bedroom and kitchen. Inevitably, it was cramped and cluttered with the ragamuffin clothes and rubbish-tip belongings of a young woman and her child struggling to survive in postwar Berlin, but Sam said it had an air of cosy eccentricity and, almost unbelievably in that place at that time, security. There was an old tiled stove that burned whatever fuel Liza could lay her hands on and doubled up as a crude cooker. There was a shelf for her medical texts, a table, as often as not littered with papers, and on the walls a few small pictures that had been given her by one of her patients.

Though there must have been many differences of detail – I had no diapers hanging from a line – in atmosphere and scale I believe it was not unlike my own little *conciergerie* in the neglected back streets of Prague. And the model I tried to recreate in my clinic in LA.

I had been obliged to leave most of my possessions behind, of course, but I gradually replaced most of the books and I bought some paintings and had others given to me by patients, including a collection of interesting charcoal sketches of scenes from *Hansel and Gretel*: darkly interwoven with the roots and branches of trees, the latticework of windows, the wicker bars of the witch's cage, with the children imprisoned within.

I even bought a good wood-burning stove.

In this environment, Adam clearly felt at home. He came here from his palace in North Rockingham, his outdoor locations, his vast, interior studios where he prowled restlessly like a beast in the circus ring, and here he would sit, tranquil, still, only his eyes roaming, taking in the objects of my room with satisfaction but also a faint, initial anxiety to be reassured that no one had moved them in his absence and they were still as he remembered them.

He went into films within a year of our escape from Prague. Sam's contacts again, of course. He started as a runner on a John Huston movie called *Sinful Davey* and Huston took a shine to him. Or maybe he just liked a privileged college kid with a lawyer father to kick around the set, it was difficult to tell with Huston. Either way, he took him on as his personal gofer on his next movie, *A Walk with Love and Death*. Then Sam lent him the money to make *The Feud*. But you can read all about this in any one of half a dozen biographies and movie magazines; I don't want to go into it now. All I will add to the story of Adam Epstein's rise to glory is this: almost every one of the films he made is rooted in the folk tales of the European forests. No matter that they are set in an American city or the Atlantic Ocean or the star system Alpha Globular, they are variations of the same old fairy tales, the

Märchen he learned at his mother's knee or, before that, in the womb.

So *Cape Death* is the story of a killer shark and a fisherman and a beautiful marine biologist from Cape Hatteras but it is also the story of the wolf and the woodcutter and Little Red Riding Hood. *Starky* is about an alien that looks like a child's toy, plays tricks on people, gets into terrible scrapes but ends up making a lonely old man very happy. Based on the story of Pinocchio. All right, I agree it does not follow the plot exactly but that is not the point. The point is that Adam's movies appeal to the same deep psychological needs and desires as the child's bedtime fairy tales and to the same fascination with the sinister, the terrifying and the grotesque. I speak as a therapist and not as a film critic but there you are, which are you more inclined to believe?

And his life was like a fairy tale, too. A series of adventures paid for by the dream factory.

Think of it. For centuries the princes who were Adam's forebears had hired artists to entertain them. Minstrels and storytellers, jesters and jongleurs, illusionists of every description had been invited to their palaces to perform their magic tricks, to provide a brief glimpse into another world, an escape from reality, from the cares of state . . . And afterwards they'd be given a few coins and some scraps from the kitchen and a place to lie down in the straw. Well, now the prince had been forced by necessity to become an entertainer but in the meantime the entertainers had become princes. More than that, they had become emperors, they had become gods, they had become legends . . . Dreams fetch a high price these days; the demand to escape from reality must be so much greater.

Brecht, who was in the same racket for a while, put it rather differently. For him, it was 'the marketplace where lies are bought'. And he the hopeful pedlar.

What is the difference between a lie and a dream? Do you know, little pig?

It was inevitable, sooner or later, that Adam would want to make the story of King Arthur, which is the greatest fairy tale of them all.

Or the story of Merlin, which is how I tend to think of it. I told you how it started, did I not, with the virgin and the Devil, but not why.

It was a conspiracy, hatched in Hell.

The aim was to bring into the world an Anti-Christ by whose evil powers humanity would be brought to destruction. But by great good fortune, when the child Merlin was born, he inherited much of his father's supernatural power but none of his wicked intent. He had his mother's good nature.

He became a great magician at the court of Uther Pendragon, performing many remarkable feats such as bringing Stonehenge from Ireland to Salisbury Plain, but the outstanding achievement of his career was helping Uther to screw the wife of the Duke of Cornwall.

This noble prince, you may remember, had had the foresight to shut his wife, Ygerne, up in the remote castle of Tintagel. But through his magic arts, Merlin turned Uther into a passing likeness of the Duke so he could enter the castle and have his way with her. Which sounds to me very much like a trick of my father's.

Arthur was the result.

As the price for his help in seducing another man's wife, Merlin took the child away with him into the forest and supervised his education and guided him to the throne when the time was right. He helped him to pull the sword out of the stone and to build Camelot and to found the order of the Knights of the Round Table who rode about the world righting wrongs and generally making themselves useful to people, particularly maidens.

Then, inexplicably, when all was going so well he fell in love with a witch, taught her his spells and got locked up in an apple tree with a pig.

Whereupon Arthur's wife promply got laid by his best friend, the Round Table fell apart and everyone more or less ended up killing each other.

This, give or take a few details, is the Arthurian legend.

But it was not the film Adam wanted to make. He wanted to make the film of the real King Arthur.

He had the idea after reading a book which claimed that the real King Arthur was a warrior chief called the Bear who'd led the British tribes against the Anglo-Saxons around the middle of the fifth century. He was fascinated by the notion that the medieval monarch of popular myth had a basis in historical reality and an entirely different image.

'I mean, forget all this knights-in-armour shit,' he instructed me, as if it was a constant preoccupation of mine. 'This was the Dark Ages, the fall of the Roman Empire, the collapse of the entire civilised world. This was fucking chaos.'

We were having breakfast on the terrace of his house in North Rockingham, where the civilised world had made an impressive comeback. A maid had just brought a fresh pot of coffee, the undergardener was spraying bugs with an organic killer and the pool boy was sucking the dead leaves off the pool with a water hoover.

Adam held the book an arm's length from his face to read the print. He still wouldn't admit he needed glasses.

'This guy was a kind of guerrilla leader, a mountain man, a tribal chief,' he said. 'He brought together the remnants of the Roman legions and the Christianised Brits and the Druids and united them against the Germans. This was the legend of Camelot.'

I detected a small historical error.

'Germans?' I said.

'Well, Anglo-Saxons,' he said. 'Same thing.'

He had a point but there were other objections.

'I don't believe anyone has ever found any historical record for the existence of this Arthur,' I pointed out.

'That's because Arthur wasn't his real name,' he said, as smugly as if he had made the discovery himself. 'His real name was Owen something but his warrior name was the Bear – they always gave them warrior names.'

The condescension of the scholar. Adam had the director's propensity for attributing every piece of original research to himself.

'And in the Celtic dialect the word for Bear is Arth.'

'Ah,' I said.

'And in the Roman it's Ursus. Arth-Ursus.'

I reached for the book and my glasses.

'And his father's warrior name was Uther Pen Dragon – which means the Terrible Head Dragon. Don't you think it would make a great movie?'

I had suspected that this was where we were heading. Adam was rarely passionate about a subject that would not make a great movie. I was about to counsel caution but my expression was sufficient of an irritant to him.

'I thought you were interested in all this stuff,' he said.

'I am,' I said.

But I am interested in the myth of King Arthur, not the spurious, or even plausible, reality. I am interested in the storytellers, the spinners of yarns – in that ambitious prelate Geoffrey of Monmouth, weaving his epic of anti-Saxon propaganda to please his Norman masters; in Chrétien, the silky musician of Troyes, playing on the lewd susceptibilities of his sex-mad countess and her even madder mother; in the ascetic monks who turned it all into a Christian morality tale. I am interested in the sex, the politics, the religion of

53

the Arthurian legend. I am interested in the need to believe in it. I am not interested in a Celtic tearaway called Bear, Son of the Terrible Head Dragon. Or at least I wasn't then.

Nor, it appeared, was anyone else. No one with any money, that is. We'd already had *Camelot*, the musical, and Borman's *Excalibur*, and the general feeling around town was that the world wasn't exactly waiting with bated breath for another movie about King Arthur, even by Adam Epstein.

Adam grew stubborn about it. It became a test of his faith in the project, his instinct for success. He decided to put his own money into it but it wasn't enough.

And so he turned to his own country.

7

THE ENCHANTED FOREST

I'm glad they put you out in the orchard. It is altogether more pleasant than the pigpen, and all the apples you can eat. We are really very fortunate. Prisons in Germany are so well appointed.

It was a jolt, of course, seeing the apple trees. As if the demon who is the particular architect of my destruction had added one more detail to the design – an afterthought.

I wish I could say I'd had a presentiment about the return to Europe. As a magician should. But I didn't. I didn't even give a thought to Magda or the son Adam had never seen. And if Adam did, he didn't speak of it.

Perhaps it was all that optimism that was flowing around at the time. We'd had the Velvet Revolution in Prague and they'd pulled down the Berlin Wall. All over Eastern Europe they were pulling down walls. It seemed a good time to be going back.

And then there was the money.

I don't know where, precisely, Adam found his pot of gold. There was talk of a banker in Frankfurt, a distant relative on his mother's side of the family . . . of film people in Munich . . . And whatever Hollywood thought about it, Bear, Son of the Terrible Head Dragon, seemed to be a popular subject in Germany.

The Arthurian legend might have been written for the

55

Germans, I've often thought, rather than the British. Or perhaps there is not so much difference between them as they both like to think. It is a story of the forest, full of dark, chthonic symbolism. No wonder it appealed so much to Jung and Wagner . . . and Hitler.

At any rate the Germans put up the money and Adam built his set in the Spessart, the great forest south of Frankfurt, which he was assured bore a striking resemblance to the landscape of late-Roman Britain. It even had wild boar. And rain.

It was raining when I arrived and Adam was standing in the replica of a fifth-century Celtic hillfort, waiting for it to stop. He was wearing an Australian stockman's coat, Texas cowboy boots and an English deerstalker hat. Small beads of water collected on the rim and dripped past his nose.

'Welcome to Camelot,' he said, without enthusiasm. 'This is summer.'

Perhaps it was the rain but I had a sudden image of him in the church of St Michael the Archangel, where we had first met, over twenty years before. He did not look so very different. There were a few lines now at the corners of his eyes and, in a certain light or when he was tired, you could see where they had begun to etch their way into his cheeks, but it would be a while before he needed major surgery. He had put on about nine kilos, perhaps, since I had found him dripping in the pew, but most of it was in his shoulders and his chest. He worked out regularly. He was obsessive about his health and travelled everywhere with a bag of vitamin supplements and body lotions and various obscure and exotic herbs that he was for ever trying to push on people, like a druggie. Have one of these, he'd say, it's got vitamins E and C and betacarotene and pure yeast and extract of bat shit, scraped at dawn from the floor of a cave in the Bolivian Yungas and dehydrated at an extremely low temperature.

I experienced no difficulty in resisting them.

'D'you have a good trip?' he said. 'How's LA?'

'Sunny,' I told him.

He shook his head in mute despair. More drips fell off his hat.

We splashed through the puddles of what was apparently the main street of Camelot, lined by a few hovels, a few hog pens . . . A wattle-and-daub Camelot for Chief Bear.

'How long can you stay?' he asked me.

I told him I was due in Prague the day after tomorrow. He looked at me carefully. It was my first trip back. Havel was in King Karl's castle and several of my old friends were in his government.

'How d'you feel about that?' he asked me.

'Nervous,' I said.

I didn't know how they'd welcome me, the exile who'd had it soft all those years in Hollywood while they were cleaning windows and being harassed by secret police and shuffled in and out of prisons. *Mea culpa, mea culpa* . . . But I am paying for it now.

'If it doesn't work out,' I said, 'I'll come back here and watch some more of the shoot.'

I'd taken a sabbatical from the practice. More guilt there, too, but not enough to stay. I felt I owed it to myself. I'd wanted to go when I saw the crowds on television, marching with their candles through Wenceslas Square, and I'd followed every move since on the news networks, read every piece of detailed analysis in the magazines as the whole massive edifice of East European Communism came crashing down, one rotten regime after another.

'It'll work out,' said Adam gently. 'I wish I could come with you.' He sounded as though he meant it.

We'd stopped under the main gate where his design team were still working, slapping mud on the walls.

'Maybe I will,' he added, in a more acerbic tone. 'Even if it stops raining, we'll never be ready on time.'

A voice from somewhere above our heads said, 'We'll be ready.'

Adam didn't even look up. I did. I saw a figure up a ladder. It wore jeans and an anorak and a bright-yellow sou'wester and only the voice told me it was a woman. Then she glanced down and I saw a cross little face, the cheeks flushed red from the wind – or embarrassment, or anger, or elements of all three. I walked on with a lingering impression of an agitated marmoset peering balefully down from the branches of a tree.

'Who was that?' I said.

'The art director,' said Adam. 'Her name's Jack.'

'Jack?' I said.

He shrugged. 'That's what the crew call her,' he said. 'For Jacqueline, I guess.'

She had been brought in at the last minute, I discovered, to replace Adam's regular art director who was off on another shoot, and she was Scottish, part of a fairly mixed bunch that included a few Americans in key position, a lot of Germans, naturally enough, almost as many Brits, a French camera operator, a Dutch clapper/loader and an Australian first assistant. The atmosphere seemed to be quite relaxed, though Adam, in his usual benign way, was doing his best to make life difficult for everyone.

Despite his desire to tell the story of the real Arthur, it seemed that the mythical king had made something of a comeback. Or perhaps it's fairer to say that the landscape of the myth had been restored. In particular, Adam wanted to recreate the atmosphere of a series of shorts entitled *The Adventures of Sir Galahad*, made by Hollywood in the fifties for the international Saturday morning minors audience, but which only he appeared to have seen. They featured a place called the Enchanted Forest where the trees had faces and could move their limbs and where the wizard Merlin and the witch Morgan le Fay and other magical creatures kept appearing at regular intervals in puffs of smoke.

I murmured something about this being difficult to square with the true history but Adam was unabashed. This was the Dark Ages when the earth magic of the Druids was still a force to be reckoned with and the gods of the natural world were far more real to people than the Christian saints. He said.

There were commercial considerations, however, of which Adam was ever aware.

'You've got to have magic,' he assured me. 'People love to believe in magic.'

Unfortunately, it didn't seem to be working for him.

Next day it was raining even harder. Adam was impossible to be around. I borrowed one of the production vehicles and took myself off to look at some of the other locations in the area.

I found the design team in a dense part of the forest throwing mud at the trees.

'Why are they doing that?' I asked one of the stand-bys.

'The governor didn't think they looked enchanted enough,' he said, in the flat, expressionless tone that film crews reserve for the whims of their directors.

Then I saw the woman in the plastic mac. She seemed to be attacking one of the trees with a stick. I moved closer and saw the 'mud' was in fact a mixture of paint and plaster and that she was drawing designs in it, the swirling, tortured contours of a figure in a painting by Munch. I saw now that several trees had been similarly treated, the natural knots and gnarls given artificial expression by a talented make-up artist so that they looked like the haunted dendroids of a children's fairy tale. Then I understood. This was the landscape of Adam's childhood: an enchanted forest where every tree had the face of a monster and there were witches hiding in the branches.

I felt it then, the warning I should have felt before, and it was still not too late. Remember, in *Don't Look Now*, when Donald Sutherland spills some red ink and it runs on to the transparency and forms the shape of the dwarf, kneeling in one of the pews of the church in Venice? I felt something of that when I looked at the faces in those trees. But I put it down to the skill of the artist – and Adam's imagination. I was meant to feel this, a sense of what the Germans call *Schrecklichkeit*, for which 'frightfulness' is a wholly inadequate translation.

So I left them to it and forgot about it and went to Prague.

I returned as a stranger. I walked the streets as Adam had, those long years ago, with my ready smile and my cautious, wondering eyes. The buildings were the same. It was still the beautiful, fairy-tale city of the winter queen but it was as if it had been touched with a magic wand and released from some binding spell. It was alive as I had never seen it before. There were young men and women with long hair and leather jackets playing guitars on the Charles Bridge. They played the protest songs of sixties America and Western Europe but they played them in celebration of being free. And there was a new ruler in the castle of King Karl and he had been elected by his people and he wrote plays. Is that not magic?

Most of my old friends seemed to be in his government, in one capacity or another. They were welcoming, they embraced me, the returned exile, but they were building a new nation and I had no part in it. Their eyes were warm but they kept darting this way and that, looking for more things to do, and sometimes they wore a hunted look I had not seen in the days when they were hunted. Some of them had put on weight, of course, but they all had this youthful vigour I was afraid I had lost, or maybe never had. Some of them wore ponytails and suits like the players in Hollywood and like them they were always on the phone. Excuse me, they would say, as it rang in the middle of a sentence.

I was not dressed right. I was dressed like a tourist. I wore blue jeans and a shirt that showed the bulge in my midriff. I had a beard. I felt like Dr Manette when he is released from the Bastille.

I asked if I could see Havel. I had been acquainted with him in the days when I was a caretaker and he a prisoner on parole. He would love to see you, they said, but he is in America. He will be back at the end of the week, maybe then . . .

So instead I went to look at the apartment block where I had lived. I went into the church of St Michael where I had met Adam. The old women were still there, still praying. There seemed to be more of them than before.

It rained.

I visited the Jewish cemetery and said my Catholic prayers for the dead. I ate carp in U Golemi where Adam had bought me lunch, but this time I ate alone and I paid for it myself.

It got better. Havel came back from America and I listened to him speak from the balcony of the People's Forum offices in the old town square and afterwards I had a message to meet him up at the castle. He looked embarrassed to be there. 'I only work here,' he said, 'I still live in the old apartment on the river.' The castle was so big, so many rooms, and still haunted by the ghosts of Masaryk and Dubček and the men who had betrayed them. He had bought a small pushbike to cycle down the long corridors, so he would not be late for meetings. I watched him cycling away for one, getting smaller and smaller, his knees sticking out as he pedalled and the presidential bodyguard bringing their guns to the salute as he disappeared through the last doorway.

I might have stayed.

I had my offers. I was tempted. There were things I could have done, I suppose.

Why did I not stay?

I phoned Adam from my hotel. He sounded pleased to hear from me but preoccupied, but then he always does when he is filming. They were way behind schedule, he said, and way over budget and he was having to use more of his own money but they had finished on location, at least, and they were moving on to shoot the interiors in studio in Munich.

'It's only an hour's flight from Prague,' I said.

'So why don't you come and join us?' he said.

So I did.

I arrived in time for the Great Flies Debacle.

Adam, in his umpteenth rewrite of the script, had dreamed up a scene where Chief Bear and the remnants of his once happy war band were feasting in the Great Hall at Camelot on the eve of Guinevere's execution for adultery. The Lancelot character was banished, the Round Table hopelessly divided and the Bear's bastard son Mordred exultant, seated at the right hand of his father. Adam intended it to be a demonic version of the Last Supper and in order to drive the point home he wanted flies. He wanted close-ups of them crawling over the food on the plates, drinking from a spilt goblet of red wine, settling on the hand of the traitor Mordred . . .

The problem was how to get them to stay in the right place. As usual, in such debates, everyone was an expert.

The props manager said you had to attract them with honey.

The camera operator said, no, what you did was, you attached them to the food with small invisible threads tied around their bodies so they could 'hover realistically'.

The Australian first assistant said, Fuck that, what you did was, you pulled off their fucking wings, that was what you did.

The make-up supervisor said he had worked with flies many times before and the trick was to put them in a refrigerator for an hour or two before the shoot so they became very sluggish and didn't move around too much.

The first seemed impressed with this; the art director less so.

She had a distinctive Scots accent and expressed herself forcefully. It was only then that I realised she was my agitated marmoset, my witch of the Enchanted Forest. She, too, had been touched by the magic wand. Under the yellow sou'wester she had been hiding a mass of, well, I will not call it golden hair but it caught the eye. Let us compromise on Titian.

No?

Are you familiar, then, with a breed of hog known as the Tamworth? That's right, the red, hairy ones. Well, it was, I suppose, a bit like that but with more of a wave in it, more of a spring. Less coarse. She wore it pulled back and tied in a scarf at the neck but it looked as if it was trying to spring out. Her features were – now I must be careful here, too, for I was going to say 'sharp' but that would give the wrong impression entirely. That would suggest shrewish, ferrety. They were not shrewish or ferrety. They were in fact quite soft but there was a sharpness in her eye, a glint. It struck sparks. Fierce, I would say, yes, she was like some Celtic warrior queen ... but now I am being fanciful and it will, besides, mean nothing to you. Let us stick to the images of the farmyard or the auction ring, with which you are better acquainted. She was about one metre sixty, weighed around fifty-five kilos, evenly distributed, there was a healthy glow to her cheeks – clearly on a good diet with plenty of vitamins, maybe she had been taking Adam's tablets – she had the light of battle in her eye and she came out fighting.

The gist of her message to the first assistant was that if he

63

wished to take more notice of the make-up supervisor than the design team, then that was his business, but she would accept no responsibility for the consequences.

I have missed a fair bit of verbiage, however.

Adam was not present for this discussion. He appeared when they were all lit and ready to shoot. The first assistant sent the second to fetch the flies from the fridge. I edged forward to see what would happen when they opened the container. The make-up supervisor was right. They didn't move around too much. The second tipped a dozen or so on to the nearest plate. They were dead. There was a moment's silence. Then someone laughed.

Not Adam.

He picked up the container of flies and walked over to the art director, who had been busy with some hangings at the far side of the set.

'What the fuck's this?' he said. He held the container under her nose.

'I'm sorry?' she said.

'When I said I wanted flies,' he said, 'I meant live flies. Flies that fly. Not dead flies that lie on their fucking asses with their little legs in the air. Or did you think no one would spot the difference?'

She looked into the container briefly and then at him. I would describe her expression as thoughtful.

'It really has fuck all to do with me,' she said, 'but I think you'll find a few of them will revive if you're prepared to wait for a few minutes.'

Adam tipped the container on to the floor at her feet. It contained many hundreds of dead flies, perhaps thousands. She did not move. Nor did Adam. I had not realised until then how angry he was. They were by now about a week behind schedule and the constant delays must have cost him millions, most of it his own money.

64

'So what do you want me to do?' he demanded. 'Stand everybody down while you give them the kiss of life?'

She told him what she thought he should do. It took only a short time but there was, yes, poetry in it. I hoped he would appreciate it. Then she walked off the set. There was a terrible silence.

I looked at the first assistant. He took a deep breath and walked up to Adam and spoke to him quietly for a moment. I saw Adam nod to himself, very slowly. There was a small twitch in his cheek where I knew he was grinding his back teeth. He glanced across at the make-up supervisor, who was trying to hide behind one of the sparks.

Then I felt something on the back of my neck. I flapped my hand and a fly fell to the floor by my feet. It was not a very lively fly but it was not a dead fly. I saw other people waving their hands at invisible tormentors.

'It's the lights,' someone said.

'Stand by to turn over,' the first yelled.

By the time they were ready to shoot, the flies were performing as God, and the director, had intended. We spent the next three hours brushing them out of our hair and fishing them from the backs of our necks as they icarused their wings in the twelve-kilowatt sun.

I saw Adam with the art director later that day. They were standing close together and he was saying something to her in a manner I had come to recognise over the years. I gathered that he had apologised and was now moving the relationship on to a more productive footing.

The marriage proposal, however, came as something of a shock.

I was back in LA when it happened but he phoned me to tell me about it. He wanted me to come over for the wedding, which was to be in Bavaria on the Chiemsee.

'But you're not to tell anyone,' he said. 'We're keeping it quiet.'

I was moved to a mild protest. I had just resumed my practice. Another absence would be most unsettling to my patients.

'Try them on Prozac,' said Adam. 'I need you there.'

So I went.

I flew to Munich where Adam was editing *Pendragon*. He sent a car to pick me up from the airport and a message to say he was working in the cutting room and would catch up with me later for dinner. He'd booked me into a small hotel near the studio recommended by his editor as being far superior to any of the grander establishments. It was a few days before Christmas and I appeared to be the only guest. I felt a desperate homesickness that was linked to a confusion about where my home really was. After twenty-two years in California I still felt like a refugee.

I went to my room and dozed. I dreamed I was in Mariánské Lázně. It was snowing and my grandmother was baking carp for Christmas Eve. There were gifts from my mother who was a glamorous film actress in Hollywood and would be arriving shortly – by reindeer sled. I heard the jangle of bells. It was the phone. Adam. If I wasn't feeling too jet-lagged, would I like to see a rough cut of the movie?

I took a cab to the studio. Adam was waiting for me with his editor, Danny Gold, whom he'd fetched over from California for the duration. He looked a little frayed at the edges. He told me his girlfriend was in England for Christmas and he was leaving straight after the viewing, whatever the director thought about it, darting a look at Adam which he pretended not to notice.

Adam said nothing to me about the marriage. I might have come over specially to see the rough cut. I wondered if I had.

66

He was nervous. He kept apologising for the quality of the print. It was only a cutting copy, it hadn't been graded or anything, it needed bringing up at least one stop and they knew it was too long.

Finally he let them run it and I could see for myself.

At first I was worried. It looked as if it didn't know if it was *Conan the Barbarian* or *The Seventh Seal*. Strong, silent warrior types in animal hides, hunched, cowled figures of monks, a bleak, haunted landscape full of burning villages and desecrated churches with the odd priest nailed to the door in the crucifixion pose or disembowelled on his own altar. Nice costumes. I liked the trees.

Then it began to get through to me. I could see what Adam was doing. In some ways it was no different from what they'd all done, everyone who'd ever touched the story since Geoffrey of Monmouth. I was familiar with Arthur as the Universal Hero, the man who'd tried to be good and to persuade his followers to be good, to rise above their ritualised blood feuds, to substitute a more civilised alternative to the primitive jungle law by which they lived and died, to eat with a knife and fork . . . but because Adam's jungle was so primitive, the life he painted so patently nasty, brutish and short, the tentative gropings of his Arthur towards the light were so much more impressive, his eventual failure so much more poignant. This Arthur was less of a king, more a man of clay (or blood, shit and piss, as Adam would later put it) but somehow, because of this, what he tried to do was more heroic. You felt at the end that despite the human frailties and failings and betrayals, despite the collapse of his towers and the crumbling of his dreams and the triumph of his enemies and the slinking, sinking back into the Dark Ages, he left more than a memory or a myth. He left the imprint of the footprints leading out of the swamp.

When it was finished and the lights came on, I sighed and nodded.

'It's good,' I said. 'I don't think you'll get your money back but it's good.'

Adam was frowning fiercely but I could see it was because he was trying not to look too pleased with himself.

'It needs a lot of work,' he said, 'but it's getting there.'

He spent half an hour talking to Danny about changes before he let him go off for his Christmas with a hug and a kiss and a gift in a shopping bag which he apologised for not wrapping properly but which he'd at least bought himself. Then he took me off to dinner.

And over dinner he told me about Jack.

I was always intrigued by Adam's ability to compartmentalise. To do several different things at once and appear to keep them all in separate boxes in his head. It is a useful facility for a film director but as a therapist I have never been convinced that it is anything more than a clever trick. The human brain is not a locker room. You cannot keep one compartment closed until you are ready to open it. I prefer to think of the brain, equally unscientifically but more in line with the teachings of my masters, as more like a series of interconnecting caves. When all is well, when one's various affairs, financial, sexual or other, appear to be in order, the contents, or residents, of these caves can be relied upon to remain more or less dormant, benign, but when there is cause for concern in a particular area the panic spreads and they all begin to agitate, to prowl like cave bears or to take off in screaming disorder like a colony of cave bats, invading all the different departments, spreading neurosis, fear and disorder . . .

A bit like the demons, when they went in through the hole in your foot.

But I confess that Adam seemed to have them all well under control – bats, bears and assorted succubi, at least for the time being.

He was in love, a difficult emotion to contain, even for one so practised. No, I am not being critical. Adam was a romantic. Another word that has been used of him is, I know, womaniser. But Adam was no Valmont, no cynical seducer. He saw no point in playing the game unless he believed himself to be in love. It was still a game. Adam was in love with being in love. But so far as I knew he had never asked anyone to marry him before – unless you count Magda, and the circumstances then were exceptional. So why was this so different? I began to piece together the various elements of the plot.

Immediately after the shoot, the pair of them had taken themselves off for a few days, touring. Adam, I should say, never took a vacation. Or if he did, he called it something else: research, looking at locations for a shoot, finding somewhere quiet to work on a script . . . But this was a vacation. They had stayed in a hotel beside the Chiemsee, they had gone skiing in the Bavarian Alps, they had stayed at country inns, at remote castles run by vampires. They had employed guides to take them to mountain huts and leave them there until morning. When the time came for Jack to return to London where she was working on a television film, Adam had gone with her. He had stayed in her apartment in a Victorian terrace in a place called Clapham, which must have been something of an experience for him, Adam's idea of a terrace being a level, paved area overlooking a swimming pool.

I was not familiar with Clapham or its terraces but the idea of Adam willingly subjecting himself to the damp, dismal miseries of November in London was not something I would previously have considered a plausible scenario. He was, however, as he said, in love.

He seemed to be amused by this but he did try to break it down for me into its component parts, as if he felt he had to explain it. He loved her common sense, he said, her dry sense of humour, her, 'taste', the way she stood up to him. There was lots more like this but I do not wish to bore you with lists. I was rather more interested in his account of a dream he said he'd had when he was staying in London with her, just before he was due to return to Germany.

In this dream, he was walking through a wood in the autumn with the leaves thick and mulchy on the ground when he saw her coming towards him. He smiled and lifted his arms to embrace her but she walked on with a polite nod and a smile as if he was a stranger and he was left staring after her, hurt and puzzled, and with a terrible sense of desolation and loss. He awoke with this feeling so sharp and painful that he tried to go to sleep again, to pick the story up where it had been broken off and to affect a better ending, to rewrite the script, as it were, but it was impossible. So he had asked her to marry him. Because of the dream.

Well, I had my own views on the subject. I immediately thought of his mother and the bears. But I also thought: he was forty-five and he'd made the movie he'd always wanted to make, so what else was there for him to do? It was time he started making children. So very practically and sensibly he'd picked a very practical, sensible young woman (with taste and a sense of humour) who was pretty enough but had both feet on the ground and plenty of breeding years left. Of course, being Adam, he'd had to put a romantic gloss on it but basically he'd chosen a homemaker and with a bit of luck she'd even do the painting and decorating herself.

You think me cynical? You are, I suspect, a sentimentalist at heart. You like nothing better than to curl up with a good romance – when you are not eating, that is, or rolling on your back in the mud. I have seen you lying there, after a session in the trough, grunting quietly to yourself with a silly smirk on your face. You are dreaming of the day your prince will come. Yes, I had a word with the deputy governor, as I said I would. A suitable mate is even now being canvassed among the local aristocracy. A stout, Westphalian boar was, I believe, your specification. 'And he'll be big and strong, the one I love . . .' Yes, well, you won't be disappointed there, my dear, though you might find it a trifle less tender than your dreams. Nasty, brutish and short, did I say?

We humans do things rather differently. Not the actual physical business, which is more or less the same, give or take a few grunts, but the build-up tends to be more elaborate. We have the Arthurian romances to thank for that, specifically the version composed by Chrétien de Troyes for his royal mistress Marie de Champagne and her formidable mother, the incomparable Eleanor (you know the one I mean, who was played so magnificently in her maturity by Katharine Hepburn in *The Lion in Winter*). Well, Eleanor and Marie, tiring of the boorish behaviour of their menfolk, desired a story of romantic seduction. Words of love accompanied by the playing of a lute. Flowers. Flattery. Foreplay . . .

Thus inspiring the obliging Chrétien to create his role models of knightly perfection.

I don't know if it worked for the men in their lives but at least a certain standard was set for future generations. We know how we're meant to behave, even if we fall woefully short of it at times, and Chrétien's blueprint has been refined by a global industry of books, films and television commercials.

But marriage is so often the antithesis of romance, as poor Eleanor and her daughter had discovered. So why do so many people appear to favour it?

I cannot give you the simple answer. I can give you the standard therapist's line, for the right price. I can tell you of the basic need to recreate the idealised one-to-one relationship with mother or father, or to erase the bitter memories of that relationship and replace it with an idyll of one's own making. But personally, I confess it has always puzzled me, possibly because of the spectacular failure rate. Were we to consider any other institution in the light of such dismal statistics I am sure there would be a widespread call for reform or abolition. I suppose it is yet another case of the triumph of hope over experience.

I kept these thoughts to myself over dinner, you'll be glad to know. I was a tolerant and kindly audience, though my attention, I must admit, began to flag over dessert. I blame the jet lag.

Next morning we drove to Prien on the Chiemsee. This was where they had fallen in love, Adam said, so this was where they were to marry.

'Why not Clapham?' I said.

We drove past one of mad Ludwig's fantasy castles on an island on the lake, a half fantasy because the men in the white coats had finally come for him, Adam said, before it was finished.

'So that is why you chose it,' I said.

Jack met us in the lobby of the hotel.

She looked wonderful. Of course. Brides do, do they not? She had let her hair down and I saw the pre-Raphaelite stunner that Adam had captured. Forget for a moment the Tamworth hog. Erase that image from your mind entirely. There is a painting by one of the original Brotherhood, William Holman Hunt, called *The Awakening Conscience*. It shows a young woman, half-dressed, rising from the knee of her lover with a look of dawning apprehension as if she has just heard her mother coming in. At least that is how it appears to me. Art historians say she is the fallen woman who has heard God knocking at the door and from what I have read about Holman Hunt they are probably right.

He used his favourite model, Annie Miller, and there is a suggestion that in the original version her features were contorted into a mask of horror as she realises what she has become. But the artist relented. Or, more likely, was persuaded by his friend Rossetti that he would never sell such an image, that he should make the face more beautiful. So the features were painted over, the horror was replaced with a kind of flushed excitement; there is apprehension, yes, but also anticipation, a sense of youthful arousal. Her red-gold hair is unbound, hanging in abundance halfway down her back, her blue eyes are opened wide, her lips parted . . .

Well, my cross little face on the top of the ladder had been painted over. Or else a switch had been made somewhere along the line while I was looking the other way. She was another of Adam's illusions.

I watched them embrace, the watcher in the wings, my apparent destiny in life. I saw them for the first time as a couple and they matched. I felt the turning of the knife in the old wound that Magda had made. But at the same time I was happy for them, can you believe that?

Jacqueline. From the French. Meaning the One Who Supplants.

I had looked it up.

She broke away from him and gave me a kiss and a big grin but her eyes, I thought, were wary and I wondered what Adam had told her about me.

'Thank you for coming,' she said. 'He needs at least one ally. I don't want him overwhelmed by us all.'

Us all.

Jack's entire family, it appeared, had flown in from Scotland. I was a little surprised that they had not insisted that the wedding should be on their home territory but I gathered that the fact that Adam was paying for it all had some bearing on the decision. They were Lowlanders, from the Galloway peninsula, and of a particularly thrifty and prudent disposition. Their ancestors were a minority Puritan sect, I was told, who had been massacred in droves by their neighbours during the religious wars of the seventeenth century. The survivors had embarked for Massachusetts or, like Jack's family, changed their religion and kept their heads down. This facility had clearly passed into the family genes. Jack's grandfather and father worked the family farm and her mother ran a market garden which seemed to be devoted mainly to the production of runner beans upon which, she told me, you could always rely. Jack had two older brothers. One was a solicitor, the other the manager of an animal-feed factory. Both upright members of the community, thirty-something going on fifty with bright, buxom wives and an indeterminate number of children with clean faces and sharp-as-a-button eyes.

They were inclined as a family to be weary of initiative. 'Nobody likes a smartarse' might have stood for the family motto, had they been the kind of family that goes in for mottoes, which they weren't. They were the kind of family that goes in for hard work, tried and trusted methods, orthodox opinions. They were not impetuous. They did not do things differently. They did not wish to stand out from the crowd. They knew that standing out from the crowd invariably led to being stoned by the mob. If any member of the family showed a glimmer of initiative or imagination or impetuosity they jumped on it quick and gave him a spade and told him to dig a trench to plant runner beans. They forgot the story of Jack and the beanstalk.

Jack was a romantic – like Adam. Along with the solid, common-sense practicality she had inherited from her Lowland forebears, there was an altogether more wild and whimsical side to her nature, an element of the ethereal, the fay . . .

It took me a while to discover this, of course. But I liked her almost at once and I think she liked me. He could have done worse, I decided.

You'd have been disappointed by the wedding. It was not at all glamorous. No celebrity guests, no publicity. The reception was in the hotel. Plenty of food and drink, you'd have liked that, at least. I made a speech. I learned to call Jack 'Jackie', which was what her family called her. Adam said he preferred it. He found it odd, he told me, fucking somebody called Jack on a regular basis. Everyone to his taste, said I.

They did not go on honeymoon. Just to bed, shortly before midnight. The family clapped politely. An uncle played the bagpipes.

Afterwards I went for a walk in the hotel gardens beside the lake. It had begun to snow. I watched it drifting down across the lights of the building. I thought, I have been here before. Then I remembered. It was in Prague, the night I first met Adam and he went back with Magda. I was glad he was not with Magda now but I felt just as lonely.

That night I had my own dream, my own portent.

I was standing on a terrace.

Not a terrace in Hollywood, nor in Clapham. This was a terrace on a hillside. It was dark and snowing and far below, dimly through the snow, I could see the lights of a city. All around me was forest, though for some reason the terrace was cleared and bare, and in the middle of it stood two figures.

One was a knight in shining armour, carrying a sword. The other wore a cowl and was familiar to me, from the movie, as the figure of Death.

Then I became aware of someone standing beside me. He was a thin, dapper gentleman of middling height and age, wearing an overcoat and a homburg hat and a white silk scarf. At first I thought he, too, was from a movie. I thought he might be Fred Astaire. But then I recognised him. He was my father, the Devil.

He ignored me. He was watching the two figures on the terrace and, after a moment, he joined them. All three men seemed to be arguing about something and although they were too far away for me to hear them, I sensed that the argument was about territory; or, to be precise, about whose territory they were on. I gathered that the knight was getting the worst of it and I knew, then, that he was Michael the Archangel from the church in Prague where I had first met Adam, though he looked less weathered, less aged. Then all three turned towards the forest as if they were waiting for something, or someone, to emerge. They were not looking in my direction and I did not think it was me they were waiting for but I thought it best not to hang about.

That is all.

There could be any number of reasons why I had this dream at this particular time, on the night of Adam's wedding. But it is inevitable, given the timing, given the subsequent history, that I should make the connection with what happened in the beech wood.

Don't you think?

8

. . . AND THE BEECH WOOD

They left the truck back at Schloss Albert in the gardens where Goethe and Schiller had once walked and where the new rock concerts were now held and made their way through the wood on foot, following a trail that someone had blazed for them earlier with slashes of luminous paint on the trunks of the trees. They didn't need their torches to find it. There was a fresh layer of snow on the ground and the reflection of the moonlight made it brighter than they might have wished.

They came out of the wood on the road beside the warning monument. They could see the obelisk, tall and black against the sky, with the red light on top. It was too dark to read the names of all those who were supposed to have died but they'd seen them before, anyway. They sprayed it with the swastika as high as they could reach and some of them pissed on it. A couple of them even took their pants down and left little piles of excrement at the foot of it.

Gerhard didn't take part in any of this, so he said later. He considered most of them to be brainless louts. He had no illusions, not about them, anyway. He walked away, across the terrace to the great bronze statue that overlooked the city. It was one of those heroic works in the Soviet style depicting a group of prisoners shortly after their liberation, with rifles they must have taken from the guards and a large flag which they waved triumphantly.

Gerhard could see the lights of the city far below. He remembered the first time he'd been up here. It was with his mother when he was only nine or ten. It was some kind of official ceremony and they'd been driven up the hill in a big black car with curtains in the back. They stood for two minutes' silence. He didn't understand any of it then, he just felt bored. He remembered his feelings better the second time, when he'd come here with the school just after his thirteenth birthday. It was part of the compulsory Youth Maturity Programme – going to Buchenwald. A measure of their capacity to become worthy citizens of the German Democratic Republic.

First they'd gone into this large exhibition hall with all these photographs on the walls showing the camp as it had been during the war. There was some sombre music by Schoenberg to put them in the right mood. Then they did the tour.

All the wooden huts where they'd kept the prisoners had gone but they'd kept the brick foundations in neat lines in this vast, empty space on top of the hill surrounded by barbed wire and watchtowers. They'd walked around in a group, not saying much, just reading the signs telling you what each building had been for and what was supposed to have happened there. There was a wind whistling through the perimeter wire and whipping up dust in little spirals. Dust devils. They all kept turning their backs into whichever direction the wind was coming from. They were all fed up but they tried to look solemn and impressed. You learned the right facial expressions in the DDR, that was one thing.

Then they went into the museum where there were more pictures and prisoners' diaries and scraps of striped prisoners' uniforms with the labels they'd had to wear: yellow for the Yids and pink for queers and red for the Communists and something else for the gippoes, he couldn't remember what the gippoes had had to wear, probably brown or black. There was a reconstruction of the inside of one of the barrack blocks with all these bunks like pigpens and a mock-up of a scaffold with a large photograph of the real one during the war with a few prisoners hanging from it. There were red spotlights on everything to give the right atmosphere and loads of signs in the usual Party jargon. It was all such obvious propaganda but they'd all had to take it in and pretend to believe in it and write an essay about their 'gut feelings' back in the lecture room while it was all still 'fresh in their minds'. Gerhard won a prize for his. It was so easy to fool them. You just had to use the right words.

They'd been taught history like dangerous animals. Savage dogs who'd rush around tearing people's throats out if you gave them the trigger word. They had to be tamed with warnings. Reminders of what could happen if they got out of control. You're animals, don't ever forget it. Look what you did, you animals. Look what happened. Rub your noses in it so you'll never forget the smell of it. That's what Buchenwald was all about. And all the rest of the warning museums and monuments throughout Germany.

They moved off again through the wood. Soon they saw the lights of the vigil outside the main entrance. There were eight or nine of them huddled round a brazier with their candles and they were singing. It sounded like some Yiddish song but it was just as likely Turkish. There were Yids *and* Turks there, according to the newspapers. They were cooking some of their greasy food, he could smell it from where he stood on the edge of the forest. He pulled the mask up over his face and began to walk forwards with the others.

The rest we know from the reports, from the eye witnesses.

Clarita Teugel had her little girl with her. She was only eight years old but she'd wanted to come and there was no school in the morning so Clarita couldn't see the harm. Besides, she thought it was important, she said, that the child knew what had happened here. But around midnight she was asleep on her feet and Clarita decided to put her to bed in the car.

She was on her way back from the car park when she saw them. It was strange, she said, that she'd been thinking what a wonderful scene it was, like a Christmas card. The singers in their long coats and scarves and hoods holding their candles around the fire with the snow-covered forest in the moonlight behind them. And when she saw this line of figures in their strange animal masks suddenly emerge from the trees it was as if they were part of the painting. For a moment she thought they were supporters, come up from Weimar to join them, but only for a moment. Then she saw the baseball bats and the pickaxe handles and the chains. She opened her mouth to scream a warning and that was when it began.

She told the police that she started forward to help, not that she could have made any difference, but then she remembered her child in the car and backed away into the shadows. She said she felt paralysed. It was as if it was all happening in the distance. Afterwards she remembered the shouts, screams and thuds and once a sharp crack like a bat hitting a hard ball. And there was a figure with the face of a bear who was flaying something on the ground with a chain, almost as if he was threshing corn. It was so unreal she could hardly believe it was happening in front of her. Then, as soon as it had begun, it was over and they weren't there any more. She thought there might have been a whistle blown but she couldn't be sure. It could have been the wind whistling through the wires.

She ran forward then. The brazier had been pushed over and one of the men, a teacher from Kreuzberg, had fallen across it. He was lying on the hot coals and there was a smell of burning. She dragged him away but his coat was smouldering. She tried to put it out with handfuls of snow but it had all turned to slush, and in the light of the fire she saw her hands were covered in blood. Then she heard the explosions and saw the other fire in the car park.

I must have read the first account of this a day or two after the wedding. It was at breakfast, I know. I was up early and alone. Then I sensed somebody standing behind me and I looked around and saw that it was Adam. He was reading it over my shoulder.

'It's started again,' he said.

I nodded. What can you say? Shocking? Terrible?

'Coffee?' I said.

'We should do something,' said Adam.

I looked up at him again, frowning. Irritably, I expect. I mean, what can you do?

'We should stay and do something,' he said.

He'd already worked out what it was.

9

GHOSTS

'Why open the wounds?' the Herr Direktor said. 'We are building the new Europe here, people do not wish to be constantly reminded of the past.' I am sure I kept my expression carefully blank but he anticipated my objection.

'Oh, I know there are some things one must not forget, but there are sufficient reminders. We even preserve the camps as warning museums. I am not sure if that is wise, but that is the decision.'

We are standing on German history. Imagine it. This is the Potsdamer Platz, centre of old Berlin: the hub of the kaiser's empire. Over there, on our right, is the Brandenburg Gate, the arch of Prussian triumphs; across to our left is the old German parliament building, the Reichstag, and in front of us – is a large rhinoceros.

The rhinoceros is apparently asleep but I am keeping a wary eye on it in case it is only pretending. We are leaning on the rails of its enclosure and they feel none too secure to me.

The rhinoceros is part of the American circus which is camped here for a season. Its tents, enclosures and trailers are laagered at one end of the Potsdamer Platz, where Hitler's Reich chancellery once stood. The centre of old Berlin is a wasteland, a site for travelling circuses and evangelists and Gipsies. It was flattened by a combination of English and

American bombs and Russian shells in 1945 and stayed flattened for half a century. The Berlin Wall ran straight through the middle of it – some chunks of it have been preserved in one corner where they were dumped by the bulldozers – and a hopeful entrepreneur, I notice, has opened an outdoor café among them. But even with the cheerful red umbrellas and their Martini logos it looks a grim old place to me, a concrete Stonehenge with graffiti, and when I walked through it earlier there were no customers.

For twenty-eight years, the Wall with its adjoining Death Strip of razor wire and land mines was as much a deterrent for developers in the West as it was for the disenchanted and desperate residents of the East. But not any more.

Now the wasteland is to become a building site and, after that, the showroom centre of the new Berlin: the hub, if not of empire, of a united Germany, even of a united Europe. The new corporate headquarters of Mercedes Benz will be here, the commercial and entertainment centre over there, and Adam's museum – where the rhinoceros is at present lying. Politics permitting.

The Museum of Year Zero.

'Everywhere in Berlin there are ghosts,' says the Herr Direktor. Everything he says sounds as if it is written for a speech, or a soundbite, rather, for he is often quoted. 'But especially here. It is a brave or possibly foolish man who would disturb them. Come I will show you where they found the bunker.'

We skirt the rhino's den and walk out on to the wasteland towards a small hillock. Paul Leibnitz is director of the city's museums and this is his particular domain. A significant portion of the city's past is buried under his feet and the historian in him longs to dig it up, while the politician hopes to bury it for ever.

'We Germans have a very difficult relationship with our

past,' he tells me, unnecessarily. 'A neurosis. We do not wish to hide it but we cannot bear to look at it too closely, either.'

He stops on the small bare hump and plants a pair of clenched fists on his hips to address me. I assume he is unaware of the significance of the pose but it might be satiric, you never know. It would be in his nature as a performer. As well as giving interviews to the media he also delivers many lectures. He is of average height with thinning hair and spectacles but he exudes a dynamic energy. He is a go-getter, an up and doer. I have been advised that his heart is in the right place, though, and that it is important to get him on my side.

'Here is the entrance to the so-called *Kutscherbunker*. Beneath our feet, under the garden of what was then the Reich chancellery, is where the SS drivers and bodyguards of Adolf Hitler sheltered during the air raids. It was discovered in 1990 when security guards were checking the area for land mines before the Pink Floyd concert to celebrate the demolition of the Wall.

'There were a number of paintings on the walls . . . you have seen the photographs?'

I nod. I know.

Under our feet there is a labyrinth of bunkers where Hitler and the staff of the Reich chancellery sheltered during the last months of the war. They were sealed up by the Russians and for fifty years lay forgotten under the Death Strip. Then the Wall came down and it was decided to hold a rock concert to celebrate.

Pink Floyd was the main attraction but there was even a band from the Red Army, it was that kind of an occasion. A celebration of hope, joy and reconciliation – a ritual burial of the past.

The site chosen was the Potsdamer Platz.

But while the security guards were checking it over for

explosives or any other nasties that might have been left there from when it was the Death Strip, they discovered a steel doorway set into concrete and buried deep in the earth.

It was the entrance to one of the wartime bunkers.

It led to a series of underground rooms which had been used by Hitler's SS drivers and bodyguards – the *Kutscherbunker*. It was exactly as they had left it in 1945 and the walls were painted with childlike representations of black-shirted warriors like knights of old holding their shields over various aspects of the German way of life – women, children, even beer drinkers in Tyrolean hats and lederhosen – while the bombs rained down. Hitler's new order of chivalry defending the German way of life from the dark Asiatic hordes.

Yes, I have seen the photographs.

'Yes. So. The photographs are taken and then the rooms are filled with sand and the bunker is sealed. Because we do not wish it to become a shrine for the neo-Nazis. You understand?'

Again, I nod. He throws out an arm. Again, the gesture is, I think, wholly unconscious.

'Over there is the entrance to the main bunker complex.'

All I can see is a block of apartments on the eastern side of the Brandenburg Gate, on the edge of the wasteland.

'This is where Adolf Hitler himself had his shelter, the so-called *Führerbunker*, and from where he conducts the last campaigns of the war. The East German authorities filled it with rubble and built a children's playground over the entrance – as a symbol of peace.'

I can see it now: the swings and the sandpit and a bright red and yellow slide. I do not think of peace but rather, obscurely, of the rhinoceros and glance over my shoulder to ensure it is not sneaking up on us. It is not.

'This is where, in the final days of the war, the bodies of Adolf Hitler and his bride, Eva Braun, were burned by the

SS guards after they had committed suicide. And also his appointed successor, the Reichsminister of Propaganda, Josef Goebbels.'

'Yes.' I nod. I know.

'And these are the bodies you wish to dig up,' says the Herr Direktor, 'these are the ghosts you wish to disturb.' He shakes his head.

'You have a museum of the Gestapo,' I point out. 'And the Museum of Resistance at the prison in Plotzensee – '

'And are they not enough?'

'This will be different.'

'Ah, yes. The technology of virtual reality. To relive the experience.' He shakes his head again. 'As if once is not enough.'

But he has given me an opening.

'We hope, by reminding people of what it was like for their parents and grandparents, to prevent it from ever happening to their children.'

'So you will recreate the conditions in the prisons, in the torture chambers of the Gestapo – ?'

'And in the bunkers. And in the bomb shelters and the basements where the people had to live all the time the Allies were bombing them. We want to show how the German people suffered, too, from all of this.'

I have been sent as a diplomat, an ambassador from Camelot. I have learned to make speeches.

'Hmmm,' says the Herr Direktor.

We walk back towards the rhinoceros. It is still sleeping. A man in a top hat has come out of one of the trailers and is practising juggling. A pair of geese stretch their necks through the bars of their enclosure to watch. Why geese, I wonder, in a circus? The juggler whips off the hat and the balls fall into it, one by one except the last, which hits the brim and falls to the dusty ground with a soft thud. The geese gently hiss. The clown picks up his ball.

'And whose "virtual reality" is this?'

'I'm sorry?'

'Who designs it? Who programs your computers? Who is to say what it was really like?'

'There will be consultants. We would hope that you yourself . . .'

I have been sent as a diplomat. I have learned to make gifts.

'Hmmm,' says the Herr Direktor.

His car is waiting on the far side of the big top. There is a small queue at the box office. A stall is selling frankfurters and beer. I can smell the mustard and the frying onions. There is even some litter blowing in the slight breeze. I look back at the untidy sprawl of the circus in its wasteland. The muddy tracks of the trailers, the straw for the animals, a heap of dung . . . I like this air of amiable seediness. It is unthreatening. I wish the Potsdamer Platz could stay like this. I like this image of the centre of Berlin. I do not want it to change, to become organised, the centre of the new Teutonia. I like the Germans when they leave things alone, like this. It is when they decide to sort things out that I worry. Possibly, this is a Czech view.

'Can I offer you a lift somewhere?'

'Thank you but I think I would quite like to walk for a while. I'd like to get a feel of the place.'

He pauses for a moment before he gets into the car.

'Well, it will not be my decision,' he says. 'Thank God.'

We both know that. But he will be consulted.

There is a silence. He still will not get into the car. Awkwardly I try to reassure him.

'If I thought it was just . . . gratuitous, a horror show, I would not, for one moment, consider . . .'

'No. I appreciate that, doctor.' He gives me an even look. He is younger than I, by about five or six years I should think, but his manner makes him seem older by at least ten. Magisterial. One of the elders of the city. He has the reputation of being a liberal.

'The name Epstein – it is Jewish, yes?'

'Yes, it is Jewish.' Not wishing to contradict the assumption, not wishing to accept the implication.

'Not that it makes any difference, you understand, but there is just the question of motivation.'

'You mean that if he were Jewish he might, possibly, feel a certain . . .?'

'Well . . .'

'That would be understandable, I think.'

'Yes.'

He stares at the ground for a moment and then up at me again with the same even look as before. It is perhaps something he practises. But then I know I misjudge him. This is difficult and he is doing his best.

'There is no question of anti-Semitism, doctor.'

'I did not for a moment – '

'If anything, it would incline the committee to be sympathetic to the proposal. There would be an element of guilt, of course, in that, but also . . . genuine sympathy. Certainly on my part.'

'Yes. I am sure – '

'But there would also be a suspicion that it might bring an element of distortion into the equation. Into the history. You understand?'

'As I said, there will be experts, historians, including German authorities on the subject.'

'So.' A small, quick smile. 'It will not be the Hollywood version.'

I spread my hands in the small, deprecating gesture of the Czech, seeing no reason, as a Czech, to distrust the Hollywood version any more than the German, or the English, or the Russian, but not, of course, being Czech, wishing to say so.

Now he is frowning.

'But I am curious, doctor. What is his motivation in this?'

I turn the gesture into a shrug. It feels very natural. I have been here six months and I am once more the *Mitteleuropäer* in the marketplace.

'Purely educational,' I assure him. He looks sceptical. 'And, of course, he was born in Germany.'

The eyebrows shoot up, the eyes widen behind the spectacles. 'Really? I did not know this.'

'In Berlin. In 1945. Until he was two years old.'

'I see.'

I see him trying to work it out. A Jewish baby in Berlin in 1945?

'He was the son of a German officer who died fighting on the Eastern front. A Prussian aristocrat: Furst von Reisenburg.'

He stares at me. Is this my idea of a joke?

'The main family estates were in the East, on the border with Poland. I think they are now on Polish territory but there was a house – a *Schloss*, I should say – and extensive lands just south of Berlin which the family used as a hunting lodge and which Mr Epstein is in the process of reclaiming from the state of Brandenburg.'

He struggles to take it in, this new image of the Prussian Junker which has so precipitately replaced whatever else he had in mind.

'So? He intends to live here, in this place?'

'He is considering it.'

'Well . . .'

He turns to get into the car and then turns again, confusedly, to shake my hand.

'I am sorry. This is a surprise to me. You must tell me more of this when next we meet, doctor. In the meantime

. . . We must wait until the committee makes its decision, I am afraid.'

I start off across the Tiergarten towards my hotel but suddenly the walk does not seem so attractive a proposition. I feel greasy, dirty, dishevelled; the air is full of dust from all the building work and the constant digging-up of roads, cables and sewers: the excavation of the bowels of East Berlin. I want to get back as fast as possible and shower and have something to eat. I have missed lunch.

There is no shortage of cabs in the eastern part of the city. It was one of the few jobs open to former members of the secret police after reunification. There is an old joke they tell in Berlin: You don't tell the taxi driver where you want to go in East Berlin, you just tell him your name and he takes you there. Unhappily, they become lost as soon as they cross over to the West.

'The Schweizerhof,' I instruct him.

He inclines his head, frowning.

'Just opposite the Zoo,' I say.

He knows the way to the Zoo.

On the way I reflect on my conversation with the director, particularly what he had said about the ghosts of the past. Despite my glib assurances, I was far from convinced that Adam's motives were as 'purely educational' as I had indicated. Ghosts have a definite commercial appeal and Adam was not unaware of that. Besides, Jewish or not, he had a personal interest to declare. They were his ghosts, too.

And mine.

So what of my motivation? What was I doing here, rooting among the bones of my past, the dust and ashes, the teeth . . . disturbing the ghosts? Curiosity? Exorcism?

I still don't know. The Calvinists believe in predestination. I, brought up as a good Catholic, must believe in choice. So

I must have chosen. Perhaps it was the guilt of the survivor, my Catholic conscience. And look where it has led me.

Perhaps the Devil had a part in it.

When I arrived at the hotel there was a message to call Frau Stobel at the office we had rented in Hardenbergstrasse. Did I have any idea where Adam was?

I had not seen Adam for a week or more. I had hardly seen him more than a dozen times in the six months or so since we had started the project. I saw less of him now that we were supposedly working together than I had seen of him before. I never knew what was happening. Never knew where he was. And for this I had given up my lucrative practice, returned to the cockpit of Europe. I was beginning to feel like a neglected wife.

'Isn't he on his way back from Frankfurt?' I said.

He'd been talking to the bankers again – and anyone else who might be of any use, even some politicians.

'I booked him on a return flight this morning,' she said, 'but he was not on it. I have checked with the airport.'

'Well, perhaps he missed it. It wouldn't be the first time.'

'I phoned the hotel where he was staying in Frankfurt. They say he checked out yesterday morning.'

'I see.'

Not seeing at all. But not yet alarmed.

'I would not be so anxious,' said Frau Stobel, 'only he had a meeting at twelve, here in the office.'

'A meeting? Who with?'

And why was I not invited?

'With the people from the *Treuhand* – about the *Schloss*.'

'Ah.' Slightly mollified. Adam's repossession claim for the Reisenburg family property was not, strictly speaking, a concern of mine.

'Have you tried the house?' I asked.

'Of course.'

Frau Stobel was tall and neat and precise and reminded me of a pencil, always kept freshly sharpened. She wore her hair pulled severely back from her face and tied in a determined knot at the back, her skin so smooth with its careful make-up I sometimes wondered if that, too, was tied in a neat bow somewhere out of sight behind her high white collar. Occasionally, when she was harassed by Adam, it looked as if it had been tied a notch too tight and begun to split in the middle between her elegantly drawn brows.

'And Jackie has no idea . . .?'

'Frau Epstein thought that he was staying in Frankfurt until this afternoon. She is expecting him back this evening.'

And Frau Stobel was picking her words with care.

'I see,' I said again. This time with more perception. So Adam had been off on some jaunt of his own for the last twenty-four hours. So far as I was concerned this was entirely in character, and yet . . . I felt a small stirring of unease. It was unlike him to miss a meeting. Or to lie to his wife.

Or was it?

10

THE HOUSE BY THE LAKE

I arrived at the house just after seven. The housekeeper, Frau Lange, opened the door.

Frau Lange was Frau Stobel's alter ego, what Frau Stobel might have been like if someone had untied the knot and let it all fall out. Not that she was relaxed, far from it, she just believed in letting her anxiety show. She was a plump, frightened pigeon of a woman, a bustler, a compulsive fluffer-up of cushions, an obsessive wiper-down of surfaces. Jackie would involuntarily flinch, she said, whenever she saw Frau Lange with the kitchen wipes, anticipating that one day, forgetful of her position, Frau Lange would reach out and wipe her, just as her mother used to when she was a brat, taking her chin firmly in one hand and removing some sticky substance from the area of her mouth while Jackie squirmed in impotent protest.

With the intuition of her kind, Frau Lange had detected a calamity in the making and she had a bottle of cleaning fluid ready to deal with it.

No, Herr Epstein was not back yet, she informed me, with just a hint of censure, but I would find Frau Epstein at the bottom of the garden, by the lake.

The house was in Wannsee, rented from some diplomat at the embassy in Washington. Not particularly grand but with a fine position on the lake and a view clear across to the

Grünewald. Jackie was sitting on the edge of a rackety wooden pier with her feet dangling above a small skiff, staring out over the water. She looked around when she heard me and tried not to look too disappointed when she saw it wasn't Adam.

'No word?' she said.

'No,' I said.

I clambered awkwardly on to the pier and sat down beside her. She put her head on my shoulder and we sat there for a moment saying nothing. The sun struck sparks off the water as it sank and I could see the moon in the sky above the Grünewald. A fine night for the bombers.

'He checked out of the hotel yesterday morning,' she said. 'He got the hotel to hire a car for him, did you know?'

Yes, I said, Frau Stobel had told me.

'I wonder what Frau Stobel hasn't told us,' she said.

This was a dangerous area for speculation. I avoided it.

'Do we know where Eric is yet?' I asked her.

Eric was Adam's minder. He was supposed to stay with him all the time. I think this was an insurance requirement. All I can say is, either he was the worst minder in the world or he and Adam had come to some sort of an arrangement early in their relationship. But maybe I maligned him. Maybe he was good at blending into the background. Maybe he disguised himself as a tree.

'Gone fishing,' said Jackie.

'Gone fishing?'

'He left a message with Frau Lange. Adam had given him the weekend off and he was going fishing. He'd be back Sunday night.' I took a moment to absorb this.

'You can't blame Eric,' said Jackie.

'The insurers might,' I said, unwisely, 'if anything . . .'

She looked at me. 'Is that what you . . .?'

'No,' I said. 'Of course not.'

But it had to be a possibility. That was what Eric was for,

after all. To guard against the kidnappers and the terrorists and the psychopaths and the sad, sick, random crazies who stalk the people in the headlines to make headlines themselves.

'And there's been a lot of publicity lately,' said Jackie, 'about the museum.'

'Well, sure,' I said, 'but – '

'A lot of people don't like it,' she said.

This was true.

'And a lot of people don't like rich Wessis who try to get their property back from people in the East.'

This also was true.

'Not so very long ago they shot the director of the *Treuhand* dead,' she said.

I shook my head.

'He's just ... doing an Adam,' I said. I had a sudden thought. 'Maybe he went to look at this property himself on the spur of the moment. You know. It's the kind of thing he does.'

'Then why didn't he call me?' she said.

But I didn't know the answer to that.

I felt the cold rising off the lake and shivered.

'Come on,' she said, using my shoulder to lever herself up, 'let's get back to the house. Frau Lange will have supper ready.'

It was growing dark. I could see the lights of the autobahn out to Potsdam. I didn't want to be sitting any longer by the lake but I didn't want to be sitting in the house either, eating up Frau Lange's stodgy food like a good boy with Jackie holding back the anger and the fear and Frau Lange fluttering in the background.

Then, as I climbed up stiffly, my knees giving me formal notice of their imminent retirement, I heard her swift intake of breath and she was away, striding down the pier without me, the planks quivering under her feet. I heard Adam's cheerful shout and saw the familiar figure striding down from the house towards us . . .

I hung back at the edge of the pier. There was a brief exchange. Then she carried on alone, back towards the house.

I went forward then and helped him up.

'Keep your head between your legs,' I advised him. 'Try to take deep breaths.'

He said something about my medical expertise which I was inclined to leave unchallenged in the circumstances. I let him apply his own therapy. There are some areas where my attentions might not be welcomed. I gazed out over the lake for a few minutes until he'd finished and then asked him if he thought he could make it back to the house. My tone was sympathetic but I am afraid the satisfaction may have shown in my face. This was something I had often wanted to do to Adam. I think he probably knew that. His reply was ungenerous.

He hobbled down to the lake and lowered himself gingerly down to the jetty.

I watched him for a moment and then sighed, pulled up my collar and walked down to sit beside him.

'How did she find out?' he said.

'You had a meeting,' I said, 'at twelve o'clock.'

He stared at me. 'Who . . .?'

I told him. His reaction seemed genuine. He let out an interesting variation on the Jewish wail he'd picked up from Sam, slamming the side of his head with the hand that wasn't clutching his nether parts.

'You forgot?' I said.

'Completely. I . . . Jesus, what an asshole!'

I thought that summed it up pretty well.

'So where were you?' I said.

He looked down at the water for a moment. Then he looked up at the sky. I waited. He sighed.

'I went to see Magda,' he said.

11

THE EXILE

W hen the long war was over and the city wall breached and broken and sold off in bits to the tourists; when the last battle was fought and lost and the losers in retreat . . . what was a poor girl to do?

Yes, I did wonder. What had Magda Krenkel been up to all those years?

Well, now we know, don't we? As much as she has chosen to tell us – and the media have discovered, though I am inclined to distrust both sources.

I still find it hard to focus on her. I see a distorted image, like the 'vulture face' of Beria, glimpsed by Yevtushenko, in the window of a limo as he cruised the streets of Moscow 'searching for a woman for the night'.

Beria? Stalin's hatchet man, the head of his secret police.

I'm sorry, I keep forgetting. You weren't around in the fifties. Besides, you're quite right, she looks nothing like a vulture. I betray my prejudice.

And she could as easily have been looking for a man, for she shared my catholic tastes and she had her choice of both, in the good old days.

Or I imagine her in her apartment that overlooked the Wall, the one the Herr Direktor pointed out to me: part of a showpiece development where only the most trusted servants of the state were permitted to reside. It was prettily landscaped with trees and shrubs and a children's playground – but you know that.

She lived alone. She had never married. Her lovers were temporary acquisitions.

One of them had made her some puppets.

He was a madman, officially categorised as such by the state. But before that, when Magda knew him, he was an artist and he made them with great skill. He made them look alive, though there was inevitably an element of caricature about them. They did not have to speak for you to feel you knew them or, at least, what they represented. For the most part you knew who was Good and who was Evil, but not always.

There was the king. He looked like a king, at any rate, though he might have been some lesser majesty like a prince. He wore a black beard tinged with grey and a tinsel crown. His face had authority but it also looked rather sad and vulnerable. There was the princess, his daughter. Or so you would think, judging from her age, though she could have been his wife. She was beautiful, of course, but there was an anxious, slightly apprehensive look in her eye as if she had just heard she was to marry the Beast. There was the wizard in his black robe flecked with silver like stars in the night sky. He had a long white beard and carried a magic wand and the face beneath his wizard's hat was fierce and noble and wise. You would feel vastly reassured to have him on your side but fear to make him your enemy. But there was a hole in his hat for the wire that came out of the top of his head and if you slid it up a little, as Magda sometimes did, you would see that he was quite bald and his forehead deeply lined with wrinkles which altered his face completely. He looked rather alarmed and apologetic as if he had screwed up badly on an important spell.

Then there was the witch. She had a wart on her nose and

100

two fangs instead of teeth. One eye was sightless, the other glaring. She did not carry a wand but a bundle of thorny twigs as if she were about to thrash someone to within an inch of his life.

'That is you, of course,' said the madman when he presented it to her.

'Thank you,' said Magda, coolly.

And there was the idiot, Igor, with his hunchback and his cyclops eye and his crooked grin.

'And that is me,' said the madman.

He didn't know how right he was, once the Stasi had finished with him.

So there was her cast of puppets waiting in the wings. She would open the curtain to take down a dress or a blouse and they would swing on their strings, limp and lifeless like those other figures she had seen, hanging from a multiple gibbet. And sometimes she would pull the strings to make them dance.

Magda used to pull a lot of strings in those days. We don't know the precise nature of her job though there has been much speculation. A petty official in the Ministry of Information, she says. A senior member of the Stasi, the papers say. Probably we'll never know. She was, of course, a psychologist by profession.

She lost the lot when the Wall came down: job, status, limousine, apartment . . . But she kept the puppets. I saw them when we met. They were symbolic of her former power and silent promptings of her determination to regain it.

And even when the Wall came down and she was cast into outer darkness, there were still a few strings she could pull. There were people who owed her favours, people whose secrets she kept.

One of them gave her a job, though not quite what she was used to, and it meant moving to a provincial city some two hundred kilometres south of Berlin.

She had a one-bedroomed unit on the eighteenth floor of a tower block. Her windows afforded her a view of other towers and distant factory chimneys and on mornings when the pollution was bad she could not see the ground below but only the tops of the towers, rising out of the smog. She rather liked this effect but she did not open the windows.

She would gaze out sometimes and imagine Adam in his own high tower with his god's-eye view over the city. She imagined his office with a great desk and panelling and expensive works of art. And all the funds at his disposal and all the people at his command, people who opened doors for him and closed them on intruders. Magda was not envious but she was, at times, resentful. She resented the years she had spent working for a lost cause while others, like him, accumulated power and privilege and riches. If that was the way the world was going, Magda had a lot of catching up to do and her beauty would not last for ever, though her anger, quite possibly, might.

And then she read about him in the newspapers and she began to pull strings. She discovered the name of the hotel he was staying in Frankfurt and picked up the phone . . .

Or so *he* said. Me, I'm not so sure. I'm not so sure he didn't ring her.

But let's accept his version of events.

He was in Frankfurt, on that we are all agreed. The city of bankers. They were impressed by Adam's plans. They suggested that he set up a trust, for tax purposes. They suggested it should be called the Reisenburg Trust. It was a good German name, a princely name. And Adam agreed because he felt it honoured his grandfather, who had been the last prince to bear the name.

The deal was struck, the papers signed; his financial advisers departed for California. Adam returned to his hotel to change for dinner.

And Magda phoned.

I wonder what she said before she came to the point. And what was his response? After twenty-five years? I find it so hard to imagine. That is why I am suspicious. And for him to drop everything like that, to change his travel plans, hire a car, drive halfway across Germany . . . to a city in the east.

I know it well. I've seen the movie.

It is the stereotype, the one they always pull out of the archives to show how bad things were when the Communists were in charge. Its brief exposure to capitalism has done little to change its appearance besides erecting a few giant hoardings to display the trinkets now available in the shops – where there *are* shops – for the natives to buy, when they have any money. They look like pictures of a different planet. There are Western cities where the streets are meaner, grimmer and grimier but none so uniformly bleak.

I am talking about a couple of years back now but I doubt it has changed much. It is a city in irreversible decline. When you turn off the autobahn you are confronted with a phalanx of barrack-block apartments with the occasional high-rise soaring from their midst like a watchtower, as if to keep a wary eye on the inmates. The city within this *cordon militaire* is largely composed of older, rather more elegant buildings, but they have either been neglected and allowed to rot or coated with a grey-brown preservative of sludge that looks rather like a mixture of dust and cobwebs bonded together with glue. Those that have escaped this dubious expedient retain a certain ravaged grace but the original stucco has fallen off in great chunks to expose raw patches of brickwork or stone like open wounds and the woodwork has not seen paint for decades. They might be derelict except that people clearly are living in them. There are curtains in the windows, even a few window boxes, and lines of washing hanging from some of the balconies.

You can take this in even when you are driving because

there is so little traffic but you have to keep an eye open for the abandoned Trabants, dumped at the side of the road like collapsed cardboard boxes, and the ancient trams that come clanging and clattering down the centre of the street, aggressively territorial. Adam thought they were trying to ram him, the drivers pop-eyed in frustration at not being able to turn off the rails. He had, of course, hired a top-of-the-range Mercedes and nothing could have more ostentatiously advertised his status as a *Besserwessi*.

He had to stop from time to time to consult the street map he had bought at a service station when he came off the autobahn. The man who had sold it to him had warned that it wouldn't be much use and he was right. The streets had been renamed after the war to honour the heroes and martyrs of the revolution and these were the names on the street map. But after the Wall came down the new regime had decided to change many of the more recognisable and objectionable ones – like Erich Honeckerstrasse – back to what they were before. Then someone discovered that these weren't the original street names. They'd been changed before, by the Nazis in the thirties to honour their own heroes and martyrs of the street fighting that had brought them to power. The resulting compromise must have required a degree of imagination, political acumen and historical knowledge rare in a city planners' department.

It was growing dark when Adam eventually found the hotel. Viewed from the outside it had a certain archaic charm, not entirely destroyed by the neon sign above the entrance. The interior was less enchanting. Adam's room was a funeral parlour with a bed instead of a coffin. But at least there was a telephone. He picked it up and then put it down again and sat on the bed to think about it. He knew that making that call was an irrevocable step, more so than making the journey from Frankfurt. For a moment he considered the alternative,

104

which was checking out of the hotel instantly and driving up to Berlin and surprising Jackie by arriving a day earlier than she was expecting him. It had many attractions but, of course, he picked up the phone and made the call.

He had not overlooked the possibility of a set-up. He had even taken the precaution of bringing one of Eric's guns with him. I'm not sure if Eric knew this. I was rather surprised he knew how to use it but he probably picked that up from the movies. Or perhaps Eric showed him in an idle moment in between practising his fly-casting.

He wondered what I would have had to say about the venture, had I known about it. He decided that one of the things I would have said was that a man approaching fifty and weighing over eighty kilos should not skate on thin ice.

In this he was entirely right.

Unhappily, skating on thin ice is precisely what attracts men of this age, whatever their weight and aptitude. It frequently takes the form of an extramarital affair or some outstanding feat of athletic prowess and invariable ends in hernia, heart attack or divorce, sometimes all three. Adam's recklessness was destined to take a different course but was motivated by the same desire to prove his continuing virility. Either that or a death wish.

He must have been aware of this: he had that much self-knowledge and a capacity for analysis for which I take at least some of the credit.

But what use is self-knowledge, you may ask, if you ignore the conclusions?

He put the gun in his briefcase and went downstairs.

The bar was full of Wessis: the managers and technicians and consultants who were 'remoulding the eastern industrial base', as he had heard it put by one of his new banker friends, and making most of the population of the east redundant in the process. They looked and sounded like expatriates in some remote corner of the Third World, suffering the inadequacies of the native culture. There was a definite celebratory atmosphere which he ascribed to the fact that it was Thursday evening and they already had their bags packed for the weekend. There wasn't a single woman among them.

He took himself off to a table in the corner of the room where he could watch the entrance – something else he'd learned from the movies. God alone knows what he thought he'd do if they appeared in the doorway in their black balaclavas: dive under the table and start shooting?

I am afraid he probably thought exactly that.

He recalled, as I did, the circumstances of their first encounter. He remembered her body better than her face: a small, compact, fit body, a peasant's body, stocky but not at all fat. He felt a sudden, surprising lust, or a memory of lust. She made love as if it was a trial of strength. He had never, before or since, enjoyed such frenzied or protracted sex. He had always made love gently in the past, but with Magda he had wanted to hold her down and thrust himself into her until she screamed, while Magda seemed equally determined to use his penis as her instrument and to ride it at her own pace and pleasure. That was why he remembered it as a wrestling match, with the honours more or less even. Her greatest delight seemed to be to exhaust him, and then revive him by goading, spurring, biting, scratching, or by contorting herself into a variety of erotic poses.

Of all her sexual accomplishments, this was the one she had most perfected. She was a shameless exhibitionist. He knew her body more intimately by the end of the second night than that of any of his previous lovers. And yet her mind – her character – remained a mystery to him. She was deliberately elusive, as if playing an elaborate game of deception with him, or as if this, too, were part of her sexual goading.

But it wasn't much use remembering her body, if he couldn't remember her face. Presumably she would not come here naked. He imagined a short, dumpy woman with a dark fuzz on her upper lip. Possibly wearing glasses, wearing . . .

Wearing a dark tailored suit and black stockings, carrying her purse tucked neatly under her arm. She stood in the entrance, poised and confident, surveying the interior of the bar, and picked him out before he had time to stand and make himself known to her. He was too busy dealing with the shock.

Magda is, of course, widely perceived to be beautiful. She has been compared in the more sensational press to Ingrid Bergman, though myself I cannot see it. In the mouth, perhaps, but look at the eyes, they are so hard, so cruelly mocking, whereas Bergman's . . . Well, there is something of fifties Hollywood about Magda, I will say. But more Crawford than Bergman, please.

Either way, I can imagine the effect on Adam if he'd been expecting something in a boiler suit with a moustache. In the past she had been so determinedly androgynous: the leather jacket, the workman's cap, the baggy trousers. He had never seen her before in a skirt. And with long brown hair down to her shoulders. She looked about thirty-five and her complexion was amazing considering the environment they were supposed to be living in. Perhaps there is something in all that pollution that is good for the skin. Perhaps they should market it.

He saw the glint of recognition and then she came over to him, briskly, a half-smile on her face.

Did they kiss, I wonder? A polite peck on both cheeks or something warmer? The last time they met they would have fucked but it was, as I later pointed out, twenty-five years ago. What is the etiquette in such circumstances?

I expect they shook hands.

107

He bought her a drink, they chatted for a while . . . My imagination fails me, I'm afraid. Perhaps she asked him about Hollywood. It has an enduring fascination for people in the old Communist bloc. I remember when I went back to Czechoslovakia after the revolution and Havel was speaking to the crowd from the balcony of the People's Forum office in the old town square. He had just been to America, to address the United Nations in New York, and thousands of us were gathered there, waiting for him to report back, to tell us how he got on with the bankers and the politicians and the people, but most of all the bankers, and he started his speech: 'Well, as you know I've just been to America and guess who I met – Paul Newman!' We all laughed but we knew he meant it.

They went into the restaurant.

I know the restaurant, too. I have not been there but I can picture it. There are many like it. The original *fin-de-siècle* mouldings have been restored and painted but badly, with a garish effect, like an old tart with too much make-up. The tables are set with style but the flowers in the centre are plastic, or perhaps silk. The menu is elaborate and flatters to deceive. There are fifty tables and as many waiters, dressed like undertakers, waiting for the rush to be buried there.

He sat as far away from the door as possible, back to the wall, briefcase at his feet. Good line of fire in all directions. Eric would have been proud of him.

Magda mocked. Not openly but it was in her eyes, as if she knew, though I expect she was only smiling a little at his discomfort. This was the Magda he remembered, always with that sardonic look, as if she knew something he didn't that gave her control of the situation.

He felt the old familiar irritation but also, rather disturbingly, its accompanying lust. He looked down at the menu and tried to focus on the pretentious descriptions and told himself that she was not at all his type and never had been. But there was something about her that both repulsed and attracted him. Not attracted, that is not the word. It was something far cruder, something that inspired a basic animal instinct to penetrate, to overcome. A desire to do it now, across the table. He had a brief, erotic vision of her stretched over it with her dress pushed up right above her breasts, wearing stockings and no underwear while he drove into her, making her writhe with pleasure . . .

He ordered the simplest dish on the menu; she the most filling. Then she told him about her troubles.

He should have been in control. She was the supplicant; he the *Besserwessi* in the business suit with the briefcase and loaded pistol inside in case she forgot who the winners were.

But Magda had a more powerful weapon. It was called guilt and she knew how to use it better than anyone.

12

THE GUILT TRIP

The name of the guilt was Gerhard Krenkel and he was Magda's son – Adam's too, according to his mother. He's in trouble, Magda had said, when she had phoned Adam in Frankfurt. I cannot say I was either shocked or surprised when Adam told me the nature of this trouble. My capacity for both had, of course, been somewhat blunted over the years. All those confessions I had heard, all those evacuations of the psyche, had prepared me for almost any form of human behaviour. Or so I thought.

I said, 'And what does this involve, precisely?'

'You mean, does he beat up immigrants, set fire to their hostels, chant *Sieg Heil* while they're burning?'

'That kind of thing.'

'God knows.'

'Doesn't Magda?'

'No. All she knows is he's running with this crowd of Nazi motherfuckers and she's worried sick.'

I said, 'And how do you feel about it?'

He said, 'Well, how do you think I feel? I'm his father, for Christ's sake.'

I withheld my opinion on this, for the time being.

I said, 'Adam, there is no genetic causality that I know that will produce Nazis.'

'Well, suck my dick,' said Adam, who was less impressed

than a Californian should be by modern psychology. It is, after all, our biggest earner after oranges. Then, more reasonably, 'But I wasn't there. All the time he was growing up. I just wasn't there.'

'And you think that's the reason for his political affiliations?'

'It could have contributed – don't you think?'

'Well, I haven't met him, but – '

'Well, I have.' This stopped me in my tracks, just as I was about to begin a short discourse on the probable psychological causes of the phenomenon of neo-Fascism in post-Cold War Europe. 'I met him this morning,' he said. 'That's why I was so late coming back.'

'I see.' What I saw was a fantastic image of the reunited family: the Hollywood father, the Communist mother and the Nazi storm-trooper son. A triptych of a confused world. I wished I had been there. 'So, what's he like?'

'Well, he's not a skinhead with a swastika tattooed on his forehead.'

'Thank goodness for small mercies,' I said.

He told me that Magda had fixed it. They had discussed it over dinner and she had phoned him at his apartment in Potsdam. I suspect there was some prior arrangement. He came down by train in the morning. For lunch, at a different restaurant. One that Magda had proposed.

'Did you take the gun?' I could not resist asking. He shook his head.

'And does he look at all . . .?'

'Like me? No. He's got ginger hair and a wimpy little moustache. He's kind of skinny. He looks . . . hungry. He probably is hungry.'

'And how did you get on?'

He considered. 'Okay. In the circumstances. He was . . . polite. A little distant. Defensive. He speaks quite good English. He's not unintelligent. He's had a reasonable education. He had a good job until reunification. He was a film editor, Milan, at the state film studios in Babelsberg.'

I said nothing.

'But he lost his job. That could be half the trouble.'

I reserved my opinion on this, too. There were other questions I wanted to ask. One was particularly pressing.

'Do you think we could go inside now?' I asked. 'I'm getting too cold to think.'

As we talked, the darkness had closed in on us. I could no longer see the opposite side of the lake, only the lights in the houses above. The black bit without any lights was the Grünewald, the eternal German forest, even this close to Berlin. We began to walk back to the house.

'And you still think you're the father,' I said, 'even now you've met him?'

'I don't know,' he said. 'But I'm not going to start questioning it now.'

'You questioned it then.'

'In my mind. With you, maybe. But not with her.'

'Why not?'

He made a noise that was not quite a laugh. 'Ego? Chivalry? Who knows? I even wrote to her . . . I said she should have the baby and we should get married and she should come and live in the West.'

This was news to me. Why had he not told me this before? I stopped walking. I even forgot the cold. For a moment.

'And she still has this letter?'

'I don't know. Maybe. She hinted as much.'

So at least we knew where we stood.

'And what has she told Gerhard, do you know?'

'What about?'

'You. Why he never saw you. You said he didn't even know who you were.'

'No. Not until a few days ago.'

'So did you tell him it was Magda's wish that you never saw him?'

'Milan, she was there with us, how could I? Besides . . . I didn't exactly put up a fight, you know.'

'And now you feel guilty about that?'

'I don't know. But I think I'd like to help him now. I think I owe him that.'

'Help him in what way?'

'I thought of involving him in what we're doing.'

'The museum?'

'Well, there may be other things. Other projects. That's why I've set up the trust.' He interpreted my silence as hostile. 'You don't think it's a good idea?'

'I am interested in why you do,' I said.

'Well, for one thing it might teach him something. About the past. His past. Germany's. Europe's. That's what it's meant to do, isn't it?'

'And you think this will make him stop being a neo-Nazi?'

'Well, it might open his eyes to what the original version was all about, for Christ's sake.'

'And it might make him go out and buy a bigger size of jackboot.'

'Okay, Milan, so what do you think I should do?'

But he knew that was cheating. Therapists are not there to tell you what you should do. This, I know, raises the question of what therapists *are* there for, but we won't go into that now.

'Some things are better not dealt with head on,' I said. 'Take sexual problems. If a client comes to me and says he is impotent, the last thing I am going to talk to him about is sex. I would want to decentralise the problem, to defocus it – '

(Yes, I know. I wish now I had chosen a different example,

114

but there you are. How was I to know? I am not all-seeing, infallible. If I was, I would not be here, in this orchard in winter, talking to a pig.)

'I don't give a damn about his sex life,' he said. 'I just don't want him to turn out like Adolf Hitler.'

Well, of course, Hitler's sex life was probably very relevant to how Hitler turned out, but I resisted the temptation to go into that now. The level of irritation in Adam's voice was rising.

'Don't try to write his script for him,' I said. 'Don't pluck him out of one cage only to put him in another.'

Adam protested that he was not thinking of putting him in a cage. Quite the reverse.

'Very well, then, a meadow, where he is forced to pick the flowers. If you do that, don't be surprised if he tramples them underfoot. Tell him, Here is the key to the lock. Open the door. Go.'

'You're on your own, kid. Hell, Milan, so what's new?'

'Give him an allowance, then, if you wish. Give him a camera and thirty rolls of film – tell him to make a movie. But let him do it himself.'

I thought of something else Adam might do, something more practical: 'You might get him an apartment here in Berlin, in Kreuzberg perhaps – I hear it's on the up. Get him away from these punks he's running with. And get him away from his mother.'

He sighed, shaking his head. 'Why did she have him, Milan? She didn't need to. It would have been easy to get an abortion in the East. She was only nineteen.'

It was a question he had asked before, many years ago. I didn't have the answer then and I didn't now. I could only make guesses.

'Maybe she felt maternal.'

'Magda?'

Now I sighed. 'I don't know her, Adam. *You* don't know her. You believe she did it to get some kind of hold over you. To keep a part of you, like some image she could stick pins into.'

'You think that's nonsense?'

'I think it is egotistical.'

'But why? Why did she? You must have some idea. Some theory.'

But I didn't. I still don't. Magda's motives will ever be a mystery to me. It would be easy to say she was mad, was always mad, but I have to do better than that. That's part of the deal.

I said, 'She's not one of my patients, Adam.' Then, reluctantly, 'There could be any number of reasons. You say she plays games, dramatises herself. Perhaps she wanted to play at being the young mother, to prove she could do it, without anyone to help her. Perhaps it has something to do with her own parentage. You said it wasn't a happy marriage.'

'That's what she told me. She said her father was a bully, an oaf.'

'And her mother turned to religion as a consolation?'

'Yes. Obsessively. But what's that got to do with it?'

'Maybe nothing. I'm just speculating. If she felt her parents had let her down, she might wish to prove she could do better.'

I hoped this was not leading me where I did not wish to go, or where I did not wish to lead Adam.

Generally speaking, I do not think it is advisable for people to try to compensate with their children for what they feel was lacking from their own childhood. It can be counterproductive. I think I told Adam this, then. If I didn't, I should have. But would it have made any difference?

'It's not going to be easy, telling people,' he said. 'They'll think I've been hiding it. Him.'

116

'You don't have to tell anyone,' I said. 'Except Jackie, of course.'

'You think I should tell Jackie?'

'What do *you* think?'

'Look, I'm asking you as my friend,' he said, 'not as my goddamn therapist. For Christ's sake stop answering my questions with another question.'

'As your friend I think you should do what you think is the right thing,' I told him. 'And if I was your therapist, which I am not, thank God, I would think you should do what you think is the right thing. So the two of us are agreed.'

'Well, la-di-da,' he said. 'And I suppose you want me to tell her about Magda, too.'

I said I thought it would be difficult not to.

He made no reply to this. We walked back towards the house. I hoped there would be a fire. Perhaps a glass of mulled wine. Just before we went in he took hold of my arm and held me back for a moment.

'I won't tell her right now,' he said. 'I'll tell her later. There are other things I have to . . . I'll tell her later. But not now.'

So what *are* you going to tell her?' I asked, in the low, urgent tones of the fellow conspirator I had suddenly become (this is the problem with being a friend; a therapist is much safer). 'About where you were?'

'I'll think of something,' he said. And then we went in.

We had wild boar for dinner.

I thought you would like to know.

With mashed potatoes, sauerkraut and gravy (Frau Lange surpassing herself in culinary mediocrity) but the wine was a decent claret, not mulled but welcome.

The atmosphere, unlike the food, was rather better than I

had expected. I put this down to the story Adam had concocted for Jackie's benefit.

He had been to Leipzig, he said, to see an old man who was in hospital with terminal cancer. He'd read about Adam's family background in the German press and written to him to say he'd been with his father at the end of the war when they were retreating from the Red Army.

'I just had to go and see him,' said Adam. 'It drove everything else clean out of my mind.'

Not bad, you think? I was quite impressed too. You have to hand it to filmmakers. None of this 'having to see a man about a dog'. But it turned out to be based on a true story, as they say. There *was* an old man – Rudi Fahrenkopf, his name was – and he *had* been with Adam's father during the war and Adam *had* been to see him in Leipzig, but six months ago.

He told me this later that evening, in his study, where we retired with brandies and Jackie safely tucked in her bed. He also showed me the diary he said the old man had given him. It was in a dirty old school exercise book – in German, of course, but Adam had had it translated and typed up.

'He died a couple of months ago,' he told me. 'His daughter let me have that. It's a bit patchy but there's some good stuff about the war and a little bit about my father.'

'You said diaries,' I reminded him.

'Ah, yes,' he said. 'There's also my mother's.'

'Your mother's?' I said. 'Liza kept a diary?' I was surprised he hadn't mentioned this before.

There were three of them, he told me, covering the first two years of the war and most of 1944. Sam had given them to him when he was about fifteen.

'I forgot I had them,' he said. 'I mean, I read bits and pieces of them at the time but they were in German and scribbled, you know, and my German's not exactly . . . but later I got them translated.'

While he was talking he was burrowing among this great pile of files and papers he'd got on his desk and – I know that you'll think this is hindsight, but – I had the idea at the time that he was trying to flummox me. I mean, Adam used to do this thing: if he had something important to tell you, or something he'd deliberately hidden from you for months, or even years, he'd tell you about it while he was doing something else – scrambling on the floor for a pen he'd dropped or pinning something on a noticeboard or throwing a basketball at your head, anything, so long as it succeeded in distracting you from the really important thing he had to tell you.

The strange thing was, it wasn't because he didn't want you to notice. It was more as if he was just trying to test you. Or, more likely, to test himself. To see if his theory or his information or anything was worth a damn thing because if it was, you'd manage to pick it out from all the shit. As he had.

He gave me the diaries. His mother's and ex-Corporal Fahrenkopf's. 'Read them,' he said, 'tell me what you think.'

'Find it,' he was saying. 'See if you can find it, as I did.'

119

13

AN OFFICER AND A GENTLEMAN

Adam's father, Conrad von Reisenburg, was a Prussian officer and gentleman, upright and noble, who always did his duty. Did you ever see Brando in *The Young Lions*? No. You missed something. The film was too stagey for me, the moral driven home like a stake through the crutch, but Brando is at his most beautiful. Short golden curls, lovely black boots . . . From the faded pictures I have seen, Conrad is not quite Brando but he's getting there.

He had a good war, by a soldier's standards, until the last day of 1943 when a piece of shell casing smashed through his ribcage and came out through his back, taking part of his right lung with it and leaving splinters of bone and metal distributed around the base of his spine. He was twenty-six, a captain in the paras and a veteran of Norway, France and Crete, but the shell that got him was fired by a Russian 166-mm howitzer and the place was Zhitomir on the eastern front.

They patched him up in the field hospital and sent him home with a trainload of the dying and the seriously wounded. He was one of almost a million casualties suffered by the *Wehrmacht* that winter. Four armies were entirely destroyed, a fifth cut off in the Crimea. Across a front of three thousand kilometres from the Black Sea to the Baltic, the Red Army was advancing on the Fatherland. I do not know whether Conrad was aware of this at the time or would have cared very much.

When you have half a lung missing and half a kilo of Russian shell in your backside, it tends to reduce your concerns to the strictly personal. I believe.

I must try not to be flippant. It is, as I am sure you understand, a protective device but I can see you find it irritating.

They took him to a hospital in Potsdam, the home of the kaisers. Imagine the black train pulling into the station with its cargo of cripples and paraplegics, the wheels of war grinding to a halt, the wreaths of steam. There is snow on the ground, snow on the trees and on the statues in the gardens of the palace of Sans Souci where the great Prussian soldier king Frederick the Great came to shed his cares and to indulge the less martial aspects of his nature, to play the cello and talk with artists and philosophers and fondle beautiful young men who had not been mutilated by war.

Here the surgeons dug into Conrad's back for the mementos of battle and discovered, somewhat to their surprise, that nothing vital had been severed. They assured him that, given time and effort and not a little pain, there was no reason why he should not walk again, though they did not expect him to run, dance or fight any more wars.

This is where he met Liza. Liza von Freyer she was then, a medical student in her final year. She was not flippant. She was, if anything, a little too serious for her own good. I have been sparing you her more serious reflections on war and pain and death. They tend to date. I think you had to be there to appreciate them.

Her diaries were not a great deal of use, as a matter of fact, either as a historical document or the basis for a film script. A young doctor at a military hospital in the middle of a war had little time for writing diaries. She used them mainly as a memory jogger with the occasional descriptive passage when the mood took her.

There was one I remember, in March '44 it must have been, when she took him out into the gardens in his wheelchair. They held hands and kissed. She recalled that there was still snow on the ground but blossom on the trees. That night another train came in. She wrote, 'The train disgorges them like some monstrous machine of war, the chewed-up bits and pieces of men.' She held another young soldier's hand. He died. She wrote, 'The Führer has called up all children over the age of ten.'

There was very little reference to Conrad, considering they were busy falling in love, but again, when you are falling in love with one man one day and putting together the bits and pieces of a trainload the next, there is little room left for romantic prose, I imagine.

She did write down when he asked her to marry him. It was 1 April. In Anglo-Saxon tradition this is All Fools' Day; I don't know whether it is in Germany also. It does not say in her diary but it should be. Only a fool would think of marriage in Germany on 1 April 1944. Or a hopeless romantic. I recall another entry in the diary, a month or so later when she had transferred to the hospital in the Flaktower in the centre of Berlin:

'Among the ruins there are branches torn from the trees and the new leaves are still growing from these shattered limbs, bursting from the bud.'

But not for long, I think.

There is one description of the war that sticks in my mind. It must have been towards the end of June. She had a couple of days' leave and was in the garden of the Reisenburgs' Berlin residence in Dahlem. She did most of her writing in gardens, hence the many references to nature. She was writing down her memory of an especially bad air raid. The Flaktower had suffered a direct hit from a whole stick of bombs; she felt the shock of the blasts in the operating theatre and all the lights went out. In the morning when she emerged and tried to make her way back to the house in Dahlem, the city was still on fire. The trees in the Zoo Gardens were burning, she wrote, even the grass was burning. There was a terrible wind full of sparks and soot. She walked with some other people towards the S-Bahn. There was a walkway through the rubble marked out with yellow tape. The wind kept blowing down window frames and sections of guttering from the ruined buildings. There was a noise of bells ringing and, she thought, of wailing people. Here and there, they would come across bodies, lying among the rubble like drunks, except that most of them were in bits. Everything was in bits. There was one body blown up on to the overhead tram lines. It hung there, she said, like a scarecrow. She joined the queue of people outside the S-Bahn, shuffling along the walkway between the two lines of tape marking the living from the dead. Unbelievably the trains were still running. 'And now I am here,' she wrote, 'and the birds are singing in the trees and the bees gathering pollen in the evening sun and there are children playing down the bottom of the garden and soon Conrad will be back with his father.'

Conrad's father was a Prussian of the old school who had served Fatherland and Kaiser in the first great war of the century and if he had any qualms about it, he didn't tell anyone. I don't think we can blame him for the rise of Hitler but he didn't do anything to stop it. Like the rest of his class he despised the little Bohemian corporal, as Hindenburg, the last of the Teutonic Knights, called him, but he hated the Poles and the Russians more. He came out of retirement to fight them as a senior officer of the *Abwehr* under Admiral Canaris but perhaps, even then, he was looking over his shoulder at the real enemy.

Liza liked him. She had not expected to but she did. He was a prince and a conservative, tall and distinguished with

124

iron-grey hair and the obligatory duelling scar, tastefully and discreetly positioned above his right eyebrow. He was one of the *alte Herren*, the old gentlemen who were born into a different world and wanted it back, but he was no despot. There was a kindly, even altruistic side to his nature. He'd taken in a number of families who'd been bombed out of Berlin. They were the children she heard playing in the garden. His house in Dahlem was full of them and their mothers and grandmothers, among whom he circulated grandly but fondly like an old patriarch.

That Sunday when Liza sat in the garden he had been to see his old friend Baron Üxkull, to plot the assassination of Adolf Hitler.

I don't know how much you know of the German officers' plot of July 1944. Not a lot, you say? Well, I won't bore you with the details. It failed.

You do know that?

Adolf Hitler did not die on 20 July 1944. The Devil would not let him; Death had nine more months to collect his dues. The gestation period of the human female, in case you did not know. Nine months to produce a child, to kill nine million more.

I am making up the number but I don't suppose it's far wrong, give or take a million or two.

It was Üxkull's nephew Claus who planted the bomb. Another beautiful young man. There were a lot of them about in Germany at that time. Adam von Trott, Ritter von Quirnheim, Conrad von Schwerin, Fritz von Schulenberg, Peter Yorck von Wartenburg, Helmuth von Moltke ... they read like the *Almanach de Gotha*, the great names of German history, sons of generals and statesmen, perfect physical conforms of the master race.

Count Claus Schenk von Stauffenberg was the most beautiful of them all, even after the war started to tear him to pieces. He had been shot up by a British fighter and lost his left eye and his right hand and two fingers off his left. He wore black gloves and a black eye patch, perfect props for the super hero.

It was he who planted the bomb.

You think that was a bad move? A man with seven missing fingers. Yes, but he was the only one with access to Hitler who was willing to kill him. The rest would only talk about it.

Stauffenberg was a knight inspired by a holy vision – to kill the Anti-Christ.

He was summoned to Hitler's battle headquarters in Poland: a wooden hut in the forest called Wolfsschanze, the Wolf's Lair. The Wolf was with his pack of generals, working out how to stop the Russians. They were all standing around a heavy oak table covered with maps. Stauffenberg had the bomb in a briefcase. Two bombs in fact. He went to the toilet to fuse them but because of the missing fingers he only managed to fuse one. It should still have been enough.

He went back into the conference room and placed the briefcase on the floor, right next to Hitler's feet as he leaned over the maps. Then he made his excuses and left.

As he walked back to the car, the bomb exploded. The hut was engulfed in smoke and flames. He did not think anyone could have survived.

But they had.

Shortly after Stauffenberg left the room, another officer had stumbled over the briefcase and pushed it further under the table. A heavy table leg, made of oak, shielded the Führer from the blast. It blew his pants off but it did not kill him. He was not even badly injured. It was the Devil's own luck.

Stauffenberg was arrested by the army. He was shot by a firing squad, standing in the courtyard of the War Ministry with three of his fellow conspirators, lit by the headlights of an army truck.

Hitler was very angry when he heard that he had been killed so cleanly and with a modicum of dignity.

But there were others. Five thousand in all were to die as a result of that bungled bomb. Not a lot, in terms of percentages. But the way they died . . .

Criminals in Germany were executed by guillotine but Hitler ordered that these criminals should be hanged like cattle. Butcher's hooks were driven into a beam in the execution chamber. Piano wire was used instead of rope. Two cameramen were detailed to record the executions on film so that Hitler could watch the suffering of the victims. They were brought into the chamber in groups and waited in turn to be hanged. Hans Ulrich, Furst von Reisenburg, was in the first batch.

They arrested his son, too. I do not know if he had been involved in the plot. It is not something that Liza mentions in her diary. The details I give you are from the history books and they do not record any part played in the uprising by Conrad von Reisenburg. He was still officially recuperating from his injuries but he had been posted, only a few days before the plot and on Stauffenberg's orders, to the Reserve Army so he may well have known about it. He certainly knew most of the plotters. They were his friends; they were of his class. So you could say he was guilty by association.

Liza's diary is blank for the three weeks after 20 July. I expect she had a lot on her mind.

Later, after the war, she told Sam about it and he told Adam. His father was imprisoned in Sachsenhausen concentration camp near Berlin and he was brought into the Gestapo headquarters in Prinz Albrechtstrasse for interrogation. There were cellars there that they used for punishment. We planned to do a reconstruction of them in our museum. Adam was particularly keen.

We do not know what happened to Conrad when he was

taken there, only that Liza went frantic trying to free him. Well, I think we could have guessed that. She tried everyone she knew who could be of influence but most of them were preparing to be arrested themselves. Then she found Maria Schenke.

Maria was a distant cousin. Also, an actress. Not brilliantly successful but in work. She worked in the state film studios in Babelsberg. More importantly she had been the lover of Josef Goebbels, the Gauleiter of Berlin and Reich Minister of Propaganda and Enlightenment. This was by no means an exceptional position. He had scores of them but it did confer the occasional favour. Liza bribed her to approach him. Then, using Maria as an intermediary, she bribed Goebbels himself. She bribed him with everything she had. Her entire inheritance, including the forests. She signed the lot over. And he signed an order for the release of Conrad von Reisenburg.

There was one condition. He was to report immediately for duty with the *Sprengkommandos*, the special explosives squads they sent in to lay the minefields and to clear them ahead of the infantry. It was a sentence of death, Goebbels's little joke.

Paul Josef Goebbels, the little joker. Let me tell you about Goebbels, he is something of an obsession of mine, with his limp and his spiteful tongue and his alley-cat charm; the ideas man, the genius of propaganda, the Prince of Lies. He was one of the few leading Nazis with pretensions to intellect. He had attended several universities. He had written novels and film scripts. Unhappily they were all rejected.

So he joined the Nazi Party.

And he met Hitler.

It was not love at first sight. Hitler did not like people who had been to university. Goebbels did not like *schlampig* little Austrians who hadn't. But they had important things in common. They were small, they felt rejected and they knew how to hook an audience. They had a great sense of theatre. The rejected artist and the rejected writer conspired to create a magnificent drama, a *Sturm und Drang* of a drama, a Wagnerian epic. With lights, sound and music they enthralled the German people and then set fire to them and most of Europe.

I can't help thinking that if someone had given them a movie camera and thirty rolls of film earlier in life, they might have saved the world an awful lot of trouble.

The interesting thing was that he started off with ideals. Unlike Hitler, who only believed in himself, young Paul Josef believed in socialism. He soon learned: probably around the time Hitler came to power and had all his close rivals shot by the SS; all those who believed in something other than him. Until then, there was a chance Goebbels might have gone along with them. But not after. From then on he was Hitler's man, body and soul.

They used to slope off to the pictures together, even during the height of the struggle for power in Berlin in '32. They both loved Greta Garbo.

They shared the same sense of humour.

Humour is the wrong word. The Germans have a better one: *Schadenfreude*, a malicious delight in other people's misfortunes. Goebbels used to tell Hitler what the Brownshirts were doing to the Jews and Hitler would roar and slap his thighs. Releasing Conrad von Reisenburg from prison for service with the *Sprengkommandos* on the eastern front was just the sort of joke that would appeal to them both.

Before he left, Conrad and Liza were married. He had been transferred to Charlottenburg Prison pending his removal to the front line and the prison chaplain married them. Then, owing to an administrative error, or some unexpected kindness, he was released on parole, on his word of honour as an officer and a gentleman, to report for duty thirty-six hours later.

So they had thirty-six hours together, two nights and a day. Thirty-six hours for the buds to open on the shattered bough.

Is this what comes of reading Liza's diaries?

Rudi Fahrenkopf's were far less lyrical. His were about food.

I suppose the only time he found to write was when they stopped somewhere, and whenever they stopped somewhere they had something to eat, or thought about what it would be like to have something to eat. The thought of eating was probably what kept Rudi Fahrenkopf alive through those last few months of war as the German army retreated across Poland. Nonetheless it is a little disconcerting to find that on 17 January, the day my history book tells me Warsaw fell, the great event in Rudi Fahrenkopf's life was that he killed a pig (I'm sorry, it happens) and roasted it over a fire made from someone's furniture. The following day they had bacon and mushrooms for breakfast.

Rudi and Conrad were in the same unit of the *Sprengkommando*. Contrary to Goebbels's expectation, and their own, their mission was no more suicidal than that of any other unit on the eastern front. The German army was too busy retreating to lay any minefields, or clear them. Instead, they blew up bridges.

Rudi calculated that his unit blew up twenty-two bridges on the long retreat to Berlin. Also two rabbit warrens. Rudi recorded that they grilled the corpses over a fire 'with a little wild garlic and sorrel'. There must have been something of the Gipsy in Rudi, either that or the master chef.

On 1 April 1945, a year since Conrad had proposed to Liza, they moved into new positions in the centre of Berlin. They were part of the inner perimeter defending the Potsdamer Platz and the Reich chancellery, now a gutted shell. They had been merged into a scratch unit comprising some old men of the *Volksturm* and a handful of twelve- to sixteen-year-old *Flakhelfers* with an 88-mm anti-aircraft gun which could be depressed to shoot at tanks. Rudi, too, was depressed. There were no more rabbit warrens, only bunkers, and it was more and more difficult to find food.

The last entry in the diary is 30 April 1945.

Nothing, it says.

I wonder if Rudi read history.

On 14 July 1789, the day the people of Paris stormed the Bastille, King Louis XVI wrote that same word in *his* diary: Nothing. Louis, passionate devotee of the chase, meant that he had failed to bag any game that day. Rudi, prime forager and master chef of the *Sprengkommandos*, meant that he had failed to find anything for the pot.

Perhaps it is a coincidence.

But on the night of 30 April 1945, in the bunker under the garden of the Reich chancellery, not a million kilometres from where they were dug in among the rubble, Adolf Hitler did what Stauffenberg and the others had failed to do nine months before. Conscious perhaps of how difficult it had proved to his enemies, he made doubly sure of it himself by crunching a cyanide pellet in his mouth while simultaneously blowing his brains out with a pistol.

So far as we know, it seemed to do the trick.

Conrad's demise is less firmly documented. Rudi makes no note of it in his diary. But he told Adam about it when they met.

They were dug into the Potsdamer Platz just south of the Brandenburger Tor. The Russians had been shelling them almost nonstop for the last two days. Once, when the smoke cleared, they could see the red flag flying from the roof of the Reichstag. They also saw the Flaktower being attacked by bombers and the guns on the roof still firing. Shortly after this, Conrad suddenly stood up and climbed out of the trench.

131

Rudi says he called to him but he didn't seem to hear. He was walking unconcernedly, as if he was out for a stroll, trailing his rifle. He got quite a long way before the machine guns found him. Rudi wasn't sure but he thought he might have been heading in the direction of the Zoo Gardens.

'What do you think?' Adam asked me, when he came in later with the brandy.

'About what particular aspect?' I said cautiously.

'About the movie,' he said.

Well, of course. I should have known. There had to be a movie, otherwise it hadn't happened.

'I don't think you should make it,' I said.

But nor did he.

He had someone else in mind.

14

AS THE WILD GOOSE FLIES . . .

I was never very happy about Lancelot.

Certainly he should never have been in the movie – *Pendragon*, I mean – not if Adam meant it to be authentic. Lancelot wasn't in any of the original stories and, personally, I've never seen the need for him. But then, of course, I'm not a woman.

Lancelot was invented at the behest of Marie de Champagne. Arthur wasn't enough of a hero for her, you see. He couldn't be. He was the husband. And in Marie's court of free love, husbands weren't heroes. Husbands were cuckolds.

So Chrétien de Troyes was prevailed upon to invent a hero more to Marie's liking and Lancelot was the result. A hero with balls – and his prick up some forbidden fruit.

I am sorry to sound so crude. But what is it about women and heroes? Why do they always have to be villains?

Well, you're a woman, of sorts, you tell me.

Was that a knowing grunt? Or a sardonic grunt? Or a *weary* grunt?

You think I am banging on a bit.

Well, you'll just have to bear with me for a moment. Emma Jung banged on about it for thirty years or so and died before she could publish, which may well happen to me, the way things are going. She was very interesting on the subject of heroes, though. One of the main prerequisites of a hero, she pointed out, was to be born in a forest and without a father; that is to say, with a father either dead or missing. The theory was that the mother consciously or subconsciously encouraged the son to take the place of the absent spouse, thus fostering the growth of heroic qualities. Either that or he turned queer. Well, it's only a theory. I'm not sure where the forest comes into it. I knew once but I've forgotten.

Lancelot had a father, of course, which is probably where he started to go wrong.

I'm not saying Lancelot was an out-and-out villain. But he was a *flawed* hero. The best you can say of him was that he tried to be good but he kept on screwing up. And he couldn't resist a bit of skirt, particularly if it was married to his best friend and sovereign lord.

That's the sort of behaviour that appears to be irresistible to women.

I mean, if they wanted a real hero and Arthur was too boring for them, with his ideas about virtue and honour and round tables and all that stuff, what was wrong with Galahad?

Galahad was the perfect knight. Beautiful, brave, all-powerful, young and virile – and Lancelot's son. But no, Galahad doesn't get past the first fence in the romantic-hero stakes.

He's just *too* perfect, that's the trouble.

A mere woman, no matter how beautiful, would never be able to deflect him from his purpose. He'd always be looking over her shoulder at the mirage of the Holy Grail, or a mirror, which is probably more likely.

For a woman, the one essential prerequisite in a hero is utter devotion – to her.

That is the main reason why Lancelot the Lover, Lancelot the Adulterer, Lancelot the Less-than-Perfect is more of a hero than Galahad the Good. And both of them are more of a hero than Arthur the Husband, Arthur the Cuckold.

To a woman, that is.

And apparently to most writers. But then they know their audience. Once Lancelot had made it into print, Arthur began to take a back seat. The macho warrior chief became a man with a grey beard and a long robe sitting on a throne.

Women, you see, can't make a hero of a man who has power over them. They want a hero who is in *their* power. Woman as wife is diminished, woman as lover is the centre of a man's entire being. Or at least he pretends she is, and that is better than nothing.

But I digress.

Callum Connolly left Los Angeles at midday. His flight was due to arrive in Berlin at ten o'clock the following morning.

This was simple enough. It was what happened to the sun that puzzled him. He worried about it all the way to the airport.

'The sun's heading over the Pacific,' he said, 'and I'm going away from it but I'll meet it coming back, right?'

His friends had thrown a leaving party for him and some of them had decided to accompany him to the airport.

'We'll never get him on the plane,' one of them said.

'He's flying already,' said another.

'He needs a downer,' said someone else. 'Who's got a downer?'

They searched their pockets for a downer. No one had a downer.

'But hang on,' he protested wildly. 'The sun doesn't move. It's *us* that's moving.'

He demanded pen and paper to work it out. He drew a big circle in the middle and labelled it 'SUN (NOT MOVING)' and he drew a small circle near it labelled 'EARTH (MOVING)' with an arrow to show the direction. He didn't know if he'd got the direction right but he didn't think it mattered. Then he drew a cross which he labelled 'PLANE' and an arrow going the opposite way from the Earth. When they reached the airport he was still trying to figure it out. He felt as if his head had turned into a clock filled with millions of moving parts made up of suns and moons and planets and aeroplanes all hurtling madly out of control, faster and faster.

'Take it off him,' someone said. 'You know what he's like. He'll start to imagine things.'

His imagination was his greatest asset but it could be a problem at times.

There was some complicated arrangement about picking up his ticket but the woman who had been his most recent lover seemed to have it all worked out.

'Is it Aer Lingus?' he asked.

'No,' she said. 'It's Virgin Atlantic. Does it matter?'

He frowned, shaking his head as if it was all a terrible mistake.

'What's its name?'

This puzzled them.

'The plane,' he said. 'What's it called?'

No one knew what the plane was called.

'I didn't know they had names,' someone said.

'Aer Lingus always call them after saints,' he said. 'They don't take any chances.'

Despite his familiarity with modern technology, his frequent use of machines such as computers, cameras, videos and other wonders of the age in which he lived, Callum Connolly remained in essence a man of the early Renaissance, teetering precariously between the material and the spiritual world. Five hundred years of scientific progress had failed to convince him of the validity of scientific explanation.

Callum knew there were valid technical reasons why an aircraft could take off, fly in a straight line eight kilometres above the earth and land safely in another continent. He also knew it was a very complicated deal worked out with God and the Devil that contained a number of clauses beyond human understanding.

Knowing this, he tried to avoid air travel whenever possible. When it was forced upon him, he endeavoured to travel Aer Lingus because of that airline's original and far-sighted practice of naming their planes after saints. He considered that the angels would think twice before letting *St Ignatius Loyola* or *St Teresa of Avila* break up in midair or hit a mountain or do any one of the utterly terrifying, mind-blowing things that Callum could imagine them doing on a bad day, when the Devil got into them. On the other hand, it might encourage the Devil to pull out all the stops. You just couldn't be sure. Still, on balance, all things considered, he preferred to put his money on the saints. On this occasion, however, the choice had not been his. His ticket had been purchased for him by the agents of some uncaring authority and they had chosen Virgin.

'I don't suppose it's short for the Virgin Mary?' he enquired hopefully.

'Is he on drugs?' asked the woman on the check-in.

'Just booze,' they lied. 'We gave him a bit of a send-off. But we're looking after him.'

'He'll have to walk on to the plane by himself,' said the woman doubtfully. 'Otherwise they won't let him go.'

This had a sobering effect on everyone except Callum. They walked him up and down the forecourt.

'I think that's the last call,' someone said.

They steered him towards the departure gate. He didn't like the way they said goodbye. It sounded as though they never expected to see him again. His lover – or was she now his ex-lover? – gave him a final passionate embrace.

'I don't want to go,' he said. 'I've changed my mind.'

'I know, dear,' she said. 'I don't want you to go, either.'

But she pushed him firmly through the departure gate.

From then on it ceased to have anything to do with him. He was processed along a series of moving belts and through ranks of machines and people who behaved like machines, smiling but firm, brooking no dissent. He found himself on the plane and he still didn't know what its name was. He asked one of the cabin staff but she didn't know either.

'What route do we take?' he demanded. If she didn't know that he was going to get off, even this late.

But she knew.

'Over the North Pole,' she told him.

This was a jolt but when he thought about it, it seemed obvious. The geography was coming back to him.

'We've done it before,' the woman assured him, confidentially. 'We could do it blindfold.'

He looked at her suspiciously, detecting a less than serious response to his concern. I am not normally like this, he wanted to tell her. My friends think of me as recklessly brave at times but flying has an unnerving effect on me. It is quite irrational of me, I know, but I have a strong resistance to being strapped into a hermetically sealed tomb filled with highly combustible aviation fuel powered by what look like giant gas lighters and driven by an unknown, unseen individual who may be perfectly competent but is as likely to be in the final stages of a terminal illness or a manic depressive who has been pushed too far, or just, like the rest of us, an average bullshitter who has done all right up to now but is about to be found out.

He had it all thought out in his mind but he knew he had as much chance of articulating it as he had of flying the plane himself.

He managed to find his seat unaided. There was a rather attractive woman sitting next to him. She had dark hair cut like a pageboy and she wore a cream linen suit with quite a short skirt. Her legs were bare and brown. He tried to pull himself together.

He looked around the rest of the upper-class section. It was almost full. Upper-class Virgin was supposed to appeal to the scruffy rich but they all looked remarkably clean, neat and well-pressed to Callum, who appeared to be the only scruffy one among them, if not rich. He wore a red-and-blue check shirt, unbuttoned, over a yellow T-shirt and black tracksuit bottoms. On his feet he wore mustard-yellow trainers with a green go-faster stripe. Comfortable clothes for a night flight to Europe and if they crashed in snow, which has to be a consideration when flying over the North Pole, he would be more easily spotted.

The doors were sealed. A member of the cabin staff demonstrated safety procedures.

This is really very dangerous, Callum wanted to tell everyone. Do not believe the commercials. They are made by people like me – in between horror movies.

With a preliminary roar, the plane began to tear down the runway. Callum shut his eyes and prayed. There were noises, inexplicable movements. They bored into the braced nerve, worse than the dentist's drill. Vibrations, shudders, a ringing noise that could be inside his head or in one of the engines. He thought he might be sick. Finally a kind of peace, a sound like the chimes of a suburban doorbell and he opened his eyes to behold two pretty women pushing the drinks trolley down the aisle towards him.

He began, fractionally, to relax.

'Going home?' his neighbour enquired, when they finally made eye contact over the champagne.

'Home?' He frowned, trying to concentrate.

'London?' she supplied helpfully.

This was very confusing. He leaned towards her, dropping his voice. 'Isn't this plane going to Berlin?'

139

'No,' she said, concernedly. 'I don't think so.'

'Shit,' he said, attempting to stand, 'they've put me on the wrong plane.'

One of the pretty women with the drinks trolley sorted it out for him. He was to change planes in London. It would be all right.

'I'm not usually like this,' he told his companion. 'I just had a bit of a farewell party.'

'That's all right,' she said kindly. 'You planning to stay long in Berlin?'

'I don't know,' he said. 'I have to see someone about a job.'

Like generations of Connollys before him.

According to his father, admittedly not the most reliable of sources, their distant ancestors were Irish soldiers of fortune, members of that elite military fraternity known as the Wild Geese who had hired themselves out for profit and honour to the Catholic princes of Europe for the best part of two centuries. Kinsmen of exiled kings and princes, his father had said. More recently and believably they had been tinkers, itinerant labourers and travelling showmen. Freelancing of one sort or another was in the blood, though at times of introspection and self-doubt, it seemed to Callum to be a hell of a way of earning a living. More often than not, in his own itinerant pursuit of profit and honour, he felt that the wild-goose chase was a more appropriate analogy.

'What about you?' he enquired politely. 'Do you work in London?'

And so they exchange the small economies of truth that are the currency of strangers who pass in the night, expecting never to meet again. We will leave them to it.

I will tell you about Callum Connolly, more reliably than he would tell you himself, though my opportunity for study was limited by time and circumstance. Unlike so many others, he was never a patient of mine and his casual confessions, though apparently candid, frequently lacked credence to my ears.

I am not saying he was a liar but he was inclined to exaggerate, to make an entertainment of his weaknesses in the hope, thereby, of diminishing their importance. It was the Celt in him, seeking always to hide in the mist.

'My father was Irish,' he told me, 'and an actor.'

But even that is only half a truth.

His father was stage Irish but not Irish-born. Camden Town was his birthplace, in London, of an Irish navvy and an English chambermaid. He married a student teacher, Callum's mother, an English rose beguiled by the blarney and deflowered at an impressionable age. She had three children by him in five years and Callum was the third. By then she was considerably less impressed but Callum was nine before she'd finally had enough of his father's fantasies and philanderings. After the divorce she took the children with her to the fell country, in the far north of England, where she had a teaching job and where, in the course of time, she met and married another whose head was in the clouds, though for more practical reasons, he being a mountain guide.

Callum's father took to drink and playing the fiddle in the pubs of Camden Town during the increasingly long and painful gaps between acting engagements until, after an evening's drinking and fiddling, he was run over by a London Transport bus, a double-decker, stepping right in front of it, according to his young female companion, while trying to explain to her the plot of *The Draughtsman's Contract*, thus taking the secret with him to the grave.

Callum tells the story, entertainingly as always, even a little proudly, so you would never guess the grief it concealed. He remembers his father carrying him home on his shoulders through the streets of north London, singing sentimental Irish ballads. Probably drunk. But he never dropped him. And he always kissed him when he put him to bed.

Callum was sentimental like his father and often cried at the movies but nowhere else, I think. He didn't let people get close enough to make him cry. Oh, they would think they were close, by the way he talked, by the way he appeared to reveal the intimate details of his life and to invite them to reveal theirs. But it was all a game: a game of charades. Guess who I am. You got it right. Now your turn. Now guess who this is. Yes, that's me, too. And I am none of them. I am the travelling player. I do my act and move on.

You think I don't like him, but that is not the case. I am simply wary of those aspects of his personality that I recognise in myself.

He once told me about a place where he had lived in London. It was a tower block on the edge of the inner city: a high-rise slum notorious for drug-dealing and vandalism where hard cases with dogs lurked on landings and where frightened old men and women ventured out with their shopping trolleys like the survivors of an endless siege, ever weary for the sound of falling shells. It had been built by a man called Erno Goldfinger, an Austrian Jew who had grown up in thirties Vienna and remembered the great apartment blocks named after the heroes and heroines of the revolution: Karl Marx Haus, Friedrich Engels Haus, Rosa Luxemburg Haus . . . wonders of their age, catering for every individual and collective need – or every need imagined by their architects. Young Erno had seen them turned into proletarian fortresses during the workers' rising of February 1934, and shelled into submission by government artillery. In his years of exile he nurtured plans of rebuilding them in a more promising environment and realised the dream in sixties London with his tower: an elegant phallus that was yet womblike in its provision of all the necessities of life.

But his enemies had grown more subtle over the years. They did not blast it with artillery. They had no need. They knew their proletariat. They moved in all the problem families, who wrecked the place as effectively as any howitzers. They destroyed everything: the four launderettes, the health centre, the bakery, the letter boxes, the lifts . . . they even closed the children's nursery on the ground floor by dropping bottles into the playground from the balconies above.

It was a microcosm of a world at war with itself: a chaos of petty warlords and their yob followers engaged in the endless pursuit of destruction for destruction's own sake.

Callum rather liked living there. He was probably the only one of the three hundred tenants who was there by choice. He called it Gormenghast and he was Titus Groan.

He had an apartment on the twenty-fifth floor, three floors from the top. He knew all about Goldfinger and shared his vision. This was how you were meant to live in the inner city in the late twentieth century, high above the city streets, the traffic, squalor and pollution. He didn't mind the war that was going on all around him. He didn't worry too much about the hard cases and the druggies. He was a little over six foot tall and had taken courses in Surviving the Streets. He had learned how to disarm a man with a knife and break his nose with the heel of his hand. These were not tricks he was ever called upon to perform. Maybe they could tell by looking at him that he knew. There were, in any case, easier victims. They tried to burgle his apartment a few times while he was out – he found the marks on the door – but he'd fitted deadlocks and lined it with steel.

He didn't go out much, anyway. Like his father before him, he was resting between jobs but he did not fiddle and he did not drink, much. He was catching up on all the movies he had missed on video. He sat on his balcony sometimes to take the air or leaned on the wall and looked down as if gazing into a distant rock pool. He felt a part of the city but detached from it, just as he liked, safely out of reach of its snares and entanglements. Like the pair of kestrels who had made their eyrie on top of the roof, in among the aerials and the satellite dishes, as if it was the top of a cliff. He would watch them hovering on the thermals beside his balcony, looking down for prey. They had made their killing fields in the wasteland along the railway line and the flyover and on the banks of the canal: the arteries of the city, far below. From time to time they swooped.

From time to time, he, too, dropped into the pool and came back with whatever he had been able to find there: food, drink, the occasional drug, a new video of an old film he hadn't seen, a woman. It was a satisfactory time of his life when he felt most at ease with himself.

But then he fell in love.

She would come back to watch videos with him, or cook – she liked cooking when she had nothing better to do. She, too, was in between jobs and sometimes she stayed for days. It was summer and she would wander around high above the city with no clothes on, leaning on the balcony munching an apple, a celestial Eve. At night they made love with the light on and the blinds open, fantasising that the whole city could see them. He watched them in the dark mirror of the window, glorying in the dual role of exhibitionist and voyeur. He took her to parties and introduced her to his friends. They began to be thought of as a regular couple.

But then he went away.

He went to Hollywood to see somebody about a job. And because he was frightened of emotional commitment. It is frequently the case with heroes.

15

YEAR ZERO, THE MOVIE

So this was the man who was to make Adam's movie. I was invited out to the house by the lake to meet him. It was a beautiful October morning, I remember, with the sun firing the glaze on the trees.

There were just the three of us, myself, Adam and Connolly. Jackie had gone to see the man from the *Treuhand* about the Reisenburg property in the east. I did not think her absence was significant at the time.

We were discussing the story line. Connolly was to write the script, it appeared, as well as direct. Adam was to produce. I was entirely in the dark about what my own role was to be.

The film was to start in 1944 when the beautiful doctor met the wounded soldier, back from the Russian front. The precise end had not yet been determined but the story would include elements of the July officers' plot, the war on the eastern front, the fall of Berlin, a good bit of sex, a lot of death and destruction and at least one brutal rape. A fairy-tale romance and a horror story, as Adam put it. Can't lose, I said; who's going to play your mother?

I was in that kind of mood.

The professional word for it is displacement.

I was feeling displaced because I had abandoned my lucrative practice and my dependent, dependable fee-paying clients to help Adam set up his Museum of Year Zero and now here we were talking about *Year Zero*, the movie. Adam insisted he wanted to do both but it seemed to me that, faced with a few bureaucratic obstacles, he had retreated into the world he knew best and I was not unnaturally peeved about it.

There were, I think, strong, objective reasons for my reservations about the project. I could understand Adam's obsession with his roots. It is a natural midlife process and something to which we adopted Americans, we long-term exiles, are inherently prone, but there is a point at which the normal crosses an invisible line into the territory of the neurotic and I feared we were lingering in the borderlands. Also, there were some dangerous or at least unpredictable animals living among these roots and I, for one, would have been a little wary of disturbing them.

There was Liza, for a start, and whatever horrors she had encountered before the arrival of the 7th Cavalry when the Reds were in control of the city.

And there was something else that I couldn't quite pin down. Something that I felt was gnawing at Adam's insides but that I needed time to discover.

Connolly, though, was all enthusiasm.

Picture the easy, boyish grin, the warm, brown eyes, the strong line of his jaw above the open-necked shirt. No, I didn't fancy him but I could see Adam did. He presented himself as a fervent disciple of the master and what can be more flattering?

But I am being unfair. Flattery is the balm of the insecure. And Adam was never insecure, not, at least, where filmmaking was concerned.

Connolly had studied the diaries and already had some ideas about the movie. The ending, he mused, would be difficult. Did we have any thoughts about it? Adam looked at me.

Well, I know where I would have ended it.

I would have ended it with a top shot of the Potsdamer

Platz through the smoke of battle and the Prussian officer and gentleman, Adam's father, lying dead amid the debris of the ruined city. But then I'm a Czech, a *Mitteleuropäer*, a realist.

Yes, a defeatist, if you like.

Adam, whatever his origins, was an American, raised in Hollywood, and Hollywood was about confidence, hope, renewal. I knew that Captain Sam would have to be in the final frame, riding into the captured city on his metal charger, in time to rescue the beautiful princess from her dark tower.

After all, if it hadn't been for the Americans, we'd still have been standing in the rubble throwing bricks at each other.

'I'm not making the movie,' I said.

We both looked at Connolly.

'Well,' said Connolly, 'it's early days yet but I'd be tempted to end with the end of Year Zero. You know, Christmastime. Hope, renewal. Sam arriving at Liza's derelict apartment with toys for the baby and maybe even a Christmas tree . . .'

Hollywood, you see. He knew which side his bread was buttered.

I was not unkind. I restrained myself. I remarked only that to Sam, being Jewish, a Christmas tree would not have had quite the sentimental appeal it clearly did for Connolly.

'I think,' said Adam, 'Sam, being Sam, would have been aware of the investment potential.'

I could see whose side he was on. I took myself off to the jetty to throw stones at the lake.

When I came back, Connolly was saying that maybe the film should be like the black antithesis of *Pendragon* with Hitler cast as Arthur's dark shadow, his fiendish reincarnation. Did Adam not think that Hitler's New Order was like some vile mockery of the whole Arthurian legend, with Berchtesgaden substituted for Camelot, the SS for the Knights of the

Round Table, might for right, and racial supremacy for chivalry?

Adam loved it, I could see. All this pseudo-Jungian stuff has always appealed to him. It's the genuine article he can't stand.

I said it was time I was getting back to the hotel.

Adam said Callum might like to share the cab. He would talk to his agent, he said. The first step was obviously a detailed treatment.

We settled into our opposite corners and smiled at each other across the expanse of leather like short-listed candidates on our way to the same awards ceremony.

'You've known Adam long?' he began.

'Twenty-five years,' I said.

'That's long,' he said.

'Yes,' I said.

'And you work with him – in the industry?'

'No,' I said. I told him about the museum project.

He expressed immediate enthusiasm. Indeed, he relaxed visibly. Museums were not movies. It clearly had not yet occurred to him that we might be competing for attention, if not for funds.

He was going out that evening, he said, with some friends he knew in Berlin. Or rather, friends of a friend. They were going to try some of the nightclubs along the Death Strip; would I care to join them?

It did not sound like my kind of evening. It sounded like the kind of evening I would go far to avoid.

God alone knows why I said yes. Or the Devil.

I was curious, I suppose, to know more about him. And curiosity, as you know, is the Devil's secret weapon, as deadly as any in his armoury.

And so I met Nicola.

16

THE DEATH STRIP

We met in a bar on the Death Strip . . .

That is how I began my statement to the police. What do you know of such places? I will try to describe it for you.

Remember the story of Sleeping Beauty – did I ever tell you that? When the witch's curse was lifted and the prince came and cleared a way through all the briars and the brambles and the cobwebs and saw the palace where Beauty lived?

Well, it was a bit like that when they pulled the Wall down, except that behind it, instead of Beauty, they found the Death Strip. It was the area the East Germans and the Russians had evacuated to make it more difficult for people to escape to the West. Some of it was wasteland, flattened by the bombs during Hitler's war and left as a killing field, sewn with land mines and raked by searchlights and machine guns mounted in the watchtowers on the Wall. But most of it was ruin: semiderelict apartment blocks, warehouses, shops and offices, as they had been thirty years ago or longer, even, because some of them hadn't been occupied since the war and were just as they had been when the Russians occupied the area in 1945: gutted shells shored up with timber, some of them with the walls ripped off to expose the insides. Ruin and wasteland . . .

When the Wall came down and they cleared away the

barbed-wire hedgerows and the people looked in, it was like looking on their own past.

The Jewish synagogue on Oranienbergstrasse had been left exactly as it had been after Kristallnacht in 1938 when the Brownshirts had rampaged through it, with the graffiti on the walls and the shards of broken glass on the floor. They found government offices with the files still in the filing cabinets. They found rooms that had been used by the Gestapo for interrogation, with the desks and the chairs still in place. And in the basements they found where the victims had been taken for torture.

The exteriors of the buildings were still scarred with the wounds of old battles: the street fighting between the Reds and the Freikorps in 1919, the Allied bombing campaign, the final assault by the Russians ... Bunkers and shelters were discovered just as they were when the survivors came out to greet the new postwar, Cold War world.

It was as if the corpse of Hitler's Germany had been exhumed by a bulldozer and people who remembered it when it was alive looked into the pit and recoiled in horror, shielding their eyes.

They wanted to cover it up as soon as possible. The city elders convened talks with planners and architects. They drew up plans to make this the showroom of Europe. They built models of what it would look like and put them on display. And while they were debating, the youth of the city, who had no memory of the past, no respect, no fear, no shame, moved into the buildings and the basements and even on to the wasteland and claimed the Death Strip for their own.

It was like a revolution except that instead of building barricades, they turned it into a playground.

Cellars were hastily transformed into bars and discos, derelict buildings into arts centres, cinemas and theatres. They wanted to have fun, to dance on the graves, to live in the present before the future turned as ugly as the past. And what fun they had.

Here was the prewar Berlin of Herr Issyvoo and his dissolute, decadent bratpack as if they had followed the Pied Piper into some secret cavern in the forest and remained there for seventy years or so through world war and Cold War, emerging when it was all over to find their old haunts very much as they had left them, just a litte more derelict, a little more knocked about by history. And it all went on much as before, as in the gloriously anarchic days of Weimar, as if nothing had happened in the meantime, as if they were self-consciously acting out the same performance with the same characters. And everyone waiting for the appearance of the lead.

So this was what happened to the Death Strip. This was what was happening when we met, in a bar just across the road from where the Wall had been.

It had once been a hairdresser's. It still had the tacky neon sign above the door and pictures in the windows of the latest hair fashions in East Berlin in 1961 when the Wall went up. And on the building opposite, there was a large mural from the same era depicting the onward march of the proletariat, the heroic faces radiating an unshakeable confidence, a skyline of factories belching a proud canopy of smoke in the background like a fleet of ironclads.

Inside they still had the original chairs and mirrors and the big, old-fashioned helmets for drying women's hair and the scars of the cigarettes trodden into the linoleum floor.

Nicky was sitting at a table in the window, smoking and drinking beer out of a bottle. She wore a black leather jacket and jeans. Her hair, which was also black, was cut short. I reckoned she was in her late twenties. I discovered later that she was twenty-four.

She greeted Callum with a hug and a kiss and gave me a

cool, practised look from under her long lashes as we shook hands. She wore a tight white body under the leather jacket; her breasts were tiny, her hips slim and lithe. I imagined she was something of a brat but I have always been attracted to that androgynous look.

Callum had told me something of her in the taxi from the hotel. They'd been at film school together in London but she had a German boyfriend called Dieter and she'd left college to join him in Berlin and help him start up a theatre company here. She was half German herself, he said, on her mother's side, and her father was loaded.

He asked after Dieter. I gathered he knew him well, they had worked together on a television drama. He had a performance that night, she said: Schiller's *Don Carlos* at Tachelas. They would meet up later but they were no longer living together, they were just good friends. She herself had given up acting, she said, and was learning to be a sculptor. She had a studio, also at Tachelas, she would show us if we liked.

We were in no hurry. We drank a couple of beers and then she took us to a cellar bar in the next block, furnished with mementos of the war, mostly in bad taste, and we had a couple more beers there and then moved on again. I couldn't decide whether I'd made the right decision or not. I hadn't done anything like this for years, probably not since the old days in Prague, and I was quite enjoying the experience of reliving my youth but I felt self-conscious and increasingly ancient. Nobody else we encountered seemed to be older than thirty, not even the barmen.

We tried to get a cab but after two or three passed us without stopping, Nicky, who couldn't stay still for a minute, suggested we walk.

We walked through dark, deserted streets bordered by buildings that looked derelict but showed glimmers of light from some of the upper windows. Nicky talked most of the way, flinging out her arms for effect but with sharp, darting glances at me, I noticed, to see how I was taking it. Callum was showing signs of restlessness. It was clear she liked an audience and it was not a role for which he was naturally suited. He told me later that she'd never been this hyper in London and he thought she must be on something. She wasn't, I later discovered. Nicky didn't need drugs. She was high on just being here, in the right place at the right time, in the *de facto* capital of Europe.

I know what you're thinking: Sally Bowles. So did I at the time and I expect there was a degree of conscious imitation – she'd read the book, she'd seen the movie. But Sally was a waif and a stray, an insecure, abandoned urchin desperately seeking a father figure or anyone who would pick up the tab. Nicky had money and confidence and a loving, supportive family back home in London. If she was living on the edge, it was because she chose to. It was a pose, a conceit. I didn't know this at the time but it didn't take me long to figure out.

The only thing she really had in common with Isherwood's louche heroine was this thing about father figures, but I didn't know that at the time, either.

The streets grew livelier as we approached the S-Bahn. The buildings were just as derelict but more of them had been turned into bars and bistros and there was a steady throng of people all moving in the same direction, like a crowd on their way to a football match. Progress was slow. The roads and most of the pavement were up to lay cable and we had to make our way along narrow walkways bordered by plastic ribbons in Day-Glo orange while the traffic was obliged to crawl along the gap between trenches and tram lines.

It's like the war, Callum said, and I remembered Liza's description in her diary when she had made her way back from the Flaktower to Conrad's father's house in Dahlem. There was even a huge hole in the middle of Oranienbergstrasse like a bomb crater filled with a mass of twisted cables. I looked down but there were no corpses.

The bodies were supplied by the Ossi prostitutes who stood like erotic sentinels at the side of the road, tall and statuesque in their uniform of short PVC jackets, G-strings and white thigh-length boots. My aesthetic appreciation was aroused and I would have liked to admire them in more detail but I suspected window-shopping was not encouraged so I continued to shuffle on with my gaze, for the most part, discreetly lowered.

The crowd all seemed to be heading for the same place: a great ruined shell of a building ablaze with light and festooned with tattered flags and banners like a fantasy castle in a war game occupied by the vagabond army.

This, it transpired, was Tachelas.

It had begun life as a prestigious department store in the early days of the last kaiser but had been left derelict since Year Zero. A row of classical statues lined the walls of what was once an elegant shopping arcade but most of them were without heads or limbs and the walls themselves bore the usual battle scars of a long, bloody century it would do well to survive. When the Wall came down, the building had been taken over by a group of artists from the West who had turned it into studios. They had opened a café, then a bar. Then a cinema, a theatre, a disco . . . even a concert hall for live bands. When we arrived the whole place was throbbing with music and pulsing with flashing lights and the besieging army was clamouring at the main entrance, despite every indication that it was already packed to bursting and dangerously close to collapse.

We had stopped at a steel door set into the ruined wall and Nicky was struggling with an immense padlock. I was beginning to give serious thought to the possibility of escape. I yearned for my quiet hotel room with a decent movie on the video channel and room service about to deliver. Then the door opened and we went in.

How can I describe it, that first impression of Nicky's studio? It is so overlaid with those later images: the horror my mind is desperately trying to block out. I have to force myself to look into this dark corner of my past, remembering it as it was – not as it became.

Dark. Yes, it was dark at first. I remember walking in and not knowing where I was. It felt spacious, though, and cold. I remember that. Then Nicky put the lights on. Neon, flickering. Then very bright, shining on . . . monstrous creatures, unidentifiable but menacingly primeval, rearing above us on their hind legs or hanging in simulated flight from the high ceiling. Smaller, even stranger shapes squatting beneath them: they might have been dwarves or goblins, demons, frightful mutants from a painting by Bosch.

The enchanted forest again, but no, this was from a different planet.

I had not thought to ask what materials she worked with. If it had crossed my mind at all, it did so as an image of clay or wood – something soft, feminine, malleable. But Nicky was a sculptor in steel, in heavy metal.

In one corner stood her forge, scattered around it the tools of her trade: picks and welders, heavy-duty batteries, oxy-acetylene cylinders, other, more obscure objects like medieval instruments of torture and on a bench stood a great black helmet with a green visor.

It was like walking into a metal menagerie or the nursery of the ogre's castle: a playroom of giant toys for a giant's offspring. Less fancifully, it had elements of the scrap-metal yard, the blacksmith's forge, an automobile repair shop . . .

I can remember walking around it, in those days of my innocence, like a child in a grotto, looking around the walls, up towards the distant ceiling. It was extraordinary, fantastic, that such a door could open into such a room. Nicky, too, was transformed but more subtly. She was less volatile but more highly charged. As if – and I am being fanciful again – as if this was where she received her energy, where she was plugged in. She was calm, composed; she had even stopped talking.

Callum did all the talking. He marvelled, enthused, he waved his arms as he strode around the huge studio praising this, questioning the identity of that. And she accepted his tributes graciously, like a princess receiving accustomed flattery, but I felt her watching me, as if waiting for my reaction, and I do not think I am being egotistical in thinking that this mattered to her far more than his. I had assumed, until then, that I was cast in the role of the avuncular third party, the gooseberry, the crowd. Now, for the first time, I saw that I was the focus of her interest. I didn't realise it was sexual; I saw it more as the student's need for the praise of her tutor, but I was pleased that she cared. I am ashamed to say that I began to pull in my stomach. The evening took on a new dimension, far more to my liking. The attractions of the hotel room were considerably diminished.

But what was I to say? I am something of a connoisseur of fine art but no critic. I do not have the words, the references . . . I think the only instant judgement one could make was that they all, in some almost magical way, expressed the power of the creatures they represented. I was about to say that, or something less pretentious, when I saw the Devil.

Dürer's Devil.

This is more difficult. I have to be careful about this. This is the shape in the dark corner that I am so scared to look upon and that haunts my dreams and my waking hours.

Perhaps I should start with the print she was copying from and that she had pinned to the wall. I had seen it before, read about it in a book of Dürer's works I had found in the university library in Prague. According to Dürer's diary of his journey to the Netherlands, he sold a copy of the original engraving on 24 November 1520. He called it *Reiter*, which means 'Horseman'. In later catalogues, it is called *Knight, Death and Devil.*

The Knight, then, is sitting bolt upright in the saddle, staring straight ahead with the visor of his helmet raised. Beside him, on a clapped-out old pony, rides Death. The Devil is walking behind them. It is not certain that the Knight is aware of the presence of his two companions, or perhaps he considers them lackeys, unworthy of his notice – his squire and his page – but you can tell by the way they are smiling that they know better. They are not his servants. He is there to serve them.

The date of the original engraving is 1513 and art historians cannot agree on the message. To me it is curiously prophetic: an allegory of the wars that were to come and the part the German soldier was to play in them, staring blindly ahead, with Death at his side and the Devil close behind.

But Nicky intended no such reference. She simply liked the Gothic imagery, she said, and all that armour and weaponry was perfect for the materials she worked in. Thus far she had completed only the figure of the Devil.

I have seen many images of the Devil and of course I have my own but Dürer's Devil is Evil personified, not as some urbane Mephisto or even a leering Pan, but the raw, primitive fear of the Beast. Its features contain elements of the goat and the wolf and, I am sorry to say, the pig. Its eyes are those of a human zombie, a psychopath on drugs. It wears a crown of fire and from the back of its head protrudes a single, enormous horn, sharp and curved like a sickle. Nicky's version was less brutish than the original but more menacing, like some evil space creature or killer robot.

'Where does this go?' I heard Callum say.

He was standing at the bottom of a staircase leading up to

a doorway, covered by plastic sheeting that moved slightly as if in a breeze.

'Come and look,' said Nicky. 'But watch where you put your feet.'

We followed her cautiously up the staircase and she drew the sheeting to one side. I felt cold air on my face and seemed to hear a clash of steel. Then we were looking down on what appeared to be an open-air theatre in the middle of a bomb site. I did not know it then but the whole of the rear of the building had collapsed, either from bomb damage during the war or because the East Germans had made a more systematic attempt to demolish it since. The space thus created was now used for exhibitions or theatrical events. There was an open stage, built of scaffolding and planks, and in the centre of the spotlight, two men in black were fighting a duel with swords.

'That's Dieter,' said Nicky.

This meant nothing to me for a moment but then Callum made a remark that reminded me it was the name of Nicky's ex-boyfriend and that this was the performance of *Don Carlos*. Have I told you this story? It is about the young prince who was son and heir to Philip II of Spain and the great hope of the liberals, who promised to end the persecution of the Jews and the Protestants and to bring peace to Europe and freedom to the rebellious Netherlands.

Dieter was playing his enemy, the reactionary Duke of Alva. He looked a swarthy tough in his mid- to late thirties with a hook nose and a beard and long hair tied back in a ponytail.

I strained to pick up the dialogue, leaning out through the plastic sheeting. The duel between prince and duke had been halted by the king's horrified courtiers. Alva turned away, sheathing his sword. He walked like a bullfighter, his back ramrod stiff but his gait delicate, as if he were stepping on eggshells. His body was wound up like a spring. I felt he could strike so swiftly and suddenly you would only see the recoil and the small, red patch where he had struck. He was superbly cast. Alva as a blond Aryan and a Fascist, as Schiller had intended: a sixteenth-century prototype Nazi who had put the Netherlands to the sword.

He seemed to stare directly up at us, over the heads of the audience. His voice carried to where we stood.

'Death is interesting,' he said.

17

THE GREEN WOMAN

I'm sorry. I've been neglecting you. You're sulking.

It must be three weeks now, yes? I hope they've been looking after you in the meantime. You don't look any thinner, if that's any consolation.

I've been ill, as a matter of fact. A severe attack of demons followed by flu. I expect my resistance was low. They moved me to the infirmary.

I try to keep up a cheerful front out here with you but back there, with my fellow criminals, it is not so easy. I had a setback in my appeal and thinking about Nicky didn't help.

I must tell you about her, though, because otherwise none of this will make any sense. And it's good practice for the appeal, if it ever happens.

So . . . Picture her in her studio in Tachelas. She is wearing a dirty blue boiler suit with a baseball cap on her head, back to front so the peak covers her neck, green goggles shield her eyes, thick leather gauntlets protect her hands, her feet are shod in heavy workmen's boots with steel toecaps. A small pickaxe is thrust through her belt –

Just give me a moment. These sudden images, what do they call them: flash frames? They happen during computer edits, I am told, when a frame from another sequence is left in the memory. I had one then. But to continue:

A red glow pulses from the mouth of the forge; the dragon is home. His stench afflicts the nostrils like the smell of burning paint. His heat warps the air. Nicky is preparing to cut the armour for her knight; a seamstress in metal, armed with a blowtorch. A yellow flame, long but limpid, drips from its spout. This is the acetylene. She adjusts the valve and the flame grows smaller but more intense with a core of blue. This is the oxygen. I know these things because Nicky explained them to me, once, with the laconic nonchalance of the expert. She stabs the metal with her blue yellow flame and makes an ugly wound. It spreads. The metal splits and falls in two sections at her feet with a great clatter that rings around the walls of the studio. She pulls off the goggles, wipes the sweat from her face with a grimy sleeve, grins at me briefly and hides again – behind a green visor, now, which covers the whole of her face. She earths the metal to a transformer with a clamp and attacks it with the arc welder. The metal glows, first yellow, then orange, then a deep, pulsing red as she welds gorget to breastplate. She steps back, pulls up the visor, considers. I watch her face. The sweat runs in little rivulets down her cheeks, beads on her nose; her expression is intense, almost fierce, her bottom lips caught between her teeth. She slams down the visor and moves in once more to the attack.

Later she takes off the boiler suit. She wears a cotton vest and pants, nothing else. She sniffs under her arms and pulls a face, strips off the underclothes and walks naked to the shower she has had built in one corner. Her body is like a dancer's, sparse but finely muscled – from heaving around all that heavy metal, I should think.

It is hard to imagine now but I liked being in Nicky's studio. I felt at home there. There was something about metal and fire that made me feel strangely comforted. Another legacy of my father's, perhaps, but I prefer to think of less sinister images:

the boy Pip eating an apple in Joe Gargery's forge; Saruman's enchanted menagerie before he went to the bad . . .

I even liked the smell of burning paint. I can smell it now – but there is that other smell in my nostrils that will ever be associated with it . . .

Another memory: she sits in the bar opposite her apartment in Kreuzberg. She wears jeans and a man's T-shirt – Dieter's? – that makes her seem even smaller than she is. She wears earrings representing sun and moon, black lipstick and long artificial fingernails – her own are short and broken – painted an almost luminous green. She drinks Budweiser out of the bottle. She holds forth about what they are doing to her beloved Berlin.

'Look at it!' Flinging a dramatic arm at the street outside with its skips and its scaffolding.

Kreuzberg was in the process of being gentrified and Nicky hated it. 'It gets more like fucking Kensington every day. Fucking *Aussenweitters*.'

She did not mean the non-Germans: the immigrants from Eastern Europe and Asia, nor, presumably, expatriates like herself. She meant the *Speisbürger* from Bonn and the south who would destroy the cosmopolitan atmosphere of Berlin and make it wholly their own.

In the days of the divided city, Kreuzberg was an enclave of West Berlin jutting into the East, bounded on three sides by the Wall and the river Spree. Blighted by its proximity to the Great Divide, it had provided cheap accommodation for immigrants, artists and students since the sixties. But now it was the geographical centre of the united city, and the civil servants and diplomats from Bonn were moving in, forcing up the rents and driving everybody else out.

This was one of the causes which Nicky embraced. There were many others. She had joined Die Grüne, who were a powerful force in Berlin politics. This may have been part of her pose but she entered into it with passion. She regularly attended their meetings and rallies. She was active in the defence of low rents, bicycle routes, traffic-free precincts and refugee hostels. She was a believer in animal rights.

She was pro-pig and anti-bacon.

I do not mean to be flippant but it was difficult for me to imagine Nicky as a political force. She was, I later discovered, a prominent member of the Anti-Nazi League and active in the defence of the immigrant community. I remember she once talked of receiving death threats but again, I am afraid, I did not take her seriously. I thought it was all part of her pose.

She had an apartment in Mittenwalderstrasse. The bar opposite was called Der Pfefferkuchenhaus – the Gingerbread House.

Another coincidence? Another warning?

There is a pattern to these things, you don't have to tell me, I'm a therapist, remember. Nicky liked the atmosphere of the Gingerbread House. What I thought kitsch, she thought camp. There is a thin dividing line and I conceded that she could discern it better than I. The young usually can, their eyes are sharper, their antennae more sensitively tuned to the mood of the moment. This was where our evenings frequently began. I could be less sure of where they would end.

Nicky was the centre of a peripatetic court in which I held the position of current royal favourite. Age, I am glad to say, was no impediment. Kreuzberg was our main stamping ground, though inevitably, as the evening wore on, we would move closer and closer to the Death Strip.

We spent a lot of time in basements. *Bunkers*, as they called them, the German making no distinction between the cellar and the bomb shelter. It was a constant reminder of the past: a *Bunker* mentality.

Many cities are obsessed with their past: London, Venice, Rome . . . my own Prague. But in Berlin it is different. What happened to Berlin this century was so terrible, so cataclysmic, you would think the Berliners would want to erase it from the collective memory, but no, they take a kind of grim pride in it. No. Pride is the wrong word; it is a combination of terror and fascination. And also humour: the humour of the gallows. They have made the horrors of the past into a tourist attraction, like the remnants of the Wall. Perhaps that is the only way they can deal with them. That is why Adam's Museum of Year Zero was such a good idea. It captured the mood entirely.

It isn't simply the bunkers or the monuments or the museums, or even the battle scars on the walls, it is more general than that. It is in the atmosphere. It is in the conversation. You can't get away from it. I remember once seeing someone fishing in the Landwehr Kanal and I asked my companion, a friend of Nicky's, if anyone ever caught anything and she said, 'I do not know. That is where they found the bodies of Rosa Luxemburg and Karl Liebknecht after the Freikorps had executed them.'

Well, yes, I suppose it is all relevant.

There are corpses everywhere in Berlin. They rise from the still waters, they push through the sidewalks. We encountered them regularly in our erratic wanderings through the bunker society of Berlin.

Around midnight, if I was lucky, we would eat. The Jewish restaurant next to the synagogue in Oranienbergstrasse was a favourite, with the added attraction of the police guard outside, in case of attack by neo-Nazis. If I was unlucky, there would be a party. Or, worse, dancing, when I would make my excuses and leave. My own antennae are finely tuned to the absurd and I was well aware of what kind of a figure I would cut in a disco.

You wince. I know.

The relationship would have been regarded as suspect, of

course, even without the outcome. A fifty-year-old man and a woman half his age. Well.

I have naturally thought a great deal about this. What might I say to a client, of either sex, of either age, who was involved in such a relationship? I might invoke the taboo of incest. If you both can deal with this, I might say, then fine, but you must be aware of that interpretation. The father/child, the teacher/pupil, both with their implied inequality. I might ask the client to consider his or her motivations. Is the relationship primarily motivated by lust on the one hand, the prospect of gain on the other?

If so, so what? You may ask.

Well, this may not be a problem in the animal world but we humans have a concept of love that is about giving, not about getting. I know, I know . . . we do delude ourselves. The reality so often falls short of the ideal, but the ideal exists and thus we are disappointed, even sickened by something that substitutes baser instincts for what we consider to be the Real Thing.

I might say all these things but . . . it was different for us.

Well, I would say that, wouldn't I?

What did we want from it, then?

Not sex. We kissed occasionally, we cuddled but we did not make love. It was not, I think, because of any lack of affection, or even inclination. I think it was because I was out of practice. I had been celibate, as I think I mentioned, for many years. I was self-conscious about my body – naked, anyway, and in certain company, in a bright light. Perhaps this is something I – we – would have overcome, given time . . .

She clearly wanted approval. And from an older man. Possibly her father held it back from her at some critical stage in her development, I don't know, but that would be one conclusion.

And me, I wanted someone to love.

I'm afraid so. It surprised me, too. But you see, I had not been in love for many years. I loved Adam, of course, but that was something else. And, besides, he had Jackie.

But I know: how could I fall in love with this chit, this poser?

Perhaps it was the boiler suit.

Whatever it was, I was distracted at a crucial time when I needed to keep my wits about me. I will say, though, in my defence, that I did keep half an eye on Callum.

It was not difficult. He, too, was part of Nicky's court, her travelling theatre, though I am sure he would not have seen it that way. He would join us most evenings in the Gingerbread House after spending the day on his script. He had moved into an apartment in Kreuzberg with Dieter, Nicky's ex, ostensibly so he could concentrate on the writing. He said it was hopeless trying to work in a hotel but I think he just liked the company. He was a very gregarious individual, always seeking distraction. I'm no expert but I didn't think he had the solitariness, the dedication to be a writer. I think he knew it, too.

'I like to visualise things but I don't really like to write them down,' he told me. 'It seems kind of . . . pedestrian. I mean, I know you've got to have a script, like a kind of blueprint, a plan you follow, but having to write it all down . . . It's just so tedious.'

I pointed out that writing things down seemed to be a fundamental requirement of the trade.

'I'm a director, really,' he said. 'It's ninety per cent bluff, you know, and hoping you don't get found out.'

But writing was different. It worried him. It was so introverted.

Well, get an introvert to do it, I said.

But he didn't want to lose control. He'd have a bash at a first draft, he said, and then he'd bring someone else in. He was surprisingly insecure. I say surprisingly because he looked so good and was at ease in most company: a handsome social animal you could take anywhere. But he had a fraction of the creative confidence of Nicky.

After three weeks he'd written just two scenes, he confessed, and they were battles. He had yet to work out a structure.

'I just don't know what the hell it's supposed to be about,' he complained to me once, 'and I can't ever pin Adam down long enough to discuss it.'

I was familiar with the problem. He tried to discuss it with me sometimes but I had too many other things on my mind to help him very much. Besides, I felt it was something he and Adam had to work out for themselves.

Dieter knew what it was about, though. It was about landing him a major part as Claus von Stauffenberg.

I betray a bias.

Dieter was an Ossi who had lived in East Berlin until the Wall came down and was desperately trying to make up for lost time in the capitalist West. He was a pushy actor-impresario with a sharp but fretful appreciation of the market economy though, ironically, the touring company he ran was heavily subsidised by the state. His relationship with Nicky was curious. He was older than she, though not as old as I, and retained the possessive instinct of the executive director who has sold his controlling interest but maintains a substantial block of shares. She was aware of this and it irritated her considerably. She was constantly sniping at him and trying to put him down while he regarded her with the smiling condescension of the former proprietor. But his eyes, I noticed, were sometimes dangerous.

He had met Callum in England. He had been in one of his television dramas – a minor role, Callum told me – and continually complained that Callum had not cast him in a feature.

'I am okay for television but not for the movies,' he said, smiling and winking at me, as if this was very amusing.

'I've only made horror films,' Callum said. 'You'd have had to play a monster.'

'So? De Niro plays Frankenstein. Klaus Kinski plays Dracula in *Nosferatu*.'

'Orlok,' said Callum, automatically.

'Excuse me?'

'Herzog's vampire was Count Orlok, not Dracula,' he said. 'At least in Murnau's original.' Callum did not lack confidence when it came to talking about movies other people had made. He was a walking encyclopedia. He seemed to have a particular interest in movies about vampires, I noticed. 'Anyway, Kinski's not pretty, nor is De Niro,' he said, 'not like you are.'

Dieter scowled but he was immensely vain and easily flattered.

'I have always wanted to play Stauffenberg,' he told me. 'In fact, I can say the part is almost made for me. He is very good-looking, you know. Wonderful body, even with the injuries. An aristocrat in every way . . .' He stroked his beard, lifting up his chin and pouting. 'I would have to shave the beard, of course, but he is even the same age as me: thirty-six. You see, I know all this. I have studied the part.'

'It's not really about Stauffenberg,' Callum insisted.

'Then who is it about?'

But Callum didn't know.

'I think it's about Adam's mother,' he said, 'or his father, or his grandfather, or his stepfather. I just don't know.'

They all wanted to know about Adam. They were familiar with his persona as the Great Hollywood Director but the papers had been full of his German identity as the lost Prince of Reisenburg.

I maintained the discretion of the confessor so they turned

to Callum. Callum, of course, knew everything there was to know about his movies but surprisingly little about the man or his background.

'You should ask him,' said Nicky. 'People usually like to talk about themselves.'

'He never stays long enough in one place for me to talk to him about anything,' Callum said. 'I never knew about this Prince of Reisenburg stuff until Dieter told me.'

'You know what this Reisenburg means in English?' Dieter asked him. Callum didn't. I waited for it. 'Travel Town,' he said. 'The town that is always away on a journey. And the prince, also, he is always away on a journey, yes?'

Gales of laughter. Whoever said the Germans have no sense of humour?

But it was a defensive humour. They found the concept of a German prince vaguely embarrassing. It belonged to the Germany of fairy-tale castles, lederhosen, beer steins and Bavarians.

Bavarians, I discovered, were created exclusively for the amusement of Berliners. The stand-up comedians we encountered on our tour of the city's revived cabaret had only to greet their audience with the customary *'Grüss Gott'* of the southerner to raise their expectations of mirth by several ratchets. Bavarians were to Berliners what Irishmen were to the English or Russians to the Czechs: funny but dangerous. Bavaria was the place of mad Ludwigs and beery peasants, of strutting Brownshirts and frenzied dictators. It was a nightmare of the past that could scare you half to death unless you got in first and laughed it back into the shadows.

Prussian princes were in the same dubious category.

'It is the one good thing about the war,' someone said. 'It sweeps away these princes and these Junkers. Except now they come back to make movies about us.'

'And does this prince have a wife?' Nicky asked.

Callum shrugged. He didn't know. He didn't seem interested. Nicky raised her eyebrows at me.

'Well?' she said.

'If he does,' I said, 'he keeps it very quiet.'

This was, after all, true. But not as quiet as he kept his son.

I'd almost forgotten about him. There'd been no more talk about him helping me with the museum project, at least. Then, one evening, I walked into the Gingerbread House and found Callum sitting talking to someone I hadn't seen before: pale and thin with ginger hair and a sad little moustache.

'This is Gerhard,' Callum said. 'Gerhard Krenkel. He's helping me with the research.'

18

THE GINGER WOLF

You can always tell an Ossi by his jeans, Nicky used to say.

She was a snob, of course, and prejudiced, partly as a result of her association with Dieter, but the ambiguity of the spoken word made it especially pertinent in Gerhard's case.

He wore Armanis, self-consciously new, with the belt threaded through the designer label so everybody could read it, a real Ossi giveaway, according to my smartarse informant. So far as the other genes were concerned, if he was Adam's son he certainly didn't wear the labels on the outside.

Nicky called him the Ginger Wolf. She said she found him creepy. Why wolf, why not fox? I asked her. She said foxes were cuddly.

Gerhard was not cuddly. And there was something of the wolf about his eyes, I suppose, if you were looking for the comparison. They were green flecked with yellow and they seemed always to be darting here and there, from one face to another, as if he were looking for some kind of an opening. Hungry, Adam had said, and he was right about the moustache, too. It was wimpish and he was constantly smoothing it with two fingers towards the corners of his mouth as if he was training it to curl around them. I did not think this would be an improvement.

I discovered that Adam had recommended him to Callum as the 'son of a friend' who had been brought up in the East and would be useful both as an interpreter and a researcher. I kept *stumm* about who he really was, of course, but I was annoyed with Adam, not just for ignoring my advice on the subject but for neglecting to inform me that he'd decided to do the exact opposite.

It was clear that Gerhard had no idea of my connection with Adam. Not at first. His eyes swept briefly across me and dismissed me as something too low down in the food chain to be worth a sniff, let alone a bite. I recognised this at once. I had seen it many times at Hollywood parties before I stopped going to them. He cottoned on pretty quick, however. I expect Callum told him. At any rate, the next time we met the eyes focused greedily. I had clearly been elevated to the status of sheep.

He began by expressing interest in the museum project but swiftly turned it into a means of pumping me about myself and Adam. I didn't mind that. I gave him the authorised biography and gently pumped back. Apart from anything else, I wanted to know what Magda had been doing all these years but I didn't want him to know that I knew who Magda was, or who he was, or thought he was. And so we cautiously traded information like a pair of Cold War spies, each trying to learn more than he gave away. I saw Nicky looking at me curiously from the far end of the table. We were in the Jewish restaurant, of all places.

He told me he'd been brought up in East Berlin by his mother who was a teacher. His father had left home when he was a baby and managed to cross over to the West. He thought he was in America but he never heard from him. When he left school he'd got a job in the cutting rooms at the state film studios in Babelsberg and he was working as an assistant film editor when the Wall came down. But then there'd been cutbacks and he was one of the people they cut. His mother, too, had lost her teaching post, he said, because she'd once been a member of the Communist Party. He said most teachers in the East had been forced to join the Party if they wanted to get on in the profession but it didn't make any difference; they were outcasts. Victims of the so-called de-stasification programme. She'd managed to find some part-time work in Halle, he said, and he'd gone on welfare.

Yes, he said, it had been tough.

I asked him how his mother knew Adam. He gave me a look then, as if he knew that I knew, or maybe because this was the most unlikely part of the story, and told me he thought they might have met at a film festival a long time ago.

Well, I knew most of this was garbage, of course, but there was enough truth in it for me to feel a degree of sympathy. I reminded myself that for one reason or another he'd had a raw deal. It wasn't his fault that he had Magda for a mother, or that he'd been raised in the East, or that he'd lost his job when the Wall came down. He was just another victim of history and even if Adam and I disagreed about the means to employ, we were both convinced that he had to be weaned from his apparent predilection for neo-Nazi skinheads who beat up on refugees.

Remember, at the time we had no idea how deeply he was involved in the movement. In fact, we only had Magda's word for it that he was involved at all and she had her own reasons for lying, or, at least, exaggerating the level of his commitment. It was her only weapon, the only string she could pull that could make Adam dance to her tune. Gerhard gave no indication to me that he had any sympathy with the neo-Nazis. Quite the contrary, in fact. He gave me the impression that he despised them. But then, I could hardly have expected anything different, not in the company we were in. Not if he wanted to keep Nicky's green fingernails out of his face.

He was particularly wary of Nicky, I noticed. Of course, he would have known about her political activities, even then. He would have known she was a threat. But at the time I assumed it was simply because he thought she didn't like him. In which assumption he was totally correct.

'What's with you and the GW?' she demanded, after she'd seen us talking together.

'We were just discussing his research for Callum,' I said.

'What research?' she said.

And that was another thing. What research?

'We're trying to find people who knew Liza and Conrad during the war,' Callum told me.

This worried me. I suppose that, as a therapist, I feel that personal history is like a minefield and you have to tread very, very carefully when you explore it. Or preferably crawl on your belly testing the soil with delicate probing instruments. It struck me that Adam was taking a lot of risks letting Callum and Gerhard loose in this particular area. It was like sending in a pair of grunts with bayonets to see what happened.

I'm sorry. Grunts. US marines. So called on account of their superior intellect, initiative and resources.

The fact is, if Adam was serious about this movie, and he seemed to be serious enough about raising the money for it, you might reasonably expect him to employ the right people for the job: a top Hollywood scriptwriter, say, and a team of qualified historical researchers. But what does he do? He picks a director of cult horror movies who's written a couple of unremarkable screenplays and a former assistant film editor in the East German state film studios who was until recently on welfare.

Apart from anything else, they made a lousy team. Callum's dislike of his eager helper was palpable. Certainly, Gerhard

176

noticed – and took appropriate action. He made friends with Dieter.

To Nicky, of course, this was entirely predictable: they were a pair of Ossis on the make. But I found it more surprising. Whatever else you might say about him, Dieter was no gauche arriviste – you couldn't spot *his* origins from his jeans. He tended to despise his former countrymen from the East – if not the women – and avoid all contact with them. If anything, I'd have expected him to make Gerhard the miserable object of his *Schadenfreude* but he seemed to reciprocate the friendship, even to the extent of defending Gerhard from Nicky's hostility.

I wondered if they'd known each other back in the DDR. They claimed not, and there was an appreciable age difference. But every time we were out on the town, Dieter would have Gerhard along. I decided, no matter how unlikely it seemed, that Dieter was being kind. Perhaps he saw something of his former self in Gerhard – the raw Ossi longing to be accepted – and wanted to help him along. Well, that's the trouble with therapists. We're always trying to see the best in people, even the guys in the black hats.

Which brings me to the ultimate question: how do you spot the baddies when they don't wear a black hat?

I know you ask yourself this frequently. I mean, here we are in this place, surrounded by them. The trustee who brought you your swill that time, when I was sick, did you know he killed his wife and her mother with a tyre lever? He'd just had a puncture and they were trying to tell him how to fix it. To look at him you'd think he was Mr Genial.

And if it's difficult for pigs, what do you think it's like for members of my profession? We are inured to shock, we are trained not to let it show, to recognise our prejudices and attempt to overcome them. We look for the light in the

177

darkness. Hannibal Lecter only ate people who were foul to him. And Hitler was a vegetarian.

And look how they were *provoked*.

I mean, can you imagine the horseshit old Hannibal had to take from all those patients of his? I can. I've heard some of it. Is it any wonder he started salivating? And how do you think young Adolf felt when he was turned down for art school in Vienna?

I dare say if they came down to the pigpen swinging a bucket of swill between them, we'd both of us be looking for the bulge in the jacket where they kept the humane killer, if we got that lucky and they couldn't lay their hands on a chainsaw. But Dieter and Gerhard came on more like the fox and the cat in Pinocchio. Remember?

'Hey diddle-de-dee, an actor's life for me.'

A pair of chancers, con artists, gold-diggers looking for the buried treasure and not too worried that it belonged to someone else. Not killers.

At least so I thought.

Let's face it, as appearances go, Gerhard was just an average dork. If he'd shaved off the ginger moustache, fastened the belt over the designer label and learned how to keep the hunger out of his eyes when he was looking at the menu, he'd have passed for a regular guy even in the Jewish restaurant in Oranienberg-strasse.

I tried to talk to him about politics a couple of times but he just gave me the party line. I don't mean the neo-Nazi party line, I mean the kind of left-liberal pap that could get you through a long evening in a bar in Kreuzberg. The second time I heard it I gave him a small hint that I'd read the personal file. The eyes looked a little hunted for a moment before he managed to change the subject.

The next time we met, he said his mother sent her regards and would I like to come to tea?

19

MAGDA

'So you chose the winning side,' she said, almost as soon as I stepped through the door. She was dressed for the role of loser and supplicant in a brown woollen dress with a neck that had lost its shape in the wash, slippers and a cardigan like an old shawl. Her hair was greasy and she was without make-up.

This was not the Magda Adam had described to me. This was the Gerhard version: the former psychology teacher in a state school who'd lost her job for once having been a member of the Communist Party. This was Magda the single mother in her late forties. This was Magda the victim.

And I was cast in the role of Victor Rat who'd deserted the sinking ship and done extremely well out of it, thank you. But perhaps that is just my guilt speaking. I'd felt the same way when I returned to Prague after the Velvet Revolution and met my old friends who had stayed on in '68. But they had been dissidents, resisters, whereas Magda . . . well, I didn't know what Magda had been, not then. That was one of the reasons I'd come.

The apartment was in Charlottenburg and very *gemütlich* with red flock wallpaper, worn Persian rugs, thick velvet curtains and an upright piano in the corner. None of it was hers, she assured me – her own tastes were far more simple (what she meant was chic) – but it had come ready furnished. I assumed that Adam was paying the rent.

'It is for Gerhard, really,' she said, 'but he has asked me to move in with him, temporarily, to keep house. Please, sit down.'

She waved me to the sofa and I sank into it to a depth of several centimetres while she stood, slightly stooped, in the middle of the room, pulled the cardigan around her and picked at the frayed edges of one of the sleeves with her fingernails. She must have been hugging herself with laughter but I wasn't to know that at the time.

'Will you have tea or coffee?' she enquired. 'I think I have both.'

I elected coffee. I could smell it percolating in the kitchen.

'*Kaffee und Küchen*,' she said, 'like a couple of old *Speisbürger*.'

We were speaking German though she spoke English fluently, I later discovered. Also Russian and Czech.

'I'll give the cake a miss,' I said, patting my stomach. She was back shortly with the coffee on a tray, and a large chocolate cake with cherries, in case I was tempted.

'Gerhard says you have been very kind to him,' she said, as she poured. 'Thank you for that.'

I inclined my head and sought for something polite to say but I couldn't find the right words for a moment. He seems a very nice boy for a Nazi? I confess I was a bit thrown by the situation. We had hardly known each other in Prague and yet we seemed to have a relationship of sorts, like the wife and the mistress who finally meet after all those years.

I muttered something about Gerhard appearing to be very interested in his work.

'It will be good for him to steep himself in this subject,' she said. 'To learn for himself instead of being taught. I am afraid the history teachers in the East were sometimes too harsh with the young. Too concerned with hammering home the lessons of the past. They aroused resentment. Why should they be blamed for the sins of the fathers?'

A certain ambiguity there, I thought, but I decided it was unconscious and let it pass. I think I had an idea at the time that she was playing a game with me but I didn't recognise its precise nature. In fact, she had a very particular purpose in inviting me to her apartment, which became clearer as time went on, but she was also permitting herself to have a little fun at my expense, a little slice of revenge. *Kaffee und Rache.*

'Gerhard mentioned that you were a teacher,' I said. 'Of psychology.'

She looked surprised. 'Did he?' She considered. 'Well, I suppose I did teach for a while,' she said, 'after university. But no, I was a civil servant. I'm afraid Gerhard is ashamed of me. He does not like to admit that I worked in the government.'

She had worked in the Ministry of Information, she said, as a press officer, mostly, though she 'tended to move a bit between departments'. For a while, in the eighties, she had worked in the film censor's office and one of their jobs had been to determine which films from the West could be shown. She had viewed most of Adam's, she said, with an almost coy smile.

'And did you let anyone else see them?' I asked.

It was not her decision, she said, still smiling, but they had, in fact, been banned. They were categorised as typical Hollywood propaganda: the triumph of the individual over the collective, the glorification of private wealth and greed. She herself had considered them 'fairly harmless, if somewhat illusory'. But her opinion did not count for much. She was far too inferior.

But now she was under investigation, she said, as if she was a war criminal.

I suppose she figured I could find this out, easily enough.

Besides, she was about to tap Adam for the money to pay a lawyer. Better to give me her version of the truth before I got it from someone else.

I asked her what she was being investigated for but she just shrugged and said it happened to everyone who had worked for the government above a certain level. They called it de-Stasification but it was just a means of kicking out the old guard and bringing their own people in. Jobs for the boys.

'It's like the southern states of America after they lost the Civil War,' she said. 'The East is full of carpetbaggers.'

There were some fundamental historic differences but I restrained myself from pointing them out. I did ask her, however, how it was that she had become a Communist, after her apparent loathing of them when we'd met in Prague.

She appeared to ponder this carefully. She had been very young then, she said, and had not known much history. The system in the East was not perfect but she had come to consider that it was 'necessary'. Communism was the only way; all other roads led to Auschwitz.

'Remember, we had seen what human beings could do to each other,' she said. 'We had seen the worst of human nature: the Beast within. We wanted to build a better society but to do that we had to change people and in the meantime there had to be controls. We had to drive out the greed and the selfish, destructive individualism in them and we had to protect them from the wolves that would otherwise prey on them.'

I wondered how she classified Honecker, or Stalin or Beria or Brezhnev – as good shepherds? But I sipped my coffee and said nothing. There would have been no point. As soon argue with a Jesuit as an unreconstructed Communist. Despite her explanation, I was surprised to find her faith quite so intact. Possibly it was the faith of the late convert. Also, I thought she probably needed to persuade herself of the rightness of the cause to justify all those years she had spent in its service.

But this was not why she had invited me for tea. I divined her purpose easily enough, I was not that stupid. She had perceived that I might be a threat to Gerhard. Therefore I was to be disarmed. To this end she painted a bleak picture of the hardships she had suffered since reunification: the defeated idealist in her lonely exile, the frustrated, ageing spinster seeking my assistance to keep her son out of bad company and to further his career. He had been in rebellion against his absent father and the liberal Western world his father represented. But now we had to help him succeed in this world so he wouldn't be seduced by those evil neo-Nazis: the displaced and the dispossessed.

I believed all this, even while I thought she was laying it on a bit thick. It seemed rational behaviour for a mother.

She wanted to know who his friends were, as any mother would. She asked me about Callum, Dieter and Nicky. Especially about Nicky. I didn't think this was significant then.

You may think me naive but remember, I didn't know the precise nature of Magda's work for the old regime in the East. We still don't. A press officer, a junior official in the film censor's office? Well, maybe, but only in her early twenties and only as a cover, if you believe those who are witnesses against her.

They say she was a lifetime member of the secret police. That she was recruited by the Stasi as a young student and sent to Prague to report on other students from East Germany who were becoming involved in the 'counter-revolution'. If that is true, it makes sense of a lot of things.

But not becoming pregnant.

Well, of course, it could have been an accident. But why keep the baby?

Is it possible that she fell in love with Adam?

It's not difficult, as I know. Perhaps she was genuinely torn between her love and her . . . ideals. Perhaps she thought to persuade him to share them. If so, his rejection must have been doubly hurtful.

When we fled Prague on the motorbike, what was going through her mind? Was she seriously contemplating leaving for the West and changed her mind at the last minute – or did she always intend to betray us at the border?

So many questions and I'll never know the answer to them. Magda remains an enigma. An evil enigma if you believe half the things she's charged with: that she was a senior interrogator for the Stasi, that she wrote the reports that classified dissidents as insane, that had them committed to asylums where they were 'normalised' with drugs and electric-shock 'therapy', the civilised methods by which we have improved upon medieval torture.

It has even been said that she took satisfaction in watching this treatment being administered, particularly if she had come to know the victims well.

Well, who knows?

My own view now is that Magda was mad. I know this is not an expression I should use as a therapist but now that I have stopped being one I can. Magda was mad as a rat and just as dangerous when cornered.

The tendency, I think, was always there but the fall of the East, the decline in her own personal fortunes and the defection, as she would see it, of her only son to the neo-Nazis had finally tipped her over the edge. Magda didn't want Gerhard to quit the neo-Nazi movement. He was her instrument of destruction, her weapon of Chaos which she would use against Adam and all those other *Besserwessis* who thought they'd won the Cold War.

The people had abandoned Communism, they had chosen a different route than the one Magda and her associates had mapped out for them. Very well, then so far as Magda was concerned they could go to the Devil. And she would help them with a firm push between the shoulder blades.

Give them another dose of Chaos, give them a glimpse of the Beast.

But I didn't know that, I had no inkling of how far she would go and how hard she could push, as I sat on the sofa in her *gemütlich* apartment in Charlottenburg and drank my *Kaffee*.

I'm afraid I even ate the cake.

20

CAMELOT

And now she has gone into politics.

This does surprise me, I'll admit.

I'd have thought that given her dubious past, even accepting her own hoovered version of it, she'd have been well advised to keep a low profile. But perhaps she decided to go for a wider audience. Maximise the support as well as the opposition.

After all, what has she got to lose?

Nicky was the first to alert me to Magda's political activities. She'd heard her speak at a rally of the German Freedom Party in Tempelhof and came back with steam coming out of her ears.

'How can she get away with that shit?' she said. 'The woman should be locked up.'

Well, quite. Though I didn't think so at the time. I was intrigued by this new image of Magda as rabble-rouser but no more inclined to take it seriously than I was Nicky's own cavortings on the stage of Berlin's diverse political cabaret.

No, it is not because they are both women. This is more a reflection on my political awareness than what you are pleased to think of as my inherent misogyny.

Mass political appeal has always been a mystery to me. I watch the old archives they show in the prison theatre.

Hitler, Mussolini, even Churchill and Kennedy and our more recent Cold War warriors. Am I missing something in the performance? Or is it a thing of the moment that does not age well and especially not on video tape?

But Magda's appeal should be obvious to an ex-therapist. She offers freedom from guilt.

Why should Germany be Europe's conscience? she argues. Why should Germans accept the refugees and the riffraff of a continent because of the unproven crimes of half a century ago?

You note the 'unproven'. Magda knows that the Big Idea also needs the Big Lie.

But I am leaping ahead.

When Nicky first spoke to me about Magda's unforeseen gift of oratory, she was little known outside a small circle of activists and probably only Nicky and her own minority group of protesters considered her at all dangerous.

'I'd like to know where she gets her money from,' Nicky said.

This did trouble me slightly. I thought immediately of Adam.

What I did not underestimate, even then, was his own vast reserve of guilt, especially over Magda and Gerhard. I decided to speak to him about it the next time I saw him but he was proving exceptionally difficult to pin down, even for Adam. He was back in Hollywood for most of November and I couldn't even reach him on the telephone. Then, early one morning, he suddenly turned up at Nicky's apartment in Mittenwalderstrasse.

I was still in bed.

'Hey, Sleeping Beauty,' she said, 'wake up, your prince has come.'

The voice penetrated several fathoms of sleep and stirred some primitive form of life. I prised open a shell to behold a blurred vision in a pale pink and blue kimono perched on the edge of the bed.

'He's in the kitchen,' said Nicky.

I was in no mood for this. It had been a hard night.

No, we had not made love. I mean a hard night on the town. We had, however, shared the same bed on our return and had it not been for the amount of beer and hock consumed, consummation might well have resulted.

But you've heard it all before.

I'm sorry. Of course you haven't. I forgot.

In Old Norse, you know, the words for 'virgin' and 'pig' are the same. And the Saxon *piga* means a maiden.

This is a sore subject, I do realise that. To resume.

'What?' I said. I may have added, 'Who?'

'Adam Epstein,' she said. 'At least that's who he says he is. In the kitchen.'

'Adam is in the kitchen?' I repeated.

He was.

Seated at the kitchen table, wearing his Jermyn Street overcoat and a faint smirk. Otherwise he looked disgustingly healthy, I noted, and had an unseasonable tan.

'Well, well,' he said.

I winced. Nicky's kitchen is not a place to venture barefoot. I peeled my sole from the linoleum and tried to avoid eye contact with the dirty dishes that obscured every other surface of the room. It was marginally preferable to look at Adam, even with the smirk. My voice, when I found it, sounded as if it had made a deeply unpleasant journey from the back of my throat with a forced diversion through the nose.

'How did you find me here?'

'It wasn't easy,' said Adam.

'Callum?'

He shrugged. 'He had an idea this was where you'd be. And I needed to talk to you.'

He had just flown in from California, he said, and was about to fly out again.

I pointed out that he could have phoned.

'I was curious,' he said. 'So. Nicky . . .?'

I said, 'There's a café across the road. Let's grab a coffee.'

We could, of course, have grabbed a coffee at Nicky's but a cup would have been more problematical. I finished dressing and took him across to the Gingerbread House.

On the way I said, 'Nicky is a sculptor. She has a work in progress based on a Dürer engraving that I think might be interesting for the lobby of the museum.'

Now why did I say that? It had crossed my mind, in fact, but it was hardly an explanation for spending the night with her. And why did I feel I needed an explanation, anyway? But I was embarrassed. I felt at a disadvantage. This irritated me.

'So I hope your curiosity is now satisfied,' I said.

'It wasn't just that,' he said. He beamed at me over the steaming coffee. He looked very pleased with himself. 'I want you to go to Prague,' he said, 'to buy the Czech state film studios.'

I expect I looked surprised. I felt surprised. Possibly my expression of surprise resembled delight. Adam certainly interpreted it as such.

'I thought you'd like that,' he said.

'Why?' I said.

He looked puzzled. 'Because you're Czech,' he said. 'Because wasn't that where your mother . . .?'

'I meant,' I said, 'why do you want me to do this?'

'Because they're up for sale,' he said. 'And it makes sense to have a studio in Europe, if we're going to make films over here.'

So it was films plural, now.

I said, 'I presume you don't mean with my own money.'

He said, 'For the trust. I want you to help with the

negotiations. There's people to see, people in government. They're probably friends of yours.'

I looked at him carefully. I had constantly to remind myself that Adam was one of the Medici who rule Hollywood. One must never underestimate the level of their ambition or their capacity to attain it.

I said, 'What put this idea into your head?'

He said, 'You did. Something you said to me once. About King Karl and his castle. Remember?'

The night we first met and I took him down by the river and told him the story in the snow. I remembered.

But I didn't quite see the relevance.

He looked at me as if I was being particularly obtuse. 'What did Hollywood do for America?' he said.

It was a little too early in the morning for a quiz game unless I'd been given the answers in advance. I believe I said something to this effect.

Adam said, 'Okay. It turned the immigrants into Americans.'

Well, I knew the theory, of course. The men who invented Hollywood, who were mostly immigrants from Middle Europe, built their success upon fairy tales and incidentally persuaded millions of their fellow immigrants to believe in happy endings. They could all be rich and successful and share in the American dream.

Arguably, Hollywood in the first half of the century did more to unite America than any temporary occupant of the White House. Adam certainly believed this.

And now he apparently hoped to emulate it in Europe.

I said, 'There was King Karl. There was also mad Ludwig.' And someone else I didn't want to mention.

He said, 'You think I'm mad.'

I shook my head. 'A European Hollywood,' I said. 'In Prague?'

'Well, why not?' he said.

Well, why not? I couldn't tell him why not.

I said, 'What about the museum?'

He swirled the dregs of his coffee in the cup.

'Adam?' I said.

'I've been thinking about that,' he said. 'I'm not sure it's you.'

'Excuse me?'

'I think you're getting a lot of opposition because you're a Czech.'

He saw my expression. 'For Christ's sake, Milan, what has got into you? I thought you'd like to go to Prague. My God, think of the possibilities!'

'I can't just drop everything,' I said. 'Besides, I'm not sure I want to get involved in all of this. It seems to be getting out of hand. What are you trying to do here? Why the hell can't you concentrate on one thing at a time?'

I had already started work on the virtual-reality models with a team of architects, designers and historians. We had been talking through the conditions in the Führerbunker during the last few days of the war. I had felt very excited by what we were doing; now I felt depressed and disheartened that Adam didn't think I was the right person for the job.

I said some of this. He sighed and said, Okay, he would go to Prague on his own. Then, of course, I felt guilty. I felt I'd let him down. I said, 'What does Jackie think about all of this?'

He said, 'I don't know.'

I said, 'Haven't you seen her? Talked it over?'

He said, 'She's out at Helmutshausen.'

This meant nothing to me.

'This house we're trying to reclaim,' he reminded me, 'in Brandenburg.'

That, too. It seemed to me that Adam was getting more

and more entangled in his roots and if he was not careful they would choke us all.

'Are you planning to live in this place?' I asked him.

'I don't know yet,' he said. 'There's a lot of work to be done.'

'And have you told her about Gerhard yet – or Magda?'

'Not yet,' he said, irritably. 'I will do. I just haven't had the time.'

I have often felt irritated with Adam but never so angry as I felt then.

He stood up. He looked very tired suddenly. 'And now I have to go to Prague.'

And so Adam went to Prague to build his Camelot and I went to Helmutshausen, to find out what he had done with his wife.

And I never asked him where Magda got her money from.

21

WHERE THE FOX
AND THE WOLF SAY GOODNIGHT

I knew I had arrived when I saw the unicorn.

It was standing on the ruin of a wall beside the road. Its horn had been broken off a few centimetres from its head and its body was scaled with a psoriasis of fungus and moss but I recognised it at once.

Of its companion, the griffin, who had been in the same family photographs, there was no sign. Nor of the great wrought-iron gates they had once guarded. Instead there was a red-and-white-striped barrier with the familiar and unequivocal words: 'EINGANG VERBOTEN.' And beyond that, half hidden among the trees, was the lodge.

It looked deserted. Most of the windows and part of the roof had been covered with corrugated iron and the parasitic climbers of the forest had laid siege to the walls. But as I stopped the car, the door opened and two soldiers came out. They wore drab, ill-fitting tunics belted at the waist and baggy pants tucked into black knee-length boots and round, flat caps with the broad red bands that distinguished them from any other army in the world.

But what were they doing here? Why weren't they back in Russia? Didn't they know the war was over?

I greeted them. In Russian.

They regarded me with suspicion.

I asked them if this was Helmutshausen.

They looked at me stonily. It could be a state secret, of course.

I said I had come to see Frau Epstein.

They said they would send for the major.

I sat in the car, pretending to study the map. The entire area had been used as a firing range by the Red Army for the best part of fifty years and was marked with the warning 'SCHUSSWEITE: DER UNBEFUGT EINGANG VERBOTEN', which I had ignored, assuming it to be redundant, the tanks and the guns and the majors to have long since departed for Mother Russia.

The two soldiers stood by the barricade, glancing towards me from time to time. They did not speak. It had stopped raining but the forest dripped. That and the crepitation of the cooling engine were the only sounds.

Then I heard the jeep. It came fast down the drive and the soldiers raised the barricade for it. The driver looked too young to be a major but he was.

'I am Major Kiselnikov,' he said.

I told him who I was and repeated that I had come to see Frau Epstein, who I believed was living in the castle.

'You are expected,' he said.

This was gratifying.

'You will follow me, please,' he said.

He turned the jeep and I followed him up the drive.

After the first few hundred metres it degenerated into little more than a track through the forest, the thin tarmac gouged in places by tank tracks as if an ogre had been cutting his teeth on it. I wondered what had happened to the game during all those years of cohabiting with the Soviet armoured corps. I had read somewhere that wildlife thrived on a firing range. At least the tanks weren't firing at *them*, unlike Adam's ancestors for the last few hundred years. The stands of forest on either side of the drive looked dense and unspoiled, except at one point where a 'tank ride' had apparently been bulldozed right through the middle. The grass was growing over it again to make a wide glade, though I could still see deep tracks in parts where the herds of armour had charged.

Then we came out of the trees and I saw the *Schloss* on a low ridge above a lake, sharply etched against the sky.

I had known what to expect from the pictures but here, in its setting, it seemed much more forbidding, much more the Gothic donjon than the French château, though both styles were discernible in its structure. Just a hunting lodge on the Polish border, Adam had said, 'where the fox and the wolf say goodnight'.

It was a saying he'd picked up in Berlin, meaning somewhere in the sticks or, to be more romantic, somewhere remote and wild and sometimes dangerous. Clearly it appealed to him. A small *castello* in Umbria would have been more to my taste but I conceded it had an eerie grandeur, like the sepia studies of Caspar David Friedrich I had in my apartment in LA. It was certainly in harmony with its bleak northern landscape and the dramatic conflict of sun and cloud.

We skirted the lake and crossed a small bridge over the stream that fed it. I caught glimpses of disturbed water where a fish, or some such creature (for all I knew, prehistoric), had briefly surfaced. Then we began to climb the ridge and became lost in the trees again and when we emerged the *Schloss* rose up directly above us.

I wasn't sure quite what function it had served since the war – Adam had suggested that the Russians might have used it for target practice but if so they must have been lousy shots. Then, as we came closer, I saw the signs of neglect and in some parts it was clearly derelict.

The drive opened out in front of the building and there was a broad flight of stone steps leading up to what was clearly the main entrance, flanked by two mythical beasts of indeterminate breed. But the major drove straight on and round the far end into a cobbled courtyard at the rear.

It was like a builders' yard, littered with their materials and trucks. A number of men in army fatigues were mixing cement, others sawing wood. And when I got out of the car and looked up I saw more of them on the roof. Jackie, of course, was halfway up a ladder.

She waved when she saw me and came down.

She was dressed pretty much as I had first seen her but wore a headscarf, Russian peasant style, instead of a sou'wester.

'Thank you, Mischa,' she said to the major with a smile. He didn't quite simper but it came close.

'Come and have some tea,' she said to me.

She led me into a room that opened directly on to the courtyard and which she said was part of the old kitchens. There was an ancient range and a tiled stove that had been here when she first came, she said, and she'd bought some basket chairs from a garden centre. Her clothes were hanging up from a rail in one corner and there was a pile of novels and paperwork on the table among the dishes and the tins of food. It reminded me of somewhere but it was a moment before I could pin it down. I had more pressing concerns. At the first break in the stream of information I said, 'What about the Russians?'

She looked surprised. 'They were here when I came,' she said.

'I assumed that,' I said. 'But aren't they supposed to be back in Russia?'

'Well, strictly speaking, yes,' she said. 'But they're clearing up the bombs.'

'The bombs?' I said.

'And the shells and things. From the range. They're the only ones who know where they are. They're pioneers. There's only forty of them. Mischa's their commander. Personally, I think

198

everyone's forgotten about them. Mischa's ambition is to be the last Russian soldier to leave Germany. The one who puts the cat out and switches off the light.'

'I see,' I said. Then, 'They didn't seem to be looking for bombs out in the courtyard. Or cats.'

'Ah, no,' she said. 'They're helping me get the place straight.'

'They live here?' I said.

'Oh, no,' she said. They lived in a barracks about ten kilometres away and came out each day to do the work she had contracted for them with Mischa. She paid them in Deutschmarks, she said, and US dollars.

'Is that strictly legal?' I asked.

'Good God, no,' she said. 'I expect we'd all be shot if anyone found out.'

This was not what I wanted to hear.

'And what happens at night?' I said.

She looked at me strangely. What did I mean?

'You don't stay here by yourself?'

She shrugged. 'Where else would I stay?'

She said Mischa had a couple of sentries posted in the lodge and they patrolled the grounds at night so there was no danger of intruders.

'And what about them?' I said. She looked at me blankly. I explained. 'You don't think they might be tempted by a woman, alone, in this place? And where do you keep this money you pay them?'

'In the bank,' she said. 'We go into town every Friday to draw it out.'

'We?'

'Me and Mischa.'

'I see. And you trust this Mischa?'

'Yes,' she said. 'Besides, who'd kill the goose that lays the golden eggs?'

I didn't know but it was probably a Russian.

'Don't worry,' she said, 'it's quite safe here. It's a castle.'

She gave me the guided tour.

She took me into the old tower, the original stronghold of Childe Helmut back in the days of Charlemagne. The stone floor was deep in bird droppings and the regurgitated corpses of small animals. I looked up through the gutted floors and though I saw no owls I imagined them, hidden among the blackened beams, peering down at me, and the Lord of Gormenghast among them with the tail of a live mouse dangling from his thin lips . . .

My bedroom was less grim, with a view out towards the lake. There were fresh flowers in a vase by the bed and a bowl of dried ones by the window. Jackie was a homemaker. All she lacked was a husband.

We rattled around the empty house, our every movement mocked with an echo. I imagined the ghosts of all those Reisenburg ancestors peering over the balustrades and retreating, sniggering, before us, down the next corridor. The rooms all looked the same. High ceilings, some elaborately moulded, wooden floors, grubby plasterwork painted a uniform cream, wood panelling darkly coated with several layers of varnish. All with a drab institutional feel. I wondered who, if anyone, had been living here for the last half-century and why.

Then, looking out of one of the windows, something caught my eye. The room we were in was right round the back of the *Schloss* where the trees grew up quite close to the walls and two or three of them seemed to be hung with long strands of glitter, like Christmas trees. Except that it wasn't glitter.

Every tree within a short distance of the building appeared to be festooned with 35-millimetre film. For a wild moment I thought it was some kind of art exhibition, a form of modern sculpture. Is this what the Russians did here?

But no, it wasn't. They made films.

'The Red Army?' I said.

'The GRU,' Jackie said knowledgeably, adding, for my benefit, 'Army intelligence.'

Mischa had told her. They had made training films here. How to follow people, how to avoid detection, how to ambush them . . . how to kill them.

I looked out of the window again and a small wind moved the film in the trees like the dead skin that is shed by snakes.

'But why decorate the trees with it?'

'Mischa says they just threw it out of the window before they left. They were drunk, apparently. They were glad they were leaving.'

I could believe that.

'And you're seriously thinking of living here?' I said.

She didn't answer for a moment. She'd been looking out of the window with me. Now she turned away.

'That depends on Adam,' she said.

'But you have discussed it with him?'

She hadn't. She hadn't seen him for over three weeks, she said, the longest since they'd been married.

'I think he's gone off me,' she said.

Despite the matter-of-fact tone, I sensed she was close to tears. I followed her down the corridor.

'Jackie,' I said. 'What's going on?'

She protested that I was his friend and confidant and she couldn't talk to me openly about him, but then she stopped walking and found a wall to lean on, beside a window. I paused behind her, waiting.

'We haven't made love for six months,' she said. 'Six months, one week, two days. I keep a note in my diary.'

After a moment I said, 'But it wasn't like that to begin with?'

She shook her head. She kept her back turned. We were at

that part of the castle that overlooks the lake and I could see a single large bird gliding down to land on the water. It should have been a swan but I rather think it was a goose.

'You think there's someone else?'

She didn't know. There had been no obvious evidence but she thought that might be the case. Didn't I?

'Well, there could be other reasons,' I said.

She turned then and challenged me to name one. I named several, off the top of my head. Hepatitis B, veneral disease, he might have discovered he was HIV positive . . .

'Thank you, Milan,' she said. 'You're a real comfort.'

'What I mean is, there could be medical problems, mental problems . . . He should talk to someone.'

Me, for instance.

She turned back to the window.

'We did talk about having a baby,' she said.

'Oh?' I said. 'When was this?'

'About six months ago.'

Or six months, one week and two days?

So was it fear of fatherhood, of his own mortality, of replacement? Possible, but unlikely. After all, he already had a son, or thought he had.

But she didn't know that.

I held my tongue. It should be Adam who told her, not I.

Then she turned again and said there was something else. Did I know she and Callum Connolly had been lovers?

She watched my reaction.

'Obviously not,' she said.

I had placed my hand on one of the walls. I needed to feel something solid. It felt cold.

'It was about a year before I met Adam,' she said. 'In London.'

She walked on and after a moment or two I followed her.

'Did Adam know?' I asked her.

202

'Oh, yes. I told him when we were in London. I said he was the only other man I'd ever met that I could ever have married.' She glanced sideways at me. 'Apart from you, of course.'

I assume she was being ironic.

'Adam was one of Callum's big heroes,' she said. 'His role model. He'd seen every film he ever made about three times over.'

Well, I knew that. But I hadn't realised the significance.

You grunt. I know you find this tediously Freudian but I happen to believe that all creative endeavour is a substitute for the real thing. So Adam's desire to involve his wife's ex-lover in a film about his mother did, yes, have a strong sexual connotation for me.

I have had a number of clients who were obsessed with their wives' previous lovers. Some hated them; some wanted to kill them; some wanted to kill their wives. But it is more common, I think, to want to like them, to feel an empathy, a warmth and respect that is not a long way removed from self-regard. And of course there is the homosexual element: the desire to make love to another man through the surrogacy of the shared female lover. But then, you will say I am displaying a prejudice.

'Did Adam discuss this with you?' I asked her. 'I mean, before he . . .'

She shook her head fiercely. 'Did he hell,' she said.

'And have you . . . challenged him with it since?'

'Have you ever challenged Adam with anything?' she said. 'He ducks and dives. He's impossible to pin down.'

There was a new cynicism about her which I didn't at all like. I shivered. A portent of disaster? And of my own powerlessness to avert it? Or perhaps it was just the cold.

We had emerged on to the courtyard and Mischa was watching us from beside one of the trucks.

'Excuse me,' she said.

I watched them talking together, wondering.

When she came back she said, 'I've invited him for supper, if that's all right with you.'

'Fine,' I said.

'He's all right, is Mischa,' she said, 'and he's lonely, but I can't have him round when I'm by myself in case he gets the wrong end of the stick.'

This, at least, was reassuring.

He came at seven in his best uniform with flowers for Jackie and a bottle of vodka for the three of us. It was the real stuff and tasted as if it was distilled from Russian boot polish.

'Electric soup,' I said, when I could breathe again.

I had heard it thus described in an account of the battle for Stalingrad but the images in my mind were of Prague in '68 and the young Red Army conscripts in their tanks. It was not easy for me to feel sociable and relaxed with someone who wore that uniform.

But the vodka helped.

It felt very strange, though, the three of us sitting round that old stove in that ancient fortress. It felt as if we were waxwork figures in a museum representing a moment of history. But which period? I wondered, if we were suddenly obliterated by a river of lava and they dug us up a thousand years hence, what would they make of us? A Czech, a Scot and a Russian found sitting at a tiled stove in a medieval castle on the German–Polish border in the last decade of the twentieth century.

What could they have been doing here?

Well, they were drinking, of course . . . They would have found the bottles.

Besides the vodka, we had two bottles of hock with our supper and finished off with Scotch whisky. We became sentimental. We exchanged stories about our homes, about our histories. Mischa spoke some English, though badly. Otherwise he spoke Russian and I translated for Jackie.

He came from St Petersburg, which he still called Leningrad, and he was older than he looked. His father had fought with the partisans against the Germans in '45 and he was still a Communist, Mischa said. Still marched with the veterans and wore the Order of Lenin pinned proudly to his lapel.

Mischa himself hated politics – and politicians. If he had any politics himself, I would say he was a libertarian, a right-wing anarchist. Most Russians are at heart. Marx wrote his revolutionary tracts for the Germans, or the British, but the wrong people got hold of the plans.

We talked about the Big Idea, the simple solution. Marx had it, so did Hitler. That was what people wanted to hear, we agreed.

'Maybe I will have the Big Idea,' Mischa said, 'when I go back to Russia. There, it is like Germany was in the twenties. The racketeers and the people who have nothing and the out-of-work soldiers and the sense of defeat. Russia is maybe right for the Big Idea. I will think about it while we are mending the roof.'

Shortly after midnight a jeep turned up for him from the barracks and he kissed us both and clung to Jackie and wept and sighed a lot before he staggered off into the night. There were no stars in the sky and the wind was from Russia, braced with ice and the bones of dead armies.

22

FOOTPRINTS IN THE SNOW

When I woke up in the morning I knew from the quality of the light that it had snowed and when I looked out of the window there was a thin but even crust on the ground broken by a single set of footprints leading down towards the lake.

And beside the lake there were two figures.

One of them was Jackie but I had to stare hard for a moment before I recognised the other. Then I knew we had problems. It was Connolly.

I had the coffee on the stove when they came in. He looked at me as though I had betrayed him.

'You might have told me,' he said.

I was confused. 'Told you what?' I said. That I had the coffee on?

'About Jackie,' he said.

I was more confused. I looked at Jackie. But she was giving nothing away. She walked over to the stove and warmed her hands on the coffee pot.

'What about Jackie?' I said.

'That she was . . . that they were married.' He looked helplessly at her but she did not turn round. She continued to warm her hands. 'That she was here.'

I thought about this for a moment. 'You mean you didn't know?' I said.

When I had seen them together by the lake I had naturally thought that he had come here especially to see her. But no. He had come to see the castle. He was interested in using it as a location for the film.

I found this hard to believe.

Gerhard had told him about it, he said.

He had no idea that Jackie would be here. No idea that she was Adam's wife. He had been standing by the lake taking photographs when she had come walking down towards him.

'Gerhard told you about it?' I said.

He said, 'We were talking about locations for the film and he said there was this place, an easy drive from Berlin. He'd heard about it when he was working at the studios in Babelsberg. They used it for some film about the Thirty Years' War.'

Could it be pure coincidence, then, that had brought Callum here? After all, how could Gerhard have known that he would find Jackie here, unless Adam had told him? And what purpose could he have hoped to achieve, except to embarrass people?

These were not questions I could ask of these two.

I said, 'How did you get past the guards?'

He said, 'What guards?'

'So much for your Russians,' I said to Jackie.

She turned round. She did not look at Callum.

'It's probably the snow,' she said.

'They're Russians,' I said. 'They're supposed to be best in snow.'

Callum looked at us both as if we were mad, or he was. He'd seen the barrier at the main gate, he said, but he'd driven round it. He hadn't seen any Russians but then he hadn't exactly been looking out for them.

We heard the sound of a truck in the courtyard.

'That'll be them,' Jackie said and went outside. While she

was gone, I explained. I don't know if he took it in or not. I expect after meeting Jackie like that, the Russian army was a minor detail.

'You haven't been in touch with her at all,' I asked him, 'since you split up?'

He shook his head. He hadn't seen or heard from her since he left London for Hollywood, he said.

'Adam Epstein,' he said. 'She married Adam Epstein.'

He kept shaking his head. He seemed dazed. Then I could see a thought had penetrated. He looked at me sharply.

'Did he know? That I was . . .'

I told him he'd have to ask Adam that.

'He did, didn't he? He fucking did.'

Jackie came in with Mischa. He glared at Callum as if he was going to take him outside and shoot him. It might have been merciful.

'I have to go and look at some problem,' Jackie said. Then she looked at Callum as if he was another.

'Will you stay for lunch?' she said.

No, he said, he wouldn't stay for lunch.

'Will you phone me?' she said.

She wrote down the number for him.

I walked him out to his car. We did not speak. But when we reached it he seemed reluctant to leave.

He looked back at the castle and shook his head again.

'What is she doing here?' he said.

Well, that was not an easy question to answer.

'Is there any way Gerhard could have known she was here?' I asked him.

'Christ knows,' he said. 'I'll find out, though, if I have to throttle it out of him.'

I wondered if I should tell him who Gerhard was but it would only have added to his problems and I saw no particular reason why I should diminish them for Gerhard.

'Did Gerhard know about you and Jackie?' I asked him.

'Not from me he didn't. D'you think I'd tell that little shit about someone I was . . .?' Then he said, 'Dieter.'

I said, 'Excuse me?'

He said, 'Dieter knew about me and Jackie. He was on the film when we met in England.'

I said, 'You mean you think Dieter told Gerhard about this and Gerhard sent you out here so you would meet her?'

He said, 'It's possible.'

I said, 'But why?'

He said, 'For the hell of it, I expect. I wouldn't put it past either of them.'

He leaned on the roof of his car and put his head down on his arms for a moment. Then he looked up.

'Why did I leave her?' he said.

'Why *did* you leave her?' I said.

He blew breath through his nostrils. It steamed in the frozen air.

'I wanted to make a movie,' he said.

It was clear that he no longer considered this a worthwhile ambition.

'And that meant leaving her?'

'It meant leaving London. I didn't think I'd be back in a hurry. So I thought we should make a clean break.'

'You didn't consider taking her with you?'

'No.' He snorted again. 'No. I wanted to be . . . unencumbered. Much good it did me. But I did love her.'

He looked at me as if challenging me to deny it. But I believed him. I wished I didn't.

He opened the car door but seemed reluctant to get in. He looked back at the castle again.

'Would have made a good location,' he said. 'For a horror movie.'

'And do you still?' I said.

'Oh, yes,' he said. 'Oh, yes. When I saw her walking down towards the lake . . . It was like . . .'

I remembered Adam's dream. But she had walked on and not looked back.

'Are you staying here with her?' he asked me.

I said only for a day or two.

'And where's Adam?'

'Here and there,' I said.

'Are they . . .?'

'I don't know,' I said. 'But – '

'Oh, don't worry,' he said. 'I'm not going to . . . Besides, I really fucked up on that. You never know what you want until it's too late.'

And the movie you made is a disaster at the box office, I thought.

But I am too cynical, as you know. The fact is, I liked him. I had not realised it until then but I had this thought, as we stood there in the snow, that we could have been friends.

If it had not been for Adam.

'What will you do now?' I asked him.

'I don't know,' he said. 'I suppose I should speak to Adam, but the way I feel at the moment I just want to get the hell out of this place, take the first plane out of Berlin.'

Perhaps that was best. If I hadn't spoken, perhaps that is what he would have done. But I did.

I felt sorry for him, to be honest. I thought he'd had a raw deal and I blamed Adam for it

I said, 'I think Adam probably thought you were the best person for the job.'

He said, 'You mean, because we both . . . because of Jackie?'

'There is that,' I said. 'He probably thinks you might have certain things in common. And if he cannot make the film himself, then you are the next best thing.'

'Like a surrogate?'

'Perhaps.'

I could see him thinking about it.

'So you think I should stay?'

I did not say that.

I said, 'That is really for you to decide. But you don't have to see Jackie again.'

'No.' He thought about that for a moment while we stood there. Then he got into the car.

I watched him drive away with a confused sense of relief mingled with regret. But relief was strongest.

When I returned to the kitchen, Jackie was there, standing by the phone, looking thoughtful.

'Adam's just rung,' she said. 'He's coming back at the end of the week. He wants us to spend Christmas here. You, too. He asked if we had any friends we wanted to invite.'

23

CHRISTMAS

At least we didn't have to look far for a tree.
Mischa brought one in from the forest in the back
of a truck and four of his men dragged it indoors and
planted it in the hall, at the foot of the stairs, a six-metre spruce
still wet from the snow. It was their parting gift. The great
uniformed bureaucracy had finally caught up with them and
they'd been given their marching orders. They were leaving
on the 20th, to be back with their families for Christmas.

Mischa was inconsolable; a great frozen drip of Slavonic
misery. We held a wake for them on the last night, all forty-six
of them, in the Great Hall. Can you imagine it? I can't and I was
there. Giving moral support. Adam was still on his way back
from Frankfurt, where he'd been having more talks with the
bankers. I was beginning to feel extremely partisan about the
Adam–Jackie relationship and so far as I was concerned Adam
was with the bankers on the wrong side of the barricades.

I can at least give you a broad picture of the evening. It was
a Brueghel, of course. Jackie had the caterers in, and a band
from Frankfurt-on-Oder. Trestle tables in a long line down
the centre of the room. Christmas crackers and funny hats.
Roast goose and capons. Gallons of wine and vodka. Seven
strapping serving wenches. Six jolly music men. Forty-six
legless Russians. Everyone got roaring drunk, of course, from
the word go and there was singing and dancing and crying.

Lots of crying, though not from the Germans who were only too glad to see the back of them – as I would have been in other circumstances.

I never thought I'd say it but I was sorry to see the Russians go. It meant there would just be the three of us for Christmas and I didn't know how I was going to cope. Mischa brought them all up to the castle the next morning before they left: in six trucks with himself leading in the jeep, the last Russians to leave Germany and all of them with hangovers. They circled the courtyard while we stood in the doorway, taking the salute. The end of an era and only a pair of bleary-eyed exiles to see it off the premises. I had to keep reminding myself it was for real.

And the *Mitteleuropäer* in me wondering how long before they were back.

'We should have had pipes,' said Jackie, watching them drive off across the head of the lake.

It was a moment or two before I realised she meant bagpipes. There were tears in her eyes.

Adam arrived that night, in a Range Rover loaded down with presents, food hampers, cases of wine – and Eric.

I had forgotten about Eric. He'd only come for one night, though. He had a flight to New York in the morning, to join his folks for Christmas. He was leaving his guns behind.

'And where's Nicky?' Adam asked me.

I told him she had gone back to see her parents in the south of England.

'So it's just us, then?' he said, thoughtfully.

I don't know whom else he'd expected. Callum Connolly?

Jackie had told him about his trip to the *Schloss*. He claimed that Callum had said nothing to him about it. He, too, had gone to spend Christmas with his family. They'd all gone rushing back to their roots, leaving us alone in the forest.

214

'I'll have a word with him when he gets back,' he said.

He clearly didn't think it was a big problem. But then he had so many other things to think about. I'd seen him like this before, of course, when he was building up to a movie. But he was beyond movies; now he was building on a grand scale. Besides the film studios, he had plans for a university. It was to be on the same site, just outside Prague: a university of the visual arts. It would be a magnet for students from all over Europe and they wouldn't just study film, theatre or painting; they would study architecture and the environment. They would be the elite who would build the Europe of the future . . .

It was all so grandiose I was inclined to treat it as pure moonshine and reach for the peanuts. But he was serious and, what is more, he was being taken seriously by the people he'd always affected to despise but secretly been desperate to impress: the bankers, the politicians, the bureaucrats – people who'd always regarded him as a Hollywood fantasist, a pedlar of dreams. But now Peter Pan was talking to the grown-ups and they were listening. This was a dream that was to become real and it was going to save Europe from repeating the mistakes of the past.

Well, no offence, but it beats hog-rearing for a high and Adam was heading way up for the stratosphere and plenty of fuel to burn.

I couldn't fault his ideals. I shared them. It was just that I wished he'd keep still for a moment and do one thing at a time. We'd come to Europe to build a museum, now we were building the future and I wasn't as sure as Adam that we could control it.

He also talked about his grandfather, the old prince, who had died such a horrible death on the butcher's hook in Plotzenzee. It had not been Adam's idea to name the trust after the House of Reisenburg – it seemed egotistical, he said

215

– but now he thought it was like an omen. Good would come out of Evil.

I always said he was a romantic but he was an overachiever, too, and it's an impressive combination.

I could see Jackie looking at him, weighing it up, torn between approval and apprehension. I think we both felt we were losing him. He was like a bubble of air that was getting bigger and bigger and floating further and further out of our reach and we could only watch it soaring over the tops of the trees, into the distance until finally it vanished out of sight, or went pop.

But at heart he was still the same Adam. Still the same kid I'd met in Prague full of wide-eyed enthusiasm, garrulous with ideas. You still wanted to hug him, hold him down, make him feel loved. But how do you hug a bubble?

The only time he slowed down was in the room Jackie had created in the old kitchen area. He would look around, almost as if he was puzzled, as if he was trying to remember something and sometimes he'd sit down by the stove and be still for a while. For at least five minutes, anyway. But I remember that Christmas as a series of events, as perpetual motion. We'd drive off to the nearest market town to listen to the carol singers in the church square and before I knew it he'd invited them all back to sing at the castle for a small bag of gold. He took us to the local dog pound because he thought Jackie needed a guard dog or at least some company when she was alone. She talked him out of loading the Range Rover with stray mongrels but he had us join in the Christmas party for the staff and we came away reeling and with the owner promising to save the next Rottweiler for us. And always he was on the phone trying to talk to people in California or New York or London or Frankfurt or Brussels and they were never there.

'What's going on?' I asked him. 'Why can't you relax?'

In the past, no matter how restless he was, he'd always

216

seemed confident. When there was a crisis on set he was always impressively calm, in control. Now there was an anxiety that I felt was entirely out of character. He seemed to be in a hurry, as if he felt there wasn't enough time to get everything done.

'There's so many things hanging in the air,' he said. 'Why do they have to have Christmas now?'

'When you're Master of the Universe,' I said, 'you can change it.'

Christmas Day was a nightmare because there was nothing for him to do, no one for him to visit and for once he felt inhibited from phoning anyone up to talk business. So he sat and twitched. Then he started trying to wire up a load of speakers he'd bought so we'd have music blaring out from every room and he got into a tangle with it and a temper and blew the fuses. All things considered, I decided I'd rather he concentrated on saving the world. We went on a long walk while dinner was cooking – we had a huge carp from Bohemia – and what with that and all the eating and drinking, he crashed out about three in the afternoon and slept through the rest of the day. Jackie and I played Scrabble.

If there was anything wrong between the two of them he didn't let it show, or even reveal he was aware of it. But I knew something wasn't working for them. There was no acrimony, no arguments. They touched, they even hugged from time to time but there was no spark, no joy. It felt sad.

Jackie seemed to spend most of her time cooking. This surprised him.

'You never cook,' he told her.

'I never cooked in California,' she said. 'Because we had a cook. I never cooked in Berlin because we had Frau Lange. The rest of the time we've been in hotels. But I like cooking, as it happens.' She went very thoughtful then. 'I used to have spells when I cooked a lot,' she said. Then

217

she looked as if she was going to burst into tears and left the room.

'What the hell's the matter with her?' said Adam.

I gave him a look.

'Jesus, what's got into you guys?' he said.

But he made a visible effort to relax and waxed lyrical over the next meal, a cassoulet. I'd have thrown it over him.

That afternoon it snowed and he worried in case the roads were blocked. He had an important meeting the following day in Prague. He stared out of the window, watching the flakes drifting down, like a little boy who can't play out. That was the thing about Adam. Even chasing fifty, you could still see the lost little boy in him. I suppose that was why we loved him, even when he fused the lights.

He figured the best thing was to have a helicopter standing by to fly him out so he had me call a hire firm in Tegel to check if they could fly in snow. They said it depended on the snow. Then he started worrying that planes wouldn't be able to land at Prague airport, so with one thing and another he decided to leave that same evening and take the night train from Berlin.

By this time I think Jackie had stopped caring.

I did manage to talk to him about Gerhard and Magda, though, before he left.

He had told Gerhard about the *Schloss*. But he couldn't believe that Gerhard had deliberately sent Callum out here to cause mischief. It must have been a misunderstanding.

'Maybe he just talked about it,' he said, 'and Callum thought it would be a good idea to come and look at it.'

He admitted he had given Magda money. An allowance, he called it. He knew nothing about her political activities and clearly he was a little shaken by them. He would get someone to look into it, he said.

But he explained that he'd thought it best to enrol Magda

as an ally, at least so far as Gerhard was concerned. They both had the same interest in weaning him from his neo-Nazi friends.

I told him I'd seen her in Berlin. He was a little shaken by that, too. He asked me what I'd thought of her.

I told him I thought she was embittered and angry but not a real problem for him. I remember the expression I used was 'essentially harmless'.

I know, That's why I thought I'd start again, with pigs.

24

STORYTIME

They turned off the main road just before the village and drove down a dirt track to the river. We know that because the police found the tyre tracks later. It was a van, they reckoned. I don't know how they know these things but I expect they were right on this occasion. You would expect them to drive a van. I imagine it looked like the kind of van that rock groups drive. They probably looked like a rock group, too: heavy metal. They drove along the side of the river for about a kilometre and parked just below the new footbridge. It was very dark down there. There was a full moon but there was a lot of cloud about. It had been snowing earlier but by then it had stopped.

It wasn't much of a river. Nothing like the Elbe or the Oder or the Neisse or the Rhine, but it had always been the border between the ancient Germanic states of Thuringia and Hesse and after the last war it became the border between East and West at this particular point. There were two villages, one on the west side of the river and the other on the east. They'd always mixed and intermarried even when one was in Thuringia and the other one in Hesse. But when the Iron Curtain came down there was no more of that. The people from the East sometimes came and stood and looked over at their relatives on the West side but no one waved or made any sign of recognition because they all knew that if the people in the East were caught waving they were in deep shit. So they just stood there, separated by the river and the lines of razor wire and the free-fire zone where they'd planted the land mines.

Like the Berliners, they, too, had their Death Strip.

The footbridge had been built in the first flush of enthusiasm for reunification. I think the army built it. But it was more symbolic than practical. They had cars now, and most of the locals would rather drive ten kilometres to the nearest roadbridge than walk a little more than a kilometre across a footbridge and up the path between the linden trees. It would have been a regressive step somehow, to walk.

The footbridge was very useful for Gerhard and his people, though. It gave them an escape route that couldn't be cut off by a police roadblock.

Of course, we don't know that Gerhard was there. We have no concrete evidence. It didn't make any sense for him to be there but then nothing Gerhard did made any sense. Gerhard wasn't about making sense, Gerhard was about Chaos, as I believe I might have said. I am not always wrong.

The hostel was on the far side of the village, in what had once been a school. The people there were mainly Romanians, plus a few from Croatia and other parts of what had once been Yugoslavia. They were all single-parent families – mothers and children. There were seven mothers and eighteen children. And four volunteers.

One of the volunteers was a nineteen-year-old music student from Weimar, working here for her summer vacation. Her name was Helga. It was her story I first read in the papers.

She had stepped out for some fresh air. It was very fuggy in the hostel at times, especially in the evenings, and too many of the mothers smoked for her liking. She walked down the garden to where the children had made a snowman. It had coals for eyes and one of them had dropped out. The snowman

looked rather sinister with its single black eye. She picked up
the fallen coal and pushed it back into the frozen socket. Then
she heard a noise out in the darkness towards the river. It
sounded like glass breaking but she thought it must be some
of the lads from the village. She felt cold suddenly and went
back indoors.

They'd put the younger children to bed after supper but
they'd let the older ones stay up late to watch a movie someone
had brought back from the video store: *Home Alone 2*, dubbed
into German. Helga thought it would be too much of a culture
shock for the kids, even if their German was up to it, but they
loved it. They were up to the point where Macaulay Culkin
finds the pigeon woman in Central Park when the first bottle
came through the window.

Helga had been warned that there was an outside chance
of something like this happening. They'd watched television
news of the attacks on the refugee hostels in Rostock, seen the
figures silhouetted against the flames, throwing petrol bombs
into the blazing buildings or with their arms raised in the Nazi
salute, chanting '*Sieg Heil, Sieg Heil*' like in the old days. But
it was the usual thing: you never thought it would happen
to you. And besides it was so rural here, so peaceful. There
was no atmosphere of violence, not like the cities. But even
if she'd been prepared there was no dealing with the shock
of that moment when the window shattered and the bottle
smashed against the floor and burst into flames.

She just stood there with her back pressed against the wall
while the flames ran across the carpet and up the curtains. She
couldn't take it in that this was real, that it was happening
here. The children were screaming and running along the
sides of the room towards the door. One of the sofas was
on fire. Then she saw that there was a child on it. The child
was on fire. She was kicking her legs and screaming and her
legs were a mass of flames. Helga came out of her trance then,

ran to her and started to beat at the flames, but they were burning her hands. Then another bottle came flying through the window, and another and another. The video was still on and Macaulay Culkin was running through Central Park in the snow with the pigeon woman and the trees were all ablaze with fairy lights for Christmas.

Three of the children were burned to death in the fire: one six-year-old boy and two girls aged eight and nine. Also one of the volunteers, a young woman from Hamburg. They were trapped in one of the upstairs rooms. Helga burned her hands. I've seen pictures. They look like claws. She used to play the violin.

It was Helga who saw the attackers. When she got out of the house, dragging two of the children with her, the flames were behind her and the light was on their faces. Except that they did not have faces. They wore masks of characters from Disney. Wolves and bears and foxes, witches and warlocks and trolls . . . That was how the police knew it was the same gang that had attacked the peace vigil in Buchenwald.

25

THE ACTRESS AND
THE REICHSMINISTER

We heard the news of the attack on the radio, just before Adam left for Prague. It was the final nail in the coffin of our Christmas, though we didn't know it was quite so personal at the time.

I was tempted to go with him but I didn't want to leave Jackie alone out there. It would have seemed like a betrayal, somehow. I decided to stay until he came back. He had a crowd of film people arriving for the New Year. I had declined an invitation to join them. I was going back to Berlin, to spend New Year's Eve with Nicky.

Next morning she phoned. She'd come back a few days early. It had been 'desperate' at home, she said. 'It rained nonstop and we played endless games of charades. You've no idea. Finally, I cracked. I said I had this deadline to meet and got on stand-by at Gatwick.'

She was back working on her sculpture: *The Companions*, as she called it. She had finished the Knight and the Devil. Now she was starting on Death.

I knew she'd had a problem with Death. In the engraving he was portrayed as an old man with a white beard and a ravaged face who rode along beside the Knight on an old nag with an egg-timer in his hand. Unlike the other characters in the composition, he did not lend himself to a sculpture in metal, so she was thinking of changing him and making him more like Death as he had been portrayed in *The Seventh Seal*. The hunched, cowled figure of Bergman's imagining lent itself more readily to her materials, she said.

There was a small pause. Then she said, 'So when are you coming back?'

'As soon as I can,' I said. 'Now that you're there.'

Quite the Lothario. Or the silly old fool. It amounts to the same thing, quite often.

When she'd rung off I took myself off for a walk round the back of the castle, to a part of the forest I'd not been before. It had stopped snowing – Adam's fears had been groundless on that score – but there was just enough of it to paint the scene. The *Schloss* rose up behind me on its cliff with the icicles hanging down from the gargoyles and the guttering and a single plume of smoke rising from one of the chimneys. As I walked through the woods, the snow dropped softly and silently from the trees in my wake and the air was full of fine droplets that brushed my face like cobwebs. I felt almost drunk with the beauty of it. Then I heard a sound, almost like an apologetic cough, I thought later, and a full-grown boar was suddenly standing there just a few metres in front of me. I hadn't seen where he had come from, he might have been there all along and I'd walked straight into him. He had tusks like sabres and a mane like a lion's and a neck like a bull ... Yes, I know I probably exaggerate, you're the expert on boars, the time you spend mooning about them, but believe me, he was a hell of a brute, a brute from Hell. What I am trying to say is that this was not your average domestic pig.

We exchanged meaningful glances.

I could see his breath in the air. I believe mine had stopped. I could sense the warmth of his blood. I felt I could reach out and touch the ridge of stiff hog's hair on his back. Though I had no such intention.

Then he was gone. He kind of sprang back on himself. A wild boar, I am told, can turn in his own length at speed, did you know that? You did. Well, anyway, that is what he did and he was gone with a rush and a flurry of snow.

I breathed again.

I stood there for quite some moments before I dared to move. Then, when the fear had receded somewhat, I was entranced by the magic of the encounter. I felt as if this was the king of the forest, exiled for all those years of the Cold War and now come back to reclaim his own. Like one of those creatures that the white queen had turned to stone in Lewis's tale of Narnia and Aslan breathed on to bring back to life.

I know. I was getting as bad as Adam. I walked on and came to a place near the castle wall where long icicles dangled down in spirals from the trees. It was extraordinary, fantastical, the way they twisted and coiled and I thought it was another bit of magic. Then, of course, I realised: this was the film the GRU had thrown out of the windows before they left. I reached up and broke a piece off – it was as brittle as brandy snaps – and held it up to the sky to see if there were any images left but they were gone, wiped clean by sun and frost as if they had never been.

When I went back indoors, Jackie was standing in the hall by the fire, looking thoughtful. She said Callum had rung. He had to talk to me urgently, he'd said. He was driving out from Berlin.

I was annoyed. I tried ringing him back but he'd already left. I was sure that whatever he had to say could have waited until I got back and that this was just an excuse to come out and see Jackie.

He arrived about midday. Jackie had washed her hair, I noted, and wore a red woollen dress with red tights and black calf-length boots that laced up the front. They sat by the fire talking about his family in England while I poured mulled wine and wished him back there.

The fairy lights were twinkling on the Christmas tree and the choir of Westminster Cathedral was trilling away on the music system, which worked perfectly now that Adam was gone, wouldn't you know.

'So,' I said, when Jackie had left us alone to prepare lunch, 'you decided to stick with it?'

He nodded. He looked decidedly shifty, I thought.

'At least until I speak to Adam,' he said, 'face to face.'

'And what did you want to talk to me about,' I said, 'that wouldn't keep?'

I felt as if I was his house master.

'I met Maria Schenke,' he said.

For a moment I didn't know who he was talking about.

'The actress,' he said. 'Liza's cousin.'

Then I remembered. The film actress from Babelsberg who'd had the affair with Goebbels and who'd used her influence with him to save Conrad von Reisenburg from the gallows.

Except that she hadn't. Not according to the story she had told Callum.

Liza had.

'Hang on,' I said. 'Before you start – where did you find this woman?'

Gerhard had found her, he said. She was in her seventies now, living in a state home for retired actors and circus performers in Potsdam. Callum had been to see her, just before leaving for Christmas, and it had been worrying him all through the vacation.

According to Maria's account, Liza had come to see her shortly after Conrad was arrested. He was facing the death penalty. His father was probably dead already. She begged Maria to intercede with the Reichsminister.

Maria felt sorry for her, she said, but could do very little.

Her influence with Goebbels was negligible. He had slept at one time or another with most of the young actresses at Babelsberg.

'Apparently he was a real charmer,' Callum told me, as if I didn't know. 'She seemed really quite fond of him, even now. She said he was a gentleman – at least with the women. And he had a great sense of humour.'

'Hysterical,' I said. 'Get on with the story.'

But he was into his subject and there was no stopping him.

'And he used to get personally involved in the movies, she said. Like, if he wasn't exactly directing them himself, he was telling the director how to do it. The Minister for Propaganda, can you imagine?'

'Yes,' I said.

'And it wasn't just so he could fuck starlets,' he went on. 'He seemed to be genuinely interested. I mean, he kept the industry going right up to the last year of the war, diverting all sorts of resources from the war effort, even using troops as extras. They kept the picture houses open all through the bombing. He reckoned it was good for morale. You know what movie they were making in the end?'

'*Frederick the Great*,' I said.

'Yes,' he said. He looked at me curiously, as if it finally got through that I might know something about it.

'I'm practically an expert,' I said. 'Year Zero and all that.'

'Ah,' he said, but it didn't stop him. 'But, you know, they were all running round in eighteenth-century costume, charging around on horseback making this movie, restaging the battles with thousands of extras from the Wehrmacht, with the bloody Red Army knocking at the doors of Berlin – '

'All that creative energy,' I said, 'and no more Jews to kill. But what did Maria tell you about Liza?'

'Oh, yes,' he said, who'd been worrying about it all over

Christmas. 'Yes, well, she says she's got fuck-all influence with the son of a bitch but she'll try and get him to see Liza. So she does and Liza cuts the deal herself. She gives him everything she's got. And I mean everything.'

'This is what Maria said?' I said.

'Yes. Exactly that.'

'"She gave him everything. And I mean everything."'

'Well – '

'Sounds like a line from one of her movies. And how did she know all this?'

'Liza told her.'

I must have looked sceptical.

'Besides, she says Liza must have known this was going to be the deal even before she went to see him. He was a notorious womaniser and she was beautiful, have you seen pictures of her? She could have been in the movies herself. It would have been inconceivable that he didn't sleep with her. That's what Maria said. You don't believe her.'

'I think she's probably a mischief-making old crow,' I said, 'but even if it's true, I don't see that it amounts to much.'

He didn't know whether to look relieved or disappointed.

'But what am I going to tell Adam?' he said. 'I mean, am I going to put it in the script or what?'

He had to fly down to Prague the next day, he said. Adam wanted to show him the studios to see what he felt about making the movie there. And there was talk of a script conference. That's why Callum had wanted to see me so urgently. He didn't know what to tell him.

'Why tell him anything?' I said. 'At least about this particular incident. Leave it ambiguous. Did she or didn't she? I mean, isn't that dramatically more interesting?'

He looked doubtful.

'Anyway,' I said, 'I'm sure Adam doesn't want to know.'

But was I?

Then he said, 'But he does know. That's what bothers me. Maria told him. He went to see her about six months ago and she told him the whole story.'

I stared at him, trying to figure it out while all sorts of nasties ran amok inside my head: bats, cave bears, demons, the lot.

'She even gave him the diaries,' he said.

'I said, 'Diaries?'

'She found them in a suitcase Liza had left with her just after the war. When the Russians were in Berlin. Maria was shacked up with this Russian officer and Liza moved in with her for a while for safety.'

It started to make sense. I'd always had that nagging doubt about Adam's story about Sam giving him the diaries when Liza died. I was sure he would have told me about them. He'd have read them, too. He spoke enough German for that. Liza had taught him.

'Well, if he does know,' I said, still trying to work it out, 'what's the problem?'

'It's the dates,' he said.

But he had to spell it out for me.

The officers' plot was on 20 July 1944. Over the next few days the arrests started – and the executions. Conrad's father, the old prince, was probably hanged on the 22nd or the 23rd, one of the first to go. Conrad was arrested on the 24th. Liza's efforts to save him happened over the next three weeks and he was released on 15 August and sent almost immediately to the Russian front.

Adam was born on 1 May 1945. I can see you starting to count. Not so easy with trotters. Let me help you. Nine months back from 1 May 1945 takes you to 1 August 1944. When Conrad was at Saxenhausen. And Liza . . .

'You're not serious?' I said.

'It's possible,' he said. 'Isn't it?'

'No,' I said. 'It's not.'

He said, 'Why not?'

And I said, 'Because – ' But then I thought better of it. 'Because she was a doctor.'

He looked at me. Now I had to spell it out.

'If she thought for one moment that she was carrying the child of . . . that man, she'd have had it aborted. She was a doctor. She had the means. She would not have let it live. Believe me.'

He still looked doubtful.

'So he was a little premature,' I said. 'My God, she had him in the Flaktower in the middle of the final Russian assault on Berlin. I don't suppose going the full distance seemed that important to her.'

'I don't think Adam's too sure about it,' he said. 'Otherwise, why didn't he tell me he'd been to see Maria Schenke?'

He had a point. Was this what was worrying Adam? It seemed impossible but . . . six months ago. I began to wonder. Then there were the diaries. They bothered me. There was something there, something I'd seen but not taken in, I was sure of it. I needed to see them again, as soon as possible, but they were in Adam's study at the house in Wannsee.

I looked at the time. It was just before one o'clock. If I went right away I could be back that night.

'When do you have to leave for Prague?' I said.

His flight was at nine the next morning.

I thought about it. I didn't want to leave him there with Jackie but I wasn't a bloody duenna. Then I thought, he has to get back to Berlin, too. Perhaps we could have lunch and then leave together.

Jackie came in. She was looking thoughtful.

'I've just seen someone,' she said, 'down by the lake.'

We looked at her.

'He was staring up at the castle,' she said.

'One of the locals?' I suggested. There was no reason for

them to stay away from the place, now the Russians were gone. It wasn't fenced in. 'Probably a walker,' I said.

'He seemed to have a camera,' she said, 'or a gun.'

We all peered out of the windows but there was no sign of anyone. All the same, suddenly I didn't feel too happy about leaving her there alone.

But I still wanted to go to Berlin. I told Jackie the whole story. I thought it might help.

'If this is what has been on his mind,' I said, 'I think I need to do something about it as soon as possible.'

'But what do you think is in the diaries?' she said.

I shook my head. 'That's what I want to look for.'

So she phoned Frau Lange and told her to let me into the house in Wannsee and Callum said he'd stay on at the castle until I got back.

This wasn't quite the reassurance I was seeking but I left anyway.

Just as I reached the autobahn, it began to snow again.

26

INSIDE THE BUNKER

By the time I reached the outskirts of Berlin I knew I wouldn't be driving back that night. The traffic was crawling along a single lane even on the autobahn and my eyes were raw from peering up the vortex of the headlights. The weather bulletins reported a blizzard sweeping in from the Baltic with gale-force winds and snowdrifts that had already made most country roads impassable.

I skirted the city and turned off for Wannsee on the western edge. I was lucky to make it to the house and Frau Lange greeted me like a lost explorer, clucking and tutting me into the study but at least offering me a welcome schnapps.

I found what I wanted almost immediately but I took a few moments to absorb it – and another glass of schnapps – before I rang Adam in Prague.

He wasn't in his hotel. I left a message for him to ring me back and then tried Jackie. It was a terrible line but at least she was there. The wind was howling round the castle walls, she said, could I hear it? I said no but I'd take her word for it.

'Did you find what you were looking for?' she said.

I told her I had. I'd tell her about it when I got back.

'Don't try tonight,' she said. 'It's too bad on the roads and we're snowed in already.'

She sounded quite pleased about it.

Then she said someone called Nicky had phoned and left

a number in Berlin for me to call her back. It was the studio at Tachelas.

'So who's this Nicky?' she added. Even with the interference I could hear the tease in her voice. She sounded far too frisky for my liking altogether.

'Just you behave yourself,' I said and I thought I heard her chuckle before she rang off.

I called Nicky.

'Where are you?' she demanded.

I told her.

'So thanks for telling me you were coming back,' she said.

I told her it was a spur-of-the-moment decision and that I would have called her.

'Would you?' She sounded doubtful. Or was it wistful? I was flattered by her need for reassurance. I am not used to playing such games. 'Well, now you're here,' she said, 'can you come over? I'm working at the studio.'

She needed to talk to me about something important, she said, and no, she couldn't talk over the phone.

I drove gingerly back into the city, sliding around the bends and nearly skidding into a tram in Oranienbergstrasse. It came hurtling out of the snow at me, bell ringing, and clattered past in a blur of light and slush. I was still shaken when I parked the car outside Tachelas. It looked deserted, its dark windows like empty eye sockets in a great ruined face. I rang the bell and banged my frozen hands on the steel door of Nicky's studio for a good minute before she opened it.

She was sorry, she hadn't heard me, she said, she had been 'chamfering a join'. She took off her welder's helmet to give me a kiss. She smelled vaguely of molten metal and burned tyre. The studio was cold as the tomb.

Appropriately, she was working on Death.

I stood before it shivering and stamping my feet. My critical faculties were numbed along with everything else in my body

236

but it did not look like Death to me. For once, I thought, her imagination had failed her, or maybe it was the materials.

'What do you think?' she said anxiously.

I told her I wasn't sure.

'Nor am I,' she said. 'It looks like a fucking monk.'

It didn't even look like a monk to me. It looked like a metal wigwam, badly made, about to topple over. I did not say this.

I said, 'Well, a monk has a sort of association with Death.'

She gave me a look and picked up the grinder.

'I just want to finish this join,' she said, 'and I'll be with you.'

She slammed down the visor of her helmet and applied the spinning disk to the metal, sending up a shower of blue sparks. I walked away to inspect the rest of the unholy trinity. The Knight sat upright on his charger with a long lance resting on his shoulder. He looked fine, I thought, and her Devil, too, was a success – a metallic monster, recognisably evil.

Perhaps she should leave them as a pair. The Good German Knight and his Dark Shadow.

Here is another story for you, one I made up myself.

On New Year's Eve 1899, the Devil held a party for members of his cabinet and their playfellows. Verdelet, his master of ceremonies, organised it. Kobal, his theatrical manager, put on a performance. Nybbas, the court fool, told jokes. Everybody got hopelessly pissed. There was some heavy gambling at the gaming tables. Asmodeus ran the bank. Then, at midnight, at the dawn of the new century, the Devil opened a book on its dominant moral propensity, which – if you were a Catholic you would know – means its most likely route to damnation. Dagon, the Devil's almoner, put his money on the internal combustion engine. Succor Benoth, his chief eunuch, spread his fairly widely on science. And a

237

young demon called Scarmiglione, the Baneful One, put his money on Germany.

The Devil was intrigued. The Germans had, thus far, been something of a disappointment to him. All those poets and composers, all those writers and philosophers and religious zealots. All that creative genius. All that noble thought. He did not himself consider the Germans a promising bet. But then he looked again and he saw the dark shadow and he thought, this young devil will go far, and he laid his money down.

Der Denker und der Henker,
der Dichter und der Richter . . .
The Thinker and the Hangman,
the Poet and the Judge . . .

Nicky stopped her grinding and I joined her as she surveyed the finished result. She shook her head.

'I'll have to start again,' she said. 'It's not scary enough. It needs, I don't know . . . What do you think it needs?'

'An egg-timer,' I said.

I was, I will admit, a trifle curt. It was very cold. I asked her if this was what she had dragged me over from Wannsee to talk about.

'Well, you are a sulky puss,' she said. But she took off her helmet and led me over to the furnace where it was warmer and poured me some Scotch whisky she had bought in the duty-free at the airport.

She wanted to talk to me about Gerhard Krenkel, she said.

'Oh, yes?' I said. As a subject, I think I would have preferred Death. 'What about him?' I said.

'Only that he's a fucking Nazi,' she said, 'that's what about him.'

I tried to look bemused. I am not a good actor.

'You don't seem very surprised,' she said.

'I just don't know what to say,' I said. This was true. 'I mean, he's never indicated any sympathies in that direction.'

'Pah,' she said. Or something like that. 'Lying little shit!'

Well, yes, but how could she be so sure?

She had her sources, she said mysteriously. But Nicky could never keep a secret. She said the Greens had a special committee monitoring the activities of leading neo-Nazis throughout Germany and she had been given fairly conclusive evidence that when he lived in Potsdam, Gerhard had been a prominent member of the organisation.

I managed to look incredulous without too much difficulty. You have to remember that at this point, I didn't think Gerhard's activities, such as they were, amounted to anything more than a kind of adolescent protest.

But there was worse to come. Nicky's mysterious contacts believed that he was a member of a *Sonderkommando* deputed to carry out attacks on refugees. They were known as the Werewolves, after the Hitler Youth fanatics who had vowed to fight on after the German surrender in 1945.

I have to confess that I thought this was garbage. Nicky was inclined to dramatise and she was always hinting at various semiclandestine activities she undertook for the Green Party. I was alarmed that she had discovered Gerhard's neo-Nazi proclivities but I couldn't believe he was involved as deeply as she was suggesting.

'Well, maybe Dieter can convince you,' she said.

'What's Dieter got to do with it?' I asked her.

I thought she looked a little shamefaced. 'He wants to talk to you,' she said. 'I've just called him. He's on his way over.'

'I thought you couldn't stand him,' I said. I admit I felt a pang of jealousy.

'I can't,' she said. 'He's a two-faced lying bastard, a fucking snake, but whatever else you say about him he's not a Nazi.'

'But what's he got to say to me?' I said.

She shrugged. He hadn't told her but he'd said it affected me personally. He was very insistent. I was beginning to be sorry I'd come back to Berlin.

He arrived about five minutes later clutching a bag full of wine and beer. He was on his way to a party, he said. He opened one of the bottles and insisted on pouring us all a glass. I thought he'd probably drunk a fair bit already. He seemed very excited.

'I want to talk to you about Gerhard Krenkel,' he said. 'He is claiming to be the son of Adam Epstein. Did you know this?'

I leaned back. 'Go on,' I said.

I could feel Nicky's gaze on my face, like the heat of the furnace, but I avoided eye contact. I was cursing myself for not anticipating this. Dieter clearly knew the whole story and he could only have got it from Gerhard or Magda. He knew about their meeting in Prague in the late sixties. He knew that Adam had visited her recently. He knew Adam was paying for Magda's apartment.

I didn't know what to say. I didn't want to let Dieter know that there was any truth in it, not until I'd talked to Adam. On the other hand, I didn't want to lie to Nicky.

I was having difficulty concentrating. From being so very cold, the studio was now unbearably hot. I was sweating and I felt drunk. I put it down to the combination of schnapps, whisky and wine. I have an idea Dieter had opened another bottle but I couldn't swear to it. I felt distanced from reality. One moment Dieter's face seemed very close, like Mephisto, I thought, whispering his temptations in the ear of Faustus. Then he seemed to be at the far side of the room, as if I was looking at him through the wrong end of a telescope.

Then something very extraordinary happened. The sculptures were moving and there was life in their eyes. They were glaring at me balefully. The Knight turned his head towards me and I saw that he didn't have any eyes, just black, empty sockets. His horse was suddenly so big it seemed to fill the whole room. I looked up at the ceiling and the Devil was there staring down at me and his metal crown had turned into a circlet of fire.

Then I went completely.

I was wandering through a corridor deep underground like Alice after she meets the white rabbit. But I knew where I was and it wasn't Wonderland. I recognised it from the discussions I had had with the historians and the archaeologists for our computer model. I was in the labyrinth of bunkers under the Reich chancellery in the last days of the war.

I kept going into rooms.

In one of them Goebbels was giving a tea party for some children and their nurses. His own children were there, all six of them, and there was a boy from the Hitler Youth playing an accordion and singing 'Die Blaue Dragoner'. He had the face of Gerhard. Magda was sitting in a corner, red-eyed, chain-smoking and drinking champagne. But I knew it wasn't Magda, it was Goebbels's wife, Mara.

I groped my way out of the room and swayed off down the corridors. People were pushing past me, their faces distorted as through a wide-angle lens, and many of them wearing masks of wolves and pigs and badgers and bears . . . I was confused. I couldn't remember this from the bunker. They swept me into a room where there was a naked woman dancing. I saw that it was Nicky and I tried to take her by the hand to pull her away but she thought I wanted to dance with her. Then everyone was dancing, all the people in masks, whirling round and round to the tune of 'Die Blaue Dragoner' and they kept barging into me and pushing me from one to another until I was out in the corridor again, feeling my way along the walls.

A woman was walking towards me. She had blonde hair

as carefully groomed as if it were a helmet and she wore a silver fox-fur coat with the lining embroidered with four-leaf clovers. Then I knew I was back in the bunker again and that this was Hitler's mistress, Eva Braun.

I knew that all these images, all these careful details, were remembered from my discussions for the museum, but I had no control over them. It was as if they had taken over my mind and were wandering around from room to room, just as I was.

And other images kept intruding, images that had no business to be there, like the people in the animal masks.

They were pushing me down the corridor again and into another room where Mara was getting her children ready for bed. They all wore long white nightgowns and the youngest had a scarf wrapped around her throat.

'That's right,' I was shouting excitedly, 'that's right, she had tonsillitis.'

She pointed at me. '*Misch, Misch, du bist ein Fisch,*' she sang.

'No, I'm not Misch,' I said, 'I'm Milan.'

But she sang on remorselessly, '*Misch, Misch, du bist ein Fisch.*'

Mara was brushing the children's hair and after she had finished she gave each one of them a chocolate. One by one they fell asleep until it came to the eldest, whose name was Helga. She wouldn't take it.

'Don't eat the chocolate,' I heard someone say and realised it was my own voice.

And then Mara was kneeling on top of her, forcing it down her throat.

Stop her, I shouted, but no one would. The people in the animal masks were standing in a circle clapping. I ran forward and tried to pull the woman away from the young girl, who I now saw was not Helga but Nicky.

242

But I didn't have the strength and Nicky was choking, her face turning blue.

I ran out of the room to fetch help and saw the doctor again in his blood-covered coat. He was standing beside an open door and I saw over his shoulder that it led into a small washroom. Inside there was an SS sergeant with a German Shepherd and four puppies. The sergeant was holding the dog and forcing open her mouth and the doctor was holding a capsule in a pair of pliers. He pushed the pliers into the dog's mouth and squeezed the ends, turning his face away, and the dog went limp in the sergeant's arms and the four puppies were barking wildly and pissing all over the place in their panic. And then the sergeant took his pistol out and shot them one after the other.

I ran into another room where a man and a woman were lying on a sofa. The woman wore a black dress with two pink roses on the neckline. She was curled up at one end of the sofa with her legs tucked under her and on a small table beside her lay a revolver and a square of pink silk chiffon and a vase with flowers in it which had been knocked over. The water was dripping on to the floor. I looked at the man. His head was hanging over the arm of the sofa, which was soaked in blood. I recognised him of course, even with the hole in his head.

Everything was now very calm and still. I could hear a dripping noise very loud in the stillness. Two lots of drips, one from the vase, one from the hole in the man's head. I looked at the blood soaking into the carpet. Or was it in my lap?

I looked up and I saw I was back in Nicky's studio.

The sculptures were no longer moving. Everything was back in its place.

I looked for Nicky and Dieter but I couldn't see them.

Then I looked at the unfinished sculpture of Dürer's Horseman. He was exactly as he should be and the Devil in position at the rear of the horse. But there was a third figure on the floor beside them.

This is one image I cannot bear to dwell on.

All I can tell you is that I knew it was Nicky and that I was no longer in the bunker and that this was not something that was happening in my head.

27

DUNGEONS AND DEMONS

W hat else? Minor details but I will try to remember them for you. I know it is important to relive the experience. I was once a therapist . . .

I was sitting on the floor with my back to the wall. I was naked. There was blood on my hands, my thighs, even my feet. I tried to get up but I couldn't make my legs work. I crawled up the wall. There was a terrible pain in my head.

What was going on in my head, apart from the pain? And the panic?

I've tried to remember, to put it all together, but there is so much I've blocked out. I've blocked out most of what had happened to Nicky, for instance. I must have looked but I can't remember what I saw, though I can remember the pictures they showed me later . . .

I remember thinking that I had been hurt. That the blood was my blood. I began to crawl across the floor towards the door. I think only then did I become aware that people were banging on it and there was a bell ringing, insistently, and this was not inside my head.

I opened the door and saw the police. I think I said, 'Thank God.'

They said I said, 'Help me, you've got to help me.'

I think I said, 'Help her, you've got to help her.'

I was shivering. I felt very cold but I was covered in sweat.

Someone put a blanket around me but it didn't stop me shivering.

The place was full of people. Someone was taking photographs.

A man came to look at me. He said he was a doctor.

I said, 'Is she dead?'

He said, 'Just look up at the ceiling.'

He shone a torch into my eyes. He took my pulse.

He said, 'I think we'd better get you to hospital.'

I said, 'Have I been hurt?'

But I thought, I haven't been hurt. This is not my blood. It is Nicky's.

A police officer came over to me. He said, 'Do you want to tell me what happened?'

I said I didn't know what had happened. I asked again if she was dead.

He said, 'Had you been drinking? Had you been taking drugs?'

I said I had drunk some Scotch whisky and some wine and before I arrived at the studio I had been given some schnapps. I said I must have passed out.

I was beginning to think more clearly. I thought, it could not have been the drink that made me pass out.

Then I remembered Dieter.

'Where is Dieter?' I said.

'Who is Dieter?' he said.

I told him. I saw that one of his colleagues was writing it down. I expected that. I wanted to be as helpful as I could. I was still trying to work it out for myself, what had happened.

It must have been Dieter, I thought. I said I did not know his address but I thought it would be in Nicky's contact book in her purse. Someone went to look for it.

I said I couldn't remember him leaving. I must have passed out by then.

246

The detective said, 'You mean from the drink?'

I said, 'I don't know.'

He asked me some other questions.

Then I was taken to hospital. They took blood and urine samples. I am still confused about all of this. It was as unreal to me as my journey through the bunker. At some stage they took me back to the police station but I can't remember when this was. It might have been hours later. It was still night, though, I remember.

The same detective was there who had questioned me earlier in the studio. He was with two other men. They told me that Nicky was dead.

I think I knew that already.

Then they cautioned me.

I said, 'Am I being arrested?'

They said, 'We just want to know what happened?'

I said, 'You'll have to tell me what happened.' I asked them if they had found Dieter.

They said they had.

Dieter had told them that he had called at the studio to collect some money that Nicky owed him. He knew she had been back to see her parents at Christmas and that her father would have given her some money and he wanted to get it from her before she spent it.

'That's not true,' I said. 'He came because he wanted to tell me something.'

'What did he want to tell you?' one of the men said.

I realised then that I couldn't say, not until I had spoken to Adam. I wondered if Dieter had known that. For the first time I began to worry that this had been thought out by someone in advance, that it had been carefully plotted.

Dieter's story made me worry even more about this.

They read his statement out to me.

He said he had booked a cab which had picked him up

from his apartment in Kreuzberg at about eight o'clock and delivered him to Nicky's studio at Tachelas. Nicky had let him in. I was there, sitting down and drinking whisky. He thought I looked 'strange', possibly drunk. I had offered him some whisky but he had declined because he had the cab waiting to take him on to a party in Dahlem. Nicky had given him the money: two hundred marks. He had left almost immediately and arrived at the party just after eight thirty.

The police had traced the cab driver, who confirmed this story. They had spoken to people at the party who confirmed that Dieter arrived there when he said he had.

The police doctor put the time of death at not earlier than nine o'clock.

There was no sign of a forced entry at the studio but the fire alarm had been ringing. This was what had alerted the police. They thought the alarm had been triggered by the blowtorch which had been left lying on the floor under a smoke detector.

Then they showed me the photographs.

She was naked and her skin was discoloured in patches. Some of it was bruising, they said, and there were burns from the blowtorch.

I was then sick.

They took me to the bathroom and waited while I cleaned myself up. Then they took me back to the interrogation room.

They said a mark had been cut into her forehead. They made me look at the photograph. It looked like a cross. This was what had caused most of the blood, they said. But the cause of death was asphyxiation. She had choked on her own vomit.

They said they had found my fingerprints on the pickaxe and the blowtorch.

I thought, Dieter must have given us drugs in the wine, but what drugs could possibly have made me do something like this? Then I thought, This is crazy, I am not thinking straight, there is nothing that would make me do something like this.

I said then that I wanted to speak to my lawyer.

They asked me who my lawyer was and I gave them Adam's name and the number of his hotel in Prague. It was an instinctive cry for help. I knew he'd be able to deal with it. He'd fix up the lawyers and he'd come back to be with me. But he wasn't there. They asked me if there was anyone else.

I began to weep. I wept for Nicky and I wept for myself.

Then I asked them to phone Jackie at the *Schloss* but they said the number was unobtainable. They said probably it was the snow; some of the lines were down. I gave them the number for her mobile phone but they had no luck with that either. It had been switched off.

Some time later I was formally charged.

And then they locked me up in a cell with my demons.

28

SNOWED UP

I'm sorry? You weren't expecting this. I promised you a fairy story, you say. Well, yes, this is true but have you not heard some of the tales of the Brothers Grimm?

Yes, I know they have handsome princes and beautiful princesses. Fairy-tale castles. Animals that speak. Pigs that fly. But there is a fair amount of violence, too, don't you think? I'm not just talking the occasional homicide. I'm talking infanticide, fratricide, drug-induced comas, cannibalism . . .

Very well. You want a little romance. I understand. Romance you shall have. What do you think was happening back at Helmutshausen, for instance, in all that snow?

Well, I wasn't there, of course. I was in a police cell, wrapped up in my blanket. But I think we can imagine it. Let's try.

Let's imagine the blizzard sweeping across lake and forest, hurling itself against the walls of the castle, howling around the turrets, pelting the windows and the walls with snow, piling it up against the doors . . .

There is a light on in one of the windows. It is warm and snug inside. They are sitting at either end of the table. She is wearing her red dress and tights and black boots. There are candles on the table. Their faces are lit by candlelight and the glow from the fire.

They are eating a goulash she has made and there is red wine. Imagine the deep, black-red fire in the glasses with the tiny golden eyes of the candles flickering in the heart of it. He lifts the glass to his lips. She is talking, animatedly, her face flushed and her eyes bright. She is more than a little drunk, more drunk than he perhaps, and happier than she has been for months.

They are remembering times past. Christmases past, when they were together. 'Do you remember?' she says.

Do you remember? The room on the twenty-fifth floor of the tower and the woman who came there, who used to make love with him in the window with the light on?

This was Jackie. Does that change your image of her? Or not?

'Remember when we brought the Christmas tree back and got it stuck in the lift?'

'And the guy with the pit-bull terrier who tried to get in with us . . .'

'Remember when we went to Kew?' she asks, in her red dress, her eyes wicked over the black-red wine.

It was the same time of year, a nowhere day between Christmas and New Year, but instead of snow there was rain, as there usually is in London. They had been to a lunchtime party near Kew and she did not like the people there and said she wanted to see the plants in the conservatory at Kew Gardens. They'd been drinking, of course. She wore a 1940s-style fitted jacket and skirt in dogtooth check, with seamed stockings and high-heeled shoes.

The conservatory was warm and steamy. Very good for the plants but very bad for thrush, she said. It is better not to wear any knickers. So she took them off.

He remembers. He groans with the memory of it, putting his head in his hands.

'We didn't,' he says.

And she says, 'Oh, but we did.'

On the bridge over the artificial stream full of golden carp.

'We were lucky we didn't fall in,' she says, 'can you imagine?'

They thought the place was empty but then they heard voices and had to take cover because he had to finish it off there and then. And did, within seconds, behind one of the palm trees.

'*Chamaedorea erumpens*,' Jackie says. She had looked at the label afterwards, so she would remember.

It is dangerous to remember such things when there is such opportunity to repeat them. There were no palm trees, it is true, but then there was no need of them for there was no one to hide from. Or so they thought at the time.

That was how it happened, he told me. He thought I might perhaps excuse him if I knew the extenuating circumstances. He didn't tell me what happened, precisely, but I think we may guess. We may imagine it.

They would have made love there and then, I think, in that warm, cosy room amid the remains of supper. They would not have gone upstairs to bed, it would have been too cold and they would have been in too much of a hurry.

So is that romantic enough for you? With the light from the candles and the fire, and the blizzard raging outside. Adultery can be romantic, as Chrétien proved in his version of the legend, though the monks insisted you must suffer for it. The whole world must suffer for it.

It blew itself out in the early hours of the morning – the blizzard, that is – and when the lovers awoke they looked out on the finished painting: a winter landscape, a scene from a fairy tale.

They were snowed in for three days. I do not think that was a problem for them. They had plenty of food and wine, plenty of fuel for the fire, plenty of exercise . . .

We have seen the pictures of them, naked apart from their boots, on the terrace, throwing snow at each other. It does seem a strange thing to do, I agree, but then she was an exhibitionist, he said, and he did not think anyone could see them. And people do run out into the snow after a sauna in Russia, I am told, and thrash each other with birch twigs.

I can imagine it might have been fun for a short while. And then they would have gone indoors again, into the warmth, to make love.

There are no pictures of them making love. That, at least, they were spared.

On the third day they spotted the photographer. It had begun to thaw a little and they were digging Callum's car out of a snowdrift. They were wearing clothes now. They stopped to embrace. She was crying.

Callum told me they had just decided that it must not continue. Not, at least, until she had talked things over with Adam and figured out whether she still had a marriage or not. So this was a goodbye embrace.

The photographer had come closer to the castle by then. Perhaps he was hoping to shoot something through the windows. The rest of the pictures were taken from the trees beside the lake, with a 600-mil lens. He wore trail skis. So when they spotted him he carried on taking pictures of Callum floundering through the snow towards him and then made off through the trees when the film was finished.

29

SCANDAL

B ut it was some time before I knew of this. You must forgive me if I appear a little confused about the order of events. They are shrouded in what I believe military men call the fog of battle. I will try to concentrate on the details as I remember them.

I appeared briefly before the magistrates in Berlin and was remanded in custody. The doors began to slam on my small life.

Each door that slammed drove me a little deeper into myself. I shut down all the extraneous emotions. I ran on emergency batteries, a small red light the only flicker of life. I felt like sailors must in a submarine that lies on the bottom of the ocean while the destroyers cruise above, searching out its position and dropping random depth charges.

Some of them did not seem so random. Some of them seemed to be aimed with alarming accuracy.

My lawyer was a man called Bocklin. I knew that he thought I was guilty. He concentrated on the drugs. Clearly he thought that they had induced me to act out of character and that this was our best case.

I said, 'No drugs will make you act out of character. But they can bring out the demon in you, the dark shadow.'

He nodded briskly. He was in his early thirties, convention-ally handsome with short blond hair and a face that glowed with health and smelled of shaving lotion. He wore glasses but I suspect they were for effect rather than necessity.

'Yes, but this was a very unusual drug,' he said. He consulted his notes. 'It has been identified as an hallucinogen known as ayahuasca, originating in the Amazon Basin.'

He looked up at me carefully.

I shook my head. I'd never heard of it. And I come from Los Angeles.

But my brisk, young lawyer had been doing his homework. 'Amazonian Indians,' he said, 'use it to liberate what they believe to be their animal souls. Under its influence they think themselves transformed into the wild beast that is the other self.'

He was still gazing at me intently through his cosmetic spectacles, as if looking for some revealing detail: the faint markings of the jaguar, perhaps, or the anaconda, or the tree sloth. He said, 'Is this the effect you yourself experienced?'

But I shook my head again. I could identify with no animal in my dream. Unless it was the German Shepherd they killed with cyanide. I did not tell him about my trip through the bunker. It would not help, I thought.

Then I thought, But what of Dürer's Beast? Perhaps I had identified with that in my dream.

He was still talking.

'The blood also revealed significant levels of alcohol in both your case and that of the deceased.'

'The alcohol I can explain,' I said.

'But not the other drug?'

'Unless it was in the wine,' I said.

'The wine. Ah, yes. Which you say was provided by this man Dieter Rauch?'

'You seem doubtful,' I said.

'No,' he said, 'not at all. It is just that there was no wine found on the premises. Nor were there any empty bottles of wine.'

I thought about this.

'Then Dieter must have taken them away with him,' I said. 'Or someone else.'

He made another note. Then he stood up and shook my hand, very briskly, and said he would keep me informed of any developments.

He asked me if there was anything I needed. Books, writing materials, food and dietary supplements, toiletries, a telephone?

I said yes to all of these and thanked him and went back into my submarine.

It must have been after this that Adam came to see me.

For once I had his undivided attention. I couldn't remember when I had last seen him so focused on a single subject.

This is not to say that he was relaxed. The way he kept trying to climb the walls of the visiting room you'd have thought he was the prisoner.

'For Christ's sake, sit down,' I said, 'you're making me nervous.'

What I meant was, he was making the guards nervous.

'How can you be so calm?' he said.

'I've considered the alternatives,' I said, 'but they've taken away my belt and my bootlaces.'

He sat down. He put his elbows on the table and his head in his hands and made the sound Sam used to make during lesser crises.

I told him this wasn't helping.

'No,' he said. 'No, you're right. Okay, let's look on the bright side.'

I waited with bated breath.

'You didn't do it. She didn't do it herself. So somebody

else had to be in that room with you. Probably more than one. Right?'

'That's one theory,' I said.

'There was no forced entry so someone had to let them in.'

I was still waiting.

'Dieter Rauch,' he said. 'It has to be.'

'Another theory is that I did it myself,' I said.

'Let them in?' he said.

'What was done to her?' I said.

He was not prepared to consider this.

'Why not?' I said.

'Because I know you,' he said, 'and I know you are not capable of a thing like this.'

'Not even in a drug-induced Dionysian frenzy?' I was quoting one of my police interrogators, clearly a scholar of classical Greek. 'Not even if I was possessed by the Devil?'

He told me not to be so stupid but I could see he was thinking about it.

'Let's go down the Dieter Rauch route first,' he said. 'We'll save the Devil for later, if all else fails, if that's all right by you?'

He said he had a team of private detectives working on the case.

'They're ex-Stasi,' he said. 'Apparently, they're the best.'

I didn't argue with him but I cannot say I shared his confidence. I have never seen any reason to believe that the secret police of the Eastern bloc were any more efficient than the agricultural workers or the manufacturers of automobiles or the distributors of essential commodities to the masses. There were just more of them.

They were checking out Dieter's alibi, he said. They were also checking out the taxi driver who claimed he had taken Dieter to Tachelas and then on to the party.

A guard announced that our time was up.

'Don't despair,' Adam told me. 'Don't give in to it. This is all crazy. We'll have you out of here in no time.'

That's what they say in the movies but this time Adam wasn't writing the script.

Three days later he was back again. I was still there.

By then he'd seen the pictures of Callum and Jackie in the scandal sheets. I, of course, had not.

But I could see he was holding something back from me. I thought it was something to do with the case. I told him he must tell me. So he did. And I knew then that I was still capable of feeling many of the emotions I thought I had switched off for the duration.

Adam had put his hand to his head and was pressing with the tips of his fingers as if he was trying to keep all the beasts in control, all the mythical monsters.

'Don't despair,' I said. 'Don't give in to it.'

He said, 'Give me one good reason why I shouldn't?'

I said, 'Josef Goebbels is not your father.'

I could feel the guards looking at me and then at each other but I didn't care. They thought I was mad anyway.

Adam said, 'What?'

I told him I knew about his conversation with Maria Schenke six months ago.

'It isn't true,' I said.

I told him what I had told Callum, that she'd have procured an abortion if she'd had the slightest doubt.

He looked hopeful for a moment. Then he frowned.

'But it was her baby, too. We can't be sure. Besides, what about the diaries?'

I said, 'What about the diaries?'

He said, 'She put a ring around August 1st. The date of conception. I was born exactly nine months later. On August 1st my father – ' He corrected himself. 'Liza's husband – was in a concentration camp. The Gestapo did not allow conjugal visits, Milan.'

I said I appreciated that but that I, too, had examined the diaries. That was why I had returned to Berlin, with such fatal consequences.

'If you look back four weeks from August 1st,' I said, 'you will see that July 4th is also ringed. Four weeks before that, May 7th. Four weeks before that, April 9th . . .'

I could see I was finally getting through to him but paranoia is a chronic disease.

'They were the dates of her period,' I said. 'August 1st was the date of her period. Even had she slept with the Devil himself it is impossible that she could have conceived at that time.'

Well, theologically I might not have been on firm ground there but I think I made my point.

'On August 15th, however,' I said, 'when she slept with your father, Conrad von Reisenburg, she would have been at her most fertile. Hence the happy, if slightly premature event, thirty-seven weeks later.'

'Jesus,' he said.

'I'm not so sure about that,' I said. 'But certainly not the Anti-Christ.'

I watched him taking it in. He looked like a man who has just been told by his doctor that the tests show the lump is benign.

He began to tell me, then, about the effect it had had on his relations with Jackie.

I said I was aware of that.

'She talked about it?'

'I observed it,' I said. 'So what now?' I asked him. 'Between the two of you?'

But he shook his head. He didn't think either of them knew. She was still at Helmutshausen. They had security there now. I hoped he didn't mean Eric. He didn't know where Connolly was.

'Why did you bring him over here?' I said. 'If you didn't want this to happen.'

'I don't know,' he said. 'Perhaps I did. Perhaps I thought she'd be better off with him. If I was . . . if I was the progeny of that . . .'

That was another thing that bothered me.

I chose my words with care. 'If you did think that, why the hell did you want to make a movie about it?'

He said, 'To find out if it was true.'

I said, 'You think a movie would tell you that?'

He said, 'Perhaps I wanted to see if other people came to the same conclusion. Perhaps I wanted to bring it out into the open, to expose it to the light.'

'Wouldn't it have been easier,' I said, 'and caused a lot less trouble all round, to have consulted a therapist?'

He smiled. It was the first time I had seen him smile for some time.

'I wonder,' I said, 'if we can now talk about the present situation.'

He stopped smiling. It was a pity but I felt I had to mention it.

'The photographer,' I said. 'How did he know?'

'What photographer?' he said. 'Know what?'

'The photographer who took the pictures of Callum and Jackie,' I said. 'How did he know they would be there? How did he know they would be . . .'

Then I said, 'Dieter.'

As Callum had said the first time he came out to the *Schloss*.

'Dieter knew,' I said.

I told Adam how he knew.

Adam said, 'But why?'

I did not know why.

'You'll have to find that out,' I said. 'You'll have to talk to your detectives. You'll have to talk to the lawyers.'

I do not know what the detectives made of it but the lawyers were not impressed. The lawyers were not interested in what had happened at the House of Helmut.

It has no bearing on the case, they said. We do not see the connection.

And nor, I admit, could I. Not then.

30

THE NATURE OF THE BEAST

My best hope, the lawyers argued, lay in the medical evidence.

The charge was manslaughter. Nicky had died by choking on her own vomit as a result of the injuries I had inflicted.

But my lawyers had assembled a weight of medical opinion, as they called it, to argue that this vomiting was as a result not of the injuries but of the amount of drugs and booze she had consumed.

They thought the state might be persuaded to accept a plea of guilty on the lesser charge of inflicting grievous bodily harm. And in mitigation, the lawyers had assembled another weight of medical opinion to argue that I had acted under the influence of a drug that made a man behave like a wild beast: the Jekyll and Hyde drug from the Amazonian rainforests. They had polished their rhetoric. They could see the headlines already. Who was I to deny them?

I knew I had not turned into a wild beast, my animal alter ego. That was a game for the lawyers to play. But I knew I was guilty. I knew because of my memory of the bunker. I knew that in my deluded state I had mistaken Nicky for Mara Goebbels and that I had tried to stop her from murdering her children. And then I had tried to burn her body, just as the SS guards had tried to burn it in the garden of the Reich chancellery with that of her husband, Paul Josef.

It was all part of my dream, my fantasy trip into virtual-reality land. But this was more fantastical and more complicated than the theories of the lawyers.

So I let them do it their way. They assembled their expert witnesses: the doctors, the psychiatrists, the narcotics experts, the anthropologists, even a witchdoctor from the rainforest. It was a circus. And I the werewolf, alone in a ring of moonshine.

It would have helped if the judge had been a romantic, or even if he had had the whisper of an imagination. But he was a no-nonsense conservative from Brunswick and the sentence was the maximum he could give. In the prison cell afterwards Adam banged his head with the flat of his hand the way Sam used to. Then he banged the walls. I seemed to be watching from another world.

'Why did you go along with that shit?' he demanded.

He did not believe that I had laid a finger on Nicky. He believed Dieter had. Or persons unknown that Dieter had let into the studio while I was under the influence of my exotic cocktail. But he could produce no evidence to back up this supposition. I pointed this out to him.

'You should have told them the real reason Dieter came to the studio,' he said.

'To tell me that Gerhard was a neo-Nazi,' I said, 'and the son of Adam Epstein?'

Where would that have got me? It would not have proved my innocence and it would have finished Adam in Germany. I did not want to destroy his dreams. For all my Bohemian cynicism, they were my dreams, too.

His grand design had survived my trip into the bunker. It had even survived the naked pictures of his wife and her lover in the newspapers. There had been a few changes in personnel, of course. A respected German historian had taken over the museum project. Callum Connolly was no longer on the payroll.

I did not know what was happening between him and Jackie.

I did not know what was happening between Adam and Jackie. I gathered that they were seeing each other. I did not know if they were sleeping together or if there was harmony between them. I was hoping he would tell me on one of his visits.

But, mostly, we talked about the past.

Now that he was liberated from the secret fear of his origins, it had renewed his interest in the father he had never known. He became the knight in shining armour, the lost hero to whom Adam could pay his uncritical homage.

But we also talked about Sam.

Sam was a realist but there were elements of the romantic in him, too. He once told me something he'd read about poets being the unacknowledged legislators of the world. He liked the sound of that. He said it was true of all storytellers, and filmmakers, too.

But Sam, as a lawyer, assumed that legislators were of benefit to the world. I, as a Middle European, knew that this depended on who the legislators were.

It was some time before Adam brought himself to tell me that he had asked Gerhard to make the movie.

'Under my supervision, of course,' he said.

Now that he no longer had any doubts about his own genealogy, he was no longer worried about Gerhard's Nazi inclinations.

It was just a phase he had been going through, a protest.

'He has some quite interesting political notions, as a matter of fact,' said Adam.

Apparently Gerhard, too, was obsessed with the Big Idea.

He thought people were tired of hearing small-minded politicians talking about inflation and trade talks and unemployment and welfare. They were waiting for the Big Idea and it didn't really matter what it was, provided it was big enough.

'So what is it going to be this time?' I asked Adam. 'Now they can no longer blame the Jews.'

I gathered that Gerhard was still thinking about it.

'Prison is a good place to think about things like that,' I said.

It was about a week before he was arrested.

31

THE ATONEMENT

It was the week I started work on the prison farm. The week we met. Late autumn with the trees almost bare and the apples lying on the ground, so rotten that even you wouldn't eat them. There was a hoarfrost, I remember, and it stayed all morning on the sides of the trees furthest from the sun. I recognised those trees as if they were people I knew from the past. The shapes were so familiar to me, the long thin branches near the tops like fingernails in need of trimming, the swollen arthritic joints. They were like old witches and wizards who had been condemned to suffer here in this shape, with their staffs and crutches and broomsticks bent and crooked and growing in on them. I felt as if they had been waiting for me to join them and that slowly, imperceptibly, I would grow to be like them.

I felt that I had walked into a familiar painting and become a part of it, though I had never possessed a painting at all like this. But I even looked for the pig and there you were, scratching your back against a tree. Ah, there is the pig, I thought.

And now I am the pigman. Milan the pigman. A role that was also waiting for me.

Until then, I had dealt well with prison, on the whole. Or at least, it had not been such a shock to the system as my friends imagined. I think this was because I had been raised in a country that was one large prison. Part of me had never escaped from it, had always expected to return there. So I was prepared for it. Or perhaps my system was already in such a state of shock I was incapable of responding to the lighter blows: the loss of freedom, the minor daily iniquities.

Apart from my visitors I had cut myself off from contact with the contemporary world outside. I did not read the newspapers or watch television. I read only books about pigs, or the past.

I felt, in some ways, as if I was retreating into the past, not just my own past but the historical past. I imagined that there was a world of chaos outside my prison walls, as at the time of the collapse of the Roman Empire when we are told that Arthur and Merlin had lived. I imagined that I was in a monastery on an island somewhere, preserving a small world of order, a chalice of peace, until the tide of chaos would reach us. But sometimes I felt it was very close, I felt it reaching through the walls, reaching into my mind, threatening to take me back to the place where the Knight and Death and the Devil waited for me to join them, to stay with them for ever.

The arrest of Gerhard brought me back to a sense of the present. Jackie phoned to tell me about it. She said that Adam was busy, talking to lawyers.

A number of neo-Nazis had been picked up in a series of what the press called dawn raids. They were charged with conspiracy offences but it was thought that most of the arrests were in connection with the attacks on Buchenwald and the refugee hostel, in both of which people had died.

'How is Adam taking it?' I asked her, carefully.

'Badly,' she said. 'He still blames himself for everything that happened to Gerhard, getting involved with these people, everything . . .'

It was the first indication I'd had that she knew Gerhard was his son. So had Adam finally told her – and if so, what were things like between Adam and Jackie now? I appreciated that this was a question that would have to keep.

When Adam next came to see me, our conversation was dominated by Gerhard.

'There's no real evidence against him,' he said. 'It's all coming from police informers. They say he was a member of the gang but they can't prove for certain that he was at either of the places where people were killed.'

I asked him what Gerhard had to say about it.

'He admits he knew some of these people and that he even went to some of their meetings in the past but he says he didn't go on any of the raids. He didn't even know about them.'

Adam was desperate to believe it, of course. The stress showed in his features. It was the first time I had noticed how much he had aged but I realised now that it must have happened since my own arrest. It was as if all his years had caught up with him in the last few months.

'You have to stop blaming yourself,' I said. 'You have to stop thinking that only you can put things right. It's pure egotism.'

But I might as well have talked to my trees. It was in his genes, it was his legacy. He thought he could put the world to rights, or at least a substantial part of it, so why should he give up with his own son?

Initially Gerhard was charged with one of the lesser offences: conspiracy to cause an affray. I suppose that was why Adam's lawyers won the appeal for bail. Adam put up the surety and appeared in court when he was remanded. Jackie said that he felt he should be there. I don't think Magda was.

Gerhard was released on a surety of two hundred thousand marks. He and Adam left the court together with the lawyers. They were surrounded by reporters and photographers. The reporters were shouting questions. Mr Epstein, is it true that you're the father? It might have been a paternity suit. In a way, I suppose it was. I've seen it all on television. It's the one thing I've watched.

He had his arm round Gerhard's shoulders as they pushed through the crowd towards the waiting Mercedes. I recognised Eric, trying to clear the way, ineffectual as ever. I didn't see what happened. You never do. Suddenly the victim is down and everyone is pushing and shouting and the cameras are all over the place. Later they go back and freeze a frame and put a circle around the assassin, the moment before. But they never capture the moment. It's as if a few vital frames are missing; a jump cut.

There were conflicting views on what happened. Some say the killer was aiming at Gerhard and Adam got in the way. Some say he saw the gun pointed at Gerhard's head and deliberately stepped in front of him. Some say that Adam himself was the target.

We'll never know, of course, because the killer was shot dead by the police. The cameras missed that moment, too, though they filmed the body lying in the street. He was a young man of Turkish origin from Kreuzberg and the member of a Muslim extremist group, the self-appointed defenders of the community, who called themselves the Grey Wolves. Callum said he used to come into the Gingerbread House sometimes for breakfast.

They showed a figure on a stretcher being lifted into an ambulance. They said it was Adam but you could not see his face. They said the bullet entered just below the left cheekbone. They said he was dead on arrival at hospital.

I was in the apple orchard when it happened. I had found a book on tree care and I was starting to prune back some of the branches.

32

THE INFORMER

O f all the blossoms, apple is my favourite. Look at it, that mass of celebrant white against the blue of the sky. No? You, of course, prefer it when the first apples fall. You have no soul, only a belly. But if eternity is a frozen moment of time, this is the moment I would choose: the moment when the apple blossom is at its most perfect, the exact moment before it begins to wither.

Yes, I am in that kind of mood.

I have had good news this morning. Dieter has cracked. He has made a new statement to the police.

And so I have another story for you.

When he was a young art student in East Berlin in the early eighties, Dieter was pressured into becoming an informer for the secret police. It happened to many people, as you know. He says that the information he gave on his fellow students was of little consequence but, of course, it is not the information that matters so much as the giving of it. It is a form of control. A way of making the puppets dance. Then one day he was summoned to meet a senior officer of the Stasi. A Major Krenkel.

Yes, this was Magda.

She required some information about one of his tutors, a brilliant artist and dissident. Again, Dieter says that the information he gave was of no consequence. Doubtless there were other informers. But shortly afterwards the artist was arrested and interrogated and declared to be in need of remedial treatment.

Yes, he was probably the artist who made Magda's puppets, I think.

He is still alive and is, I believe, one of the people who have made statements concerning her and her activities for the old regime.

But let us stick to Dieter's story.

Dieter says that while he was directing a production of Schiller's *Don Carlos* at Tachelas, Magda came to see him. She was of course no longer a senior officer of the Stasi. But she reminded him of the time when she was and when he had been an informer.

He was naturally loath for anyone else to know this.

She required a service of him. A very small service. She understood that he had met her son, Gerhard. She was anxious, as any good mother, to protect her son from undesirable elements. There were certain people, she said, with whom he had become acquainted in Potsdam who had links with the neo-Nazi movement. She would be eternally grateful if Dieter would befriend Gerhard himself and keep a brotherly eye on him and inform her of his connections with these undesirables.

It seemed wise not to refuse her. Also an act of kindness. And these people in Potsdam were no friends of Dieter.

But then Magda became interested in others, in people who were in Dieter's own circle of acquaintances. Among them were Nicky, Callum and I. She demanded regular reports on our activities.

It is disturbing to know that our nightly excursions into the Death Strip were monitored by Magda. I feel now what it is like to be one of her puppets.

Gradually her demands upon Dieter increased.

Then, shortly before Christmas, the Christmas that I spent

272

at Helmutshausen, she told him that he must arrange a meeting with Nicky and me in her studio. He was to ensure that we were in a sufficiently euphoric state. Then he was to open the door to let some people in . . .

There were four of them. He recognised at least two as acquaintances of Gerhard's from Potsdam. They are among those who have since been charged with the killings at Buchenwald and the hostel in Hesse.

He claims that he had no idea they would use violence.

He had been told that they would arrange us in certain postures and in certain costumes and then take photographs. He assumed this was to ensure future compliance with Magda's wishes. He claims that he was horrified when he heard of Nicky's death. It has been on his conscience ever since.

Of course he is also afraid.

He has been in hiding all winter, since the first arrests. He fears that the movement already believe him to be one of the people who informed upon them. I don't know what kind of deal he has struck with the state. I do not particularly care.

So that is Dieter's story.

I don't know if it is true. I expect, like most stories, it contains a degree of truth and myth.

I expect Magda will deny it. I expect she will say that she had no motive for such a crime, unlike Dieter himself, who had been Nicky's lover and might be said to have been jealous of her relationship with me.

Dieter says that she perceived Nicky as a threat because of her political activities, that she became alarmed when he informed her that Nicky had discovered Gerhard's links with the neo-Nazi movement and the people responsible for the attacks.

But I am not so sure.

I wonder if she cared that much about Nicky. I wonder if she even cared about Gerhard.

I have thought very carefully about this. I have said she was mad but there was a certain twisted logic at work. I have tried to analyse it.

I think her real motive was revenge.

Magda had made her choice a long time ago at that border crossing in Czechoslovakia. Maybe before that, before the three of us left Prague together. But she made the wrong choice. She chose the losing side. All those years in the service of the state only to see it crumble away, to face penury, imprisonment and, even more hurtful to her, the loss of her power over others. And we were the winners, the *Besserwessis* who picked up the pieces. Adam with his new young wife, his castle in the forest, his ambitious plans – and I his closest friend, his counsellor . . .

She meant to bring us down, to prove her power over us, to make us suffer.

Let me tell you another story. Just a short one. The one that Kleist told about the puppet-maker who believed that only puppets and gods made any kind of sense. Human beings were nonsense. They had lost their connection to the Great Scheme of Things.

Magda's great skill is in perceiving the hidden wires that protrude from people and connecting them to the Great Scheme of Things. And if there is no scheme, if the gods are dead, or sleeping, or impotent, then Magda will jerk the strings anyway, just for the hell of it, to make the puppets dance.

But it is only a theory.

Magda, of course, has said nothing.

She is too busy making speeches.

33

THE MERLIN

Jackie says Dieter's evidence will finish her. I hope she is right. For the present, I am more concerned with the effect it will have on my own judges.

The auguries are hopeful. The prison authorities permit me to have visitors whenever I wish, within reason, just as they permit me to stay out here all day talking to you. I think these are indications of their belief in my innocence and that I will soon be released.

Jackie is coming to see me this afternoon.

She asked me how I would feel if she brought Callum with her. I said I would feel fine. This is probably an exaggeration but it is a sign that her own wounds are healing.

She has asked him to make the film that Adam wanted him to make. If nothing else, it will be good therapy for them both.

The child she is carrying is Adam's, she says. Not Callum's. He was conceived the night Gerhard was arrested. I am glad but he will never replace Adam, not for me, at least.

She intends to bring him up at Helmutshausen. She is thinking of turning the old *Schloss* into a children's home and a hostel. For refugees from the east. She wants me to live and work there. She says my skills will be useful.

I think she means as a therapist. But I have given up being

a therapist, a wise man. I am a tree surgeon now, I am the pigman.

I can't imagine leaving this place. I think I am afraid to think about it. Perhaps I will go back to Prague. I can imagine walking along the Charles Bridge, the bridge of martyred saints, a place of grief and redemption. But I've had enough of darkness and torment. I can do my grieving here, among the apple blossom, for Adam and for Nicky and for myself.

Did I really believe I had killed her, or was that my guilt finding its outward expression at last?

Guilt for being born. For being who I am, the Devil's son.

Didn't you guess?

Why do you think I was so sure that Adam was not? Don't you think I would have recognised my own brother, or half-brother, as he would have been?

Besides, it would have been too much of a coincidence, even for one of my stories.

But I am as sure as I can be of my own fathering, which is as sure as anyone can be. I have seen the pictures of them together when he came to the studios outside Prague the day of my conception: Paul Josef Goebbels and my mother. It was the last day of the shoot and they are drinking champagne with their arms around each other. She is even wearing her nun's costume. How could he ever have resisted her?

Do I really see myself as Merlin? A difficult question. I have had patients who think they are the Christ, or the reincarnation of famous kings or queens, but never Merlin. Yet I recognise it as a similar delusion.

And there, I have said it – a delusion.

But perhaps every age must have its Merlin.

Some people think it is a title, you know. He was not Merlin, but *the* Merlin. As in the Wizard, or the Shaman.

Perhaps there was more than one. Perhaps there still are.

We need our Merlins just as we need our Arthurs and our Lancelots and our Galahads, our Morgan le Fays and our Mordreds and the whole pervasive clan, just as we need the delusions, the myths, the Camelots.

Adam regarded *Pendragon* as the finest film he had ever made and wanted it to be his epitaph. He told me that in Munich when we had just seen the rough cut and we were about to drive to his wedding.

'Why do we believe in the dream of Camelot,' he asked me, 'when we know, rationally, that it was only war games for restless knights and gossip for idle gentlewomen?'

'You tell me,' I said. 'You made the movie.'

'It was about men who aspired to be gods,' he said, 'and the human weaknesses that drove them back into the swamp. The lechery, the violence, the betrayals . . .'

He was taking it personally, you see, even then. This is the trouble with egotists.

There is one more thing. I have not forgotten my promise. I have taken it up at the highest level, with the prison governor himself. I am sorry for the delay but it was unavoidable. There was an outbreak of swine fever in the local farms and I am determined to choose a healthy partner for you. It is so important, of course, who the father is.